CHANGING FLAGS

CHANGING FLAGS

A NOVEL OF THE BATTALION
OF ST. PATRICK

RAY HERBECK, JR.

FIVE STAR
A part of Gale, a Cengage Company

GALE
A Cengage Company

LIBRARY OF CONGRESS CATALOGING-IN-PUBLICATION DATA

Names: Herbeck, Ray, Jr., author.
Title: Changing flags : a novel of the battalion of St. Patrick / Ray Herbeck Jr.
Description: First edition. | Waterville, Maine : Five Star, [2022] | Identifiers: LCCN 2021025292 | ISBN 9781432889173 (hardcover)
Subjects: LCSH: Riley, John, 1817—Fiction. | Mexico. Ejército. Batallón de San Patricio—Fiction. | Mexican War, 1846-1848—Fiction. | LCGFT: Biographical fiction. | Historical fiction.
Classification: LCC PS3608.E7263 C48 2022 | DDC 813/.6—dc23
LC record available at https://lccn.loc.gov/2021025292

First Edition. First Printing: January 2022
Find us on Facebook—https://www.facebook.com/FiveStarCengage
Visit our website—http://www.gale.cengage.com/fivestar
Contact Five Star Publishing at FiveStar@cengage.com

Printed in Mexico
Print Number: 01   Print Year: 2022

CHANGING FLAGS

Prologue
WASHINGTON CITY
THE PRESIDENT'S OFFICE
JANUARY 12, 1846

He felt deliciously notorious for keeping his own counsel, as if secrecy were an enticing relish that would enhance his otherwise bland personality. And that perfectly suited President James Polk, a pleasantly haunted chief executive.

"I learned that from you, sir," Polk said in his soft Tennessee drawl, sounding almost like a prayer. He had arranged for this meeting purposely at a very late hour, not caring if it suggested sinister purpose. "You are the only one I can trust to keep my confidence."

Long ago, office seekers and staff had departed the President's House, the official name Polk preferred to the more colloquial White House. Not a servant remained on duty. His adoring but overly chatty wife, Sarah, already had retired. And the two weary Marines on guard outside would remain in the freezing winter air, pacing the portico and shivering in overcoats. There would be no one to pry into, report, or record what might transpire or even if a meeting took place.

"I treasure these moments alone together," Polk admitted. "They validate my plans on how to expand the nation and complete your work." No surprise to Polk, there was no response: nobody else was in the room.

He stood looking up reverently at a gilt framed portrait of President Andrew Jackson in his military uniform, glittering with gold trimmed collar and sword belt. Polk personally had hung the martial portrait of General Jackson behind his desk. It

7

was draped in black crepe though nearly a year after Jackson's death. Polk still grieved.

As Polk waited fitfully in his second story office, flickering amber light from the candle chandelier and oil lamps cast a warm if fragile glow off the portrait as well as new, shining appointments. Jackson had not succeeded in getting brighter, more steady gas lines laid back in 1829. Polk swore to complete that chore before he left office after first finishing more important aspects of Jackson's legacy. In the basics, the small room remained unchanged from Jackson's tenure. But Polk's desk, armchair, and side chairs now were in the currently popular antique French style, encrusted with shimmering gold leaf. Jackson himself had installed the gilded eagle cornices above the gold silk curtains. More gold décor was appropriate, Polk believed, for an imperial presidency that would crown the vision of the great man.

"Excuse me, sir," he said apologetically, "but my two best generals are arriving." The rhythmic clatter of horse hooves outside drew him to the window, its thin panes no defense against noise. "You must help me decide which one to choose," Polk continued louder from the window, as if the portrait of Jackson might hear him better.

Below he watched the solitary figure of Brigadier General Zachary Taylor rein up his plodding horse, Old Whitey, by the portico. He dismounted easily, leaving his famous if dumpy steed with a Marine guard. Taylor was wrapped in a plain, practical dark blue military overcoat. He could pass for a disheveled private, Polk thought.

"His simple attire tells us much, doesn't it, sir?" Polk continued. "But perhaps for this mission, simple is best. We shall see."

The rolling crunch of heavy carriage wheels atop crusted ice on the drive announced the arrival of his second guest, Major

General Winfield Scott, straining an ornate brougham coach handled by a black driver in livery. It slowed to a halt. Scott remained inside until a Marine sprang to the door, opened it, and stiffly saluted as Scott's immense bulk emerged. He glowed in the moonlight from his gilt encrusted overcoat as he strode, all pomp and ceremony, to the portico.

"This shall be a study in contrasts, sir," Polk observed. He almost cracked what passed for a smile with him. The harpies of the press whined that after a year in office they could find in him nary a trace of a sense of humor. Yet he saw his present situation cause for a good laugh, if only he could risk one. He never allowed himself to reveal what he found funny: it could give someone political advantage. After all, no one knew he still found it amusing that he had been elected, not even Sarah.

Eleventh President of the United States at age 49, James Polk was the youngest to date, though he looked older with his slender, diminutive stature and full head of graying hair. He wore it longer and swept back, as had Jackson. His face was hawk-nosed and thin, also like that of Jackson. Some dared to call him "Young Hickory." Never mind what they intended; Polk took it as a compliment.

"Together, sir, we shall surprise and surpass them all," Polk vowed, returning to his desk and again addressing the portrait.

A crafty political operative, Polk used his unintimidating stature to seem ineffectual and unobtrusive. As a new president, he was so seldom noticed when he attended state functions that Sarah was moved to force attention from the crowd. As official hostess, she ordered that the Marine Corps band play an old Scottish martial air, "Hail to the Chief," as he made his entrances.

"Thank God, sir," Polk mused, "they do not play bagpipes, so plebeian. Brass imparts the more regal tone."

Nobody thought the Democrats would nominate Polk for the

election of 1844, let alone that he'd be elected, simply because so few knew his name. In the end, it worked to his advantage. He was known as "the dark horse" candidate, the nation's first, a safe unknown among contentious rivals. As a slaveholder from Tennessee, also home state of his late mentor, he could have faced vehement opposition. Many remained incensed over Jackson's expansion of federal power, even though "Old Hickory" had been out of office since the mid-1830s.

And with the recent admission of Texas into the union as a slave state, concern also arose about the future slave status of Oregon. Great Britain was rattling its heavy broadsword over that frontier's boundaries with British North America, unofficially known as Canada. If necessary, Polk boldly had declared, he would deal with the British as had Jackson in the War of 1812: the cry became "54° 40 or Fight!" This latitudinal line in the sand would extend the United States claim on Oregon up to Alaska. At Jackson's urging, Polk proclaimed that he would risk war for the territorial integrity of the nation. And he further avowed that if elected he would not stand for re-election, to better focus on the nation's pressing business. With Jackson's public endorsement, he won. But some still wondered who in truth he was and what he envisioned.

"You never told your officers what your plans were until the last moment," Polk whispered to the portrait, suddenly aware of approaching bootsteps in the hall. "And you never lost a battle."

His hands free from political shackles, he would take the next step in his mission tonight. Polk believed that while he must entertain a risk of war with more powerful Britain, he must manufacture an actual war with weaker Mexico. Like a suddenly righteous strumpet, Mexico haughtily had rebuffed his generous offer of money to purchase what he wanted, the so-called "disputed territory." He saw the Rio Grande and its natural harbor at Matamoros as the best defensible border against possible British invasion over Oregon.

But Mexico insisted that the Nueces River, hundreds of miles inland and more vulnerable, was the true boundary of Texas. Polk saw war as his only recourse. Besides, he silently crowed, war would hide his true goal: Polk hungered for the Mexican state of California. It would complete Jackson's national vision. Like Jackson, Polk believed it was the will of God, expediently labeled "manifest destiny," that this country span from the Atlantic to the Pacific. Toward that end, anything could be justified. Polk might even compromise on Oregon just to hold Britain at bay.

He likened his smug moralism to that of the Crusaders, who also fought for something pre-ordained by God, acquisition of the Holy Land. Similarly, Polk was driven, some said obsessed, to complete Jackson's work. To do what to him must be done, Polk this night would choose which of the country's two most qualified generals might best provoke Mexico. Polk believed in his soul it would be a tidy war easily won. He only worried that Mexico would not find courage enough to fight.

"Help me choose wisely, sir," Polk concluded quietly, casting a sidelong glance at his two guests. They had not heard him, he was sure, as they hastily removed overcoats and warmed themselves at Jackson's old stove, perched in a sandbox in front of the bricked-up fireplace. The red glow from its glassed door bathed their faces in even more of a ruddy winter hue. Though both were in their sixties with silver gray hair, they could not be more different.

At six feet, five inches tall and three hundred pounds, Major General Winfield Scott towered above his squat rival, Brigadier General Zachary Taylor. Scott gloried even at this late hour in his dark-blue, full-dress uniform, glorious with gilt buttons, epaulettes, and sword belt, personifying his nickname, "Old Fuss and Feathers."

Taylor, fresh from army forts out west, looked plain, rumpled, and unkempt. With his field uniform still flecked with mud, craggy Taylor looked every bit his soldier nickname, "Old Rough and Ready." Though both were members of the opposition Whig Party and both from the South, neither was particularly political. But, Polk knew, victory could change that.

Possibly making a Whig general into a military hero was a chance he had to take. Whomever he chose must be counted on to do his duty in a politically blameless fashion; in a manner that would force Mexico to start this war and enflame national anger, to swamp party lines in a wave of righteous retribution. Of course, he would not reveal this was his true purpose tonight. He could handle political complications down the road. Right now, he needed secrecy.

"Gentlemen let me be plain," Polk opened. "What we say here tonight must remain within these walls and go no further." His hands fidgeted with a document as he watched the two sit and eye one another, intrigued. Taylor relaxed into a slack-jawed gaze, as if to say, "All right, fire when ready." Scott unleashed a suspicious stare, as if he doubted Polk had ever spoken "plain" anytime in his life.

"I must invoke your sense of honor," Polk appealed. "Give me your solemn word that nothing of what we discuss, not even the fact that we met, will be spoken of or written down, anywhere, ever."

"Mr. President, ain't that a bit like askin' us to buy a pig in a sack before takin' a peek?" Taylor ventured in his slow, Louisiana twang. Wide-eyed Scott cleared his throat, probably for dramatic effect, Polk thought.

"First, sir, you must at the least assure us that what you ask will not put the republic in danger," Scott intoned, an edge to his mild, Tidewater drawl.

"What I ask only will strengthen our country," Polk asserted, "and make it eminently more secure." Scott looked at Taylor, who shrugged a nod.

"This is most unusual, sir," Scott cautioned. "But on those assurances, we agree to absolute secrecy."

"Excellent, gentlemen," Polk sighed, feeling enormous relief. He handed the document to Scott. "Tomorrow morning I shall send this order to Secretary of War Marcy," Polk said, noting that Scott already was reading it. "It instructs him to dispatch with all haste four thousand soldiers to the mouth of the Rio Grande in Texas, opposite Matamoros, Mexico. This must be done to assert our territorial rights and to defend our border." He paused for effect. "One of you shall command." Polk eyed his quarry with veiled amusement as they exchanged looks of surprise, concern, and, predictably, competition. Scott passed the order to Taylor.

"It's about time, Mr. President," Taylor asserted curtly, giving the page a cursory glance and handing it back to Polk. "Greasers been runnin' roughshod over that damn borderland, playin' hell with the Republic of Texas for nine years. Well, Texas belongs to us now. Seems to me we got to shit or get out of th' damn outhouse." He spat tobacco juice into a gleaming brass spittoon.

Prepared for Taylor's legendary vulgar profanity, Polk merely offered a wan smile and an agreeable nod. Jackson had been as unschooled and uncouth as Taylor, Polk knew. Military victories had propelled him into high office.

He turned to Scott, who was glaring in stern disapproval at his subordinate. But Polk knew that Scott, every portly inch a Virginia gentleman, would not reprimand him in front of Polk. Taylor was simple; Scott, complicated.

"If we position troops down there, Mr. President," Scott warned, "Mexico has said it will view it as an act of war. Are you prepared for that eventuality?"

"General, should not the question truly be, are you prepared?" Polk evaded with a sly twinkle in his eye. "A novice such as I must rely on your fabled experience in these matters of the military." Polk knew that by feeding the massive ego of Scott, he would be throwing down a gauntlet at the feet of the scrappy Taylor.

Scott had won major victories in the War of 1812 and emerged top soldier. Then he almost singlehandedly re-invented the United States Army. Scott forged a small but highly trained professional force in the fires of frontier expansion. He populated his eight infantry regiments with officers schooled at the fledgling Military Academy at West Point. And he literally wrote the book by which they lived, the drill manual known as "Scott's Infantry Tactics," though much had been adapted from British manuals.

Polk did find it worrisome that Scott openly had criticized President Jackson for his Seminole Indian War of 1835. He had labeled it unjust and unwarranted. But in the end, he did his duty. And Polk knew he would do the same in the current crisis. He was counting on it.

"We already stand stretched in a thin line, Mr. President," Scott observed, "but we will do what we must, as always. To move in a timely manner, though, the regular troops must come from our frontier garrisons, up and down the Mississippi River." He looked at Taylor pointedly. "We will draw your own 6th Infantry from Fort Jessup, Louisiana; the rest, from Fort Snelling in Minnesota, Fort Mackinac in Michigan, and Forts Gibson and Scott in the Indian Territory." Polk could see that Scott exulted in having a fort named after him.

"There're no better soldiers anywhere, Mr. President," Taylor bragged. "My boys can whip every damn greaser that comes our way." He added almost whimsically, "That is, if fightin' actually breaks out." Taylor may suspect, Polk thought, but if he does, he did not seem to care. He may even be hoping for it.

"But will that leave our pioneer settlements out there defenseless?" Polk wondered.

He feared political backlash from Indian uprisings, always possible since Jackson forcibly re-settled the so-called Five Civilized Tribes out west from their eastern haunts. The Seminole War had been long and brutal.

"We would reinforce from our eastern garrisons," Scott affirmed. "Things could become prickly, though, if Britain chooses to fight over Oregon."

"Let 'em come!" Taylor blurted with what seemed to Polk lethal glee. "My boys'll give 'em the runnin' shits all th'way back to Bristol." Scott again tossed him a disapproving look. No matter; Polk thought Taylor held promise.

Cagey and unconventional, Taylor had won both his rank and the Seminole War during Jackson's term with a surprise attack through swamps at Lake Okeechobee in Florida. Since Polk considered Mexicans only slightly more civilized than the savage Seminoles, he felt Taylor might do. But more importantly to Polk, President Jackson admired Taylor, calling him the right man to fight the British over Canada, had war erupted in a previous border dispute.

"Well, it should not come to that," Polk soothed. "Britain has other little wars to contend with right now. Besides, Mexico will raise a mighty hue and cry but never fire a shot. They are all brag."

"With due respect, Mr. President," Scott cautioned, "Mexico has fifty thousand men under arms: we have barely eight thousand. That kind of superiority has been known to embolden even the timidest of soldiers." Polk knew that Scott did not trust him because of his penchant for secrecy. "Sir, do you want war?" he pressed.

"My plan is sound and simple: strengthen our border,

General Scott, and force Mexico to back down and concede our land. I do not want to start a war," Polk lied convincingly. "But be prepared, if Mexico starts one." Scott drilled into him with piercing eyes. Polk did not blink. He merely showed the slightest hint of a smile.

"Every general begins his battle with a sound plan, sir," Scott replied in a tone hinting at condescension. "But it all goes wrong once the first shot is fired."

"Damn right, sir," Taylor interjected. "That's why you got to be prepared for what you don't know might be comin' at you." Scott and Polk exchanged quizzical looks. Taylor made a hasty sign of the cross and rolled his eyes.

"Ah-h-h . . . General Taylor makes a curious point, sir," Scott explained. "I believe he means you must consider how Mexico's national religion may figure in any possible conflict." Polk was brought up straight: this was new.

"Half our army is immigrants, Mr. President," Taylor expounded. "And more than half of them are Irish Catholic. They may be damn Papists, talk in a helluva funny way, and drink too much, but by God they do love a good fight. They make our best soldiers despite how we've treated their kind, what with th' riots and all." Taylor again spat into the spittoon, making it ring this time.

Polk squirmed at mention of riots that erupted in the 1830s and could again anytime the economy took a downturn. Native born Americans felt threatened by Irish immigrants who would work hard and for less money.

And they were still arriving here by the thousands, fleeing starvation in their homeland due to the ongoing potato famine. Their shops here had been looted and Catholic churches burned. Even now, it was hard for anyone Irish to find decent work. Well, Polk thought, now more could join the army.

"I understand that Mexico is a Catholic country, gentlemen,"

Polk replied. "But I fail to see how that could affect our army. Catholics happily have slaughtered others and each other for centuries for whatever cause paid them. Our money is good. Why would they not do their duty for us?"

"Mr. President, that question cannot yet be answered," Scott observed. "I hope we never find out." He looked at Taylor, who again shrugged. "In any event, we must now recruit more of them and other immigrants, as well. Our regiments are undermanned. Training takes time. If war breaks out, as you observed, we must be prepared."

Scott seems superb at logistics, Polk thought. "Toward your point, General, I intend to ask Congress to authorize funding for four more regular infantry regiments," he said. "And I will ask the states to raise and equip volunteer regiments for federal service, if necessary."

"Volunteers?" Taylor sneered, sounding as if Polk had given a name to a new disease. "You can't count on them for anythin' other than runnin', Mr. President," he growled, "and runnin' don't win fights."

"That is, if fighting even occurs. Correct, Mr. President?" Scott probed.

Polk perceived that Scott was growing more suspicious. His conscience might prove troublesome. Taylor, however, seemed not to care one way or the other, so long as he saw action. Taylor knew that combat offered his only sure path to promotion, perhaps to the rank of major general like Scott. If the Mexicans pushed, Taylor would shove back harder. And Scott could be counted on to supply him with enough troops and materiel to get the job done.

Polk had made his decision.

CHAPTER 1
MACKINAC, MICHIGAN
FEBRUARY 1, 1846

Black and blue clouds rolled like bruised fists across the choppy, gray lake. Looking battered but still ready for a good brawl, they took aim straight for town with what seemed to him an arrogant swagger. They were much like himself, Riley thought— seasoned warriors, drifting from one fight to the next. They called no place home and were faithful to nothing but the code of conflict that carried them around the world. Now, that same code would spirit him home to Ireland, though his purpose remained murky. He could not see beyond his need to fill an indefinable, aching void. The longing nagged at him like some dutiful woman too shrill to be ignored. Maybe she had been forgotten inside his mental barracks footlocker too long, like so many other inconvenient memories tossed there, safely hidden.

With the cynical eye of a soldier who had seen too much, Riley surveyed Mackinac's familiar, odorous waterfront bowels from the seat of a rolling farm wagon. Clad now not in a uniform but faded laborer's clothes and an immigrant cap, he nevertheless felt envy as a column of United States infantry swung past to brass band music: "Green Grows the Laurel," a popular drinking song in three-quarter time.

"Only Yanks would swing off to 'war' to a waltz," Riley scoffed, his light brogue adding lilt to the sarcasm. Years among the Brits had dulled his Irish edge, he knew, but there was still no mistaking his roots. He took a swig from his pewter flask, engraved with an Irish harp and the Gaelic motto, "Erin Go

Bragh." He offered it to Judge O'Malley, driving in the seat beside him.

"Sure and your puny sense of humor is surpassed only by your profoundly poor judgment," O'Malley said in his usual deadpan style. His heavy brogue added weight to what he intended as a warning. Graying O'Malley, straining to look elegant in a battered top hat and threadbare tailcoat, was used to getting his way: he handled legal affairs for Mackinac's downtrodden Irish minority.

Betraying his bittersweet love for soldiering, Riley merely laughed, continuing to tap his toe instinctively as the troops marched down to the docks amid cheers. "Don't they look sharp," he said, thinking them oddly pretty in clean, sky-blue uniforms piped in white, hair cropped close, young faces smooth and shaven. "Give it time," he predicted. The military brass band, brave in bright-red jackets, blared from the post office porch.

"Don't like that color for musicians, though," Riley opined. "Too damn cheerful. That's one thing the Brits got right," he added. "Their uniforms are more somber, closer to brick."

"Closer to blood," O'Malley observed, "as you know better than most."

"Got to admit," Riley forged on, ignoring O'Malley's inference, "I won't be missing much about this place." He saw the rough frontier village as rife with Yank hypocrisy. Merchants, saloon keepers, sailors, and whores had brightened the darkening streets in boldly colored capes or checked overcoats, bracing for whatever punches the gathering storm might throw. "Tain't no mere weather gonna deny them waving farewell to their reason for existence," he said, a judgment he held for all garrison towns.

"Just like you," O'Malley replied in caustic reprimand, "they got what they think good reason for taking their own 'Queen's shilling.' "

"Leastwise their President Polk is boosting business for them," Riley countered with a grin, "and for me!" O'Malley shook his head in dismay.

Mackinac clung precariously to the shore of feisty Lake Huron in the shadow of old Fort Mackinac, looming above on a bluff. With rotgut liquor, journeyman food, delightfully obliging women, and a sturdy wharf, the town gleaned its livelihood from the garrison. Now the lads were departing by ship for what amounted to merely a card game of brag in Riley's mind. But the town, like this entire cocky nation, looked on it more as a crusade sanctioned by God Himself. They might be partly right, he smiled. In his own loose fashion, he had been praying for such an opportunity to get out, go home, and start over.

Riley dismissed O'Malley's dark banter and returned his gaze to the crowded streets, teeming with what he saw as the broken promise of young America. Here and there he spotted a rouged harlot who would acknowledge him with a knowing smile. He would doff his cap with a wink, drawing a giggle. These girls were the only thing American that had lived up to Riley's expectations. To him, America had proven she was nothing more than a tantalizing tease that lured him here but then failed to deliver. All he ever found as a civilian was menial work more suited to a slave with pay barely above subsistence.

"Sure and this ain't nothing but nativism," Riley avowed, "running amok in the streets." He felt ensnared by what he saw as a raging patriotic fever, sure to prove deadly. He spied a Protestant preacher, severe in black frock coat and slouch hat, standing near the post office. He aroused martial spirit in his gathered faithful with Bible in one hand and upraised sword in the other. As he recounted "the blessings of expanding freedom into heathen lands," Riley noted a group of Potawatami Indians in white man hand-me-downs watching the troops in stoic silence. Riley had battled savages like them around the world in Queen Victoria's endless little wars. He doubted if any felt "blessed" after losing.

As the preacher exulted in "securing the blessings of freedom for our own citizens," Riley studied a slave catcher, dressed peculiarly Southern in white straw hat and dingy linen coat. He was taking leave of a constable on horseback and holding a rope to a manacled, sullen black runaway in tow atop a mule. No doubt, down South one would collect a reward and the other again become "property." For an instant, Riley's eyes locked with those of the dusky runaway.

Many times, Riley had seen those same eyes, brown pools of bottomless seething anger. In India, he saw them in sooty black faces down the barrel of his musket, just before pulling the trigger. In China, they were set in wispy yellow faces that fell before thrusts of his bayonet. And he sighted them in biscuit-brown faces down cannon tubes in Afghanistan, an instant before a fiery blast sent them to whatever heaven the heathens sought. He still saw them in restless dreams, frozen in grotesque, glassy, and opaque stares from faces contorted in death across smoky fields. Battles never truly end, he admitted.

Somehow this felt different. Here was a runaway simply wanting to escape his personal hell and start over, much like Riley. In a rare moment of insight, Riley thought he might have much in common with this hapless black. Perhaps, in the end, it all had less to do with color of skin and more with yearning of soul. He comforted himself with his code that a professional soldier should not agonize over such issues. The preacher ended by condemning "the dead hand of the Catholic Church," drawing a bigoted roar from the crowd.

"There's the boardinghouse just ahead," Riley announced. He bristled at sight of the sign beside its glass door: Rooms—No

Irish Need Apply. He felt as black as the runaway.

O'Malley reined up the wagon in front. Riley hopped down and yanked a carpetbag from the wagon bed. After setting the brake, O'Malley slid down beside him. Frail and shriveled, O'Malley looked tiny beside Riley. A robust, weathered twenty-eight, Riley stood a head taller at more than six feet with a solid frame of tested muscle. Riley knew he was perceived as intimidating. He used it.

"Thanks for the lift but I'll walk the rest of the way. These poor old dogs ain't yet forgot the drill," Riley chirped. He playfully marched in place to the music like some overgrown ragamuffin, about to tag along with the children parading behind the departing infantry.

"Faith only a lunatic believes his own blarney," O'Malley marveled.

"Been searching for the right path back home," said Riley, nodding at the troops. "And here it up and slugs me in the face."

"The last time I checked, County Galway was still in Ireland, not Mexico," cracked O'Malley.

"And sure it's 'Texas,' not 'Mexico,' " Riley said. O'Malley rolled his eyes. Riley nodded at the door. "Your new 'immigrant wards,' your honor."

A teenage, raven-haired Irish colleen and her red-headed younger brother were being pushed to the wagon by an unkempt manager, one cheek bulging and the cuffs of his plaid trousers spattered with tobacco juice. Dark tresses flowed down the sides of her distressed face and cascaded wildly over her shoulders, avoiding her every effort to tuck them up quickly beneath a green bonnet. As her glowering brother loaded baggage, Riley sauntered around the front. He stood near the manager and whistled along with the jaunty melody of the band, watching the parade. Shrugging off Riley, the manager confronted O'Malley.

"Judge, my thanks for taking in these two rascals," the manager said after spitting. He grinned, baring tobacco-stained teeth. "I can't have Popers under my roof. No decent folk'll stay here otherwise."

The girl suddenly lost her composure. A tear traced down her alabaster cheek, and she choked back a sob. O'Malley and Riley traded dark looks as O'Malley offered her a handkerchief.

"Never let the bastards see you cry, dear," O'Malley said, smiling, "or worse, the native born." The landlord glared.

"There are ports in Texas with ships," Riley observed, picking up his earlier theme. He yanked his flask, unscrewing the cap. "On the way, I'll earn ship's passage doing what I do best." Riley downed a healthy swig.

"Now, would that be drinking or fighting," O'Malley asked playfully, "which in two years' working for me is all I've known you to do?"

Riley had carefully re-screwed the cap and replaced the flask in his pocket. He saw that the brother and sister had climbed safely into the wagon. Without warning, he unleashed a brutal left uppercut to the landlord's jaw, lifting him off his feet, then instantly slamming him back into the boardinghouse wall with a powerful right cross. Out cold, the manager crumpled into a drooling heap beneath the No Irish sign.

"That'd be soldiering," Riley hissed. He stepped to the astonished but grateful colleen with a bow, kissed her gloved hand, and held onto it, as if finding something precious he had lost long ago after hiding it in his "footlocker."

"Thank you, kind sir," she said, sobbing in a whisper of a brogue. "America is not at all what I had expected."

" 'Tis everything you could ever want, darlin', if you're a native born bastard," said Riley, a gleam in his piercing blue eyes.

She smiled weakly and squirmed a little, not uncomfortable

with the seat but rather the language. A hint of rose flushed her cheeks.

"Our money is almost gone," she whimpered, fighting back more tears. "What will our pa say should he learn we ended up on the streets?"

"Judge O'Malley here helps Irish like us who wash ashore only to find their dreams gone wayward," he said. Riley tenderly gave her hand to O'Malley, as close to a father as he had known. She and her brother would be in kind hands.

"Yours is the dream of a madman!" O'Malley pressed, his only recognition of the assault being a discreet nod of approval. He pulled Riley out of earshot of the siblings. "I'm blessed if there won't be war. You'll be more trapped than you think you are now!"

"Been the fate of the regular soldier since he first stepped off on the left foot. Nobody knows what to do with him once the fighting stops, least of all his own self," Riley admitted uncomfortably, coming closer to truth than he would like. He gestured at the marching troops and enthusiastic crowd, cheering them on as the music played. "He's pissed on in peace but worshipped in war."

"And executed if he deserts," O'Malley whispered.

"Once you taste adultery, judge, can you ever stop?!" Riley teased. "Besides, they can kill you for desertion only when the politicos declare it a 'war' good and proper. This'll be nothing but a flexing of muscle." He picked up his carpetbag and pointed to a banner spanning the street that read, "Manifest Destiny! Ho! For Mexico!"

"If it's this nation's self-declared 'destiny' to steal its neighbor's land, and such larceny pays my way back home, I'm taking it," he declared, "just like I took the Queen's shilling."

"Another army of occupation," growled O'Malley. "At least that British coin fed your family on your home soil, that is until they packed you off to steal somebody else's."

"So nothing's changed, has it?!" Riley quipped.

"It all changed when you left the lobsterbacks in Canada just for to find America's 'pot of gold,' " O'Malley snapped. "There's a price to be paid for breaking any vow, marital or military. I remember pulling you out of that rowboat, and a sorry wet rag of a soldier you were."

"And I found no gold, did I? Because it's locked safe inside the damn bank marked 'No Irish Need Apply.' So now I'm joining a different army just to get myself back home!" Riley affirmed. "In my mind, it's simple justice."

" 'Simple' as in 'simple minded!' Faith it is unholy!" O'Malley said.

"As if the bloody British were saints?!" Riley could only smile at how the old man could be so naive. Soldiering to Riley had become nothing but a business. Expert services went to the highest bidder, and "Queen Vickie" paid top dollar. Step over the rotting corpses and march on. "The blessed, nagging challenge of my entire existence has been how best to pay for it," Riley confessed in a patronizing tone. "Soldiering for the sake of the shilling is more honest than any cause trumped up by a damn politico." He pointed at the banners proclaiming the quest, to secure disputed borderland in the new state of Texas. "I keep it pure, just 'holy' enough for me, O'Malley. I'm in it for the money, not the morality."

"Mexico claims that land as its own," argued O'Malley. "They'll fight if our troops go traipsing across it. And didn't we do the same back home, when the Brits come in so high and mighty?"

"Ancient history," said Riley. "Now half the British army's Irish, just like this one, except for the arrogant bastard officers, of course."

"Half less one in both cases, soon enough," O'Malley said

26

quietly. "And that one's marching off to war, he is!"

"These lads'll march home without a shot fired, after this lad marches home in a different direction," Riley insisted. He pulled a folded letter from his carpetbag and handed it to O'Malley. "Please send this to my mum and sis back home, along with my last wages," he requested. He started hiking up the hill.

"The 'dream' you're chasing is a nightmare, John Riley!" O'Malley yelled, flailing his arms in a fruitless appeal.

"Then let me wake up in uniform with my former rank . . . or die!" Riley yelled, laughing.

He strode up the high bluff looming above the street. On top sat the bastion of Fort Mackinac, built by the British during the War of 1812 but American ever since. Riley smiled at the delicious irony. He watched its huge garrison flag being lowered for sunset to the haunting bugle tune "To the Color," hypnotic in its catchy, joyous melody. He started to whistle along. He turned to see O'Malley disappear slowly from his view. He did not realize that with each step he took uphill, the gathering gloomy fog from the incoming storm was wrapping itself around Riley like a shroud.

Fort Mackinac was a sturdy rectangle of stone buildings and log blockhouses, palisades little improved since its days as a British outpost. When Riley crossed the bustling parade ground minutes later, he immersed himself in the immigrant stew that comprised the regular U.S. Army. As troops loaded wagons, hitched horses to artillery limbers with cannons and drilled, he heard thick accents: German, Scots, British, Polish, Swedish, and, most prevalent, Irish. The soldiers looked "garrison perfect" in grooming and uniform as they prepared to leave. Riley cast his discerning eye at one squad drilling just outside the headquarters offices. He strode past and bounded onto the shaded porch.

Leaning against a post, he fortified himself with a discreet swig. He studied the company sergeant. The top soldier could be the same age as Riley but looked ill. His skin had the dull gray pallor of a lead musket ball. Though he bawled crisp commands from the manual of arms with authority, his voice often cracked. And he was racked by a deep, wheezing cough. Taking note, Riley stepped into the open doorway of an office marked "Capt. Moses Merrill, Co. K."

In his mid-thirties, Merrill stood lean and fit in a tight-fitting, dark-blue military frock, the white stripe up his sky-blue trousers an unmistakable totem of power. He looked unusually affable for an officer, perhaps due to the bushy sideburns stretching to the bottom of his jaw. He worked at a map on the rear wall, back to the door. Unseen, Riley paused to survey the office.

A military flintlock musket hung on a side wall with gleaming bayonet affixed to the muzzle; beneath it was a framed diploma from the United States Military Academy at West Point. A half-packed campaign chest and trunk cluttered the floor. Riley focused on the map that held Merrill's attention.

It showed the small "United States of 1844" compared to the huge expanse of "Mexico" west of the Mississippi River. "Texas" had been outlined in red paint with "Statehood 1845" scrawled across it. Merrill had marked the borderland "Disputed" and shaded it with crossed lines. The wide band lay between the Nueces and Rio Grande and stretched all the way north to the Arkansas River. Merrill was plotting a course down the Mississippi to New Orleans and along the Gulf Coast to a red *X* marked "Port Isabel." A short distance inland was a circle marked "Ft. Texas—Camp," just across the Rio Grande from "Matamoros," Mexico. Riley rapped on the door frame.

"Top of the evening, Captain, from your next top soldier," Riley announced cheerfully. Merrill turned, judging him just another civilian laborer.

"If you want work, see my sergeant. He's just outside, sir," Merrill replied in a civil tone, but wary. Riley stepped closer and spoke in a whisper.

"Not for long I'm sorry to say, sir," he said reverently. "He's got himself the wet cough. You'll soon be needing a steady hand to make the lads 'stand to,' should the greasers give you a go down in Texas." Riley nodded at the map.

"That may be," Merrill said, mildly amused. He suspected something at Riley's use of "stand to," a British command. "But our Colonel McIntosh is possessed of a peculiar notion. I can only promote persons in U.S. uniform."

"A slight technicality, sir," Riley said, smiling and leaning on the desk, "what two professionals such as us can easily overcome."

Merrill let a knowing smile escape his control. His bushy sideburns rippled, giving him the look of a mirthful chipmunk. He desperately needed new recruits. He was being pressured by higher command.

"You have the air of an old soldier, sir," Merrill said. "So you must know that I cannot knowingly enlist a deserter, even one of exceptional merit."

Riley hid a moment of panic behind his steady gaze, holding Merrill transfixed. He did not think himself "old" in a time when reaching sixty was considered blessed; at best, Riley was "middle aged." The drill cadence being called by the sergeant outside sparked an idea. Riley grabbed the musket on the wall with its attached bayonet. Now Merrill hid his own moment of panic.

"I can understand your fear, sir," said Riley. He heard the sergeant outside bawl the next command, "Carry arms!" Riley wielded the musket like an expert. He aroused Merrill's curiosity. "When a man boasts on soldiering, it begs the question, 'If you loved it, why'd you leave it?!' " Riley executed the next command, "Present arms!"

Merrill was intrigued. He came out from behind his desk to inspect Riley. He looked him up and down, walking around him as Riley continued to execute the demanding maneuvers of "Scott's Drill," the U.S. Army standard. Riley knew it was based upon the British manual with which he was on intimate terms.

"Toes turned out at 45 degrees," Merrill observed. "Little finger against the feather spring," he added, scrutinizing Riley's left hand. Riley performed the next command, "Shoulder arms!" and slapped the stock of his musket with his palm. "Smartly done, sir!" Merrill exclaimed. "And can you read?"

"And write, sir, as any sergeant must," Riley said.

"A literate civilian who knows the drill perfectly," Merrill mused, "and who is willing to swear he is not a deserter from any army?" He took an enlistment form from his desktop and slid it across toward Riley.

"Long wanted to soldier, sir," Riley said with a gleam in his eye, "but wondered if I was too dull to catch onto the craft." The final command, "Charge bayonet!" was shouted outside. Riley unleashed a guttural yell and dropped the musket into the correct lethal stance waist high, leveling the bayonet at Merrill's chest. Merrill recognized the steely look of a professional soldier in Riley's eyes.

"I get the point, sir," Merrill cracked with a smile, unflinching. Riley nodded, put the musket down and filled out the form: "Height," six feet, two inches; "Hair," brown; "Eyes," blue; "Age," 28. As he signed the paper, Riley felt a wave of relief wash away the constant aching tightness in his neck.

"Report to our quartermaster for your uniform," Merrill said. "My company embarks at dawn tomorrow on the last ship for Texas, or is it Mexico? Call it what you will," he said, eyeing the map. "It's all the land of Democratic humbuggery." Riley stood to attention and saluted with his palm facing outward, returned by Merrill. "Convenient, isn't it, that the British salute is identical to ours?" he added suggestively.

Merrill's look let Riley know that he had guessed his secret. But somehow, Riley felt he could trust this ramrod straight American, a unique feeling for him toward any officer.

"You might say, sir," said Riley, clearing his throat, "that of the army of her majesty the Queen, the private has become a 'distant admirer.' " Riley knew that enlisted men must reference themselves to officers in the third person. He turned on his heels and marched toward the door.

"Private John Riley!" Merrill snapped, looking at the enlistment form. Riley stopped and executed an about face. Merrill stared at him hard. "Do not 'distance' yourself from this army."

"The private don't know enough to start over at nothing else, sir," Riley said soothingly, "and the Good Lord knows he's tried. He can honestly promise you that he'll be retiring with stripes, sir—or not at all." Riley expected that the extra pay for three stripes would amount quickly to sea passage home from some Texas port or Matamoros. Until he could afford to "go missing," he believed, all he had to do was give it time.

"I can promise you such a promotion if your skills merit it, Riley. Bloodline or birthright hold no water here, unlike some armies with which we apparently are both familiar," Merrill said. He stared at his new ward with mixed emotions. Riley looked to be a prime recruit, a seasoned veteran who could steady the ranks of Merrill's "fresh fish" if they came under fire. He also knew now that Riley had deserted the British, probably from Canada. Perhaps this was a bargain cut with the Devil, he thought, but needs must. "Just give it time, Private," Merrill warned.

"That's exactly what the private plans to do, sir," piped Riley. He again saluted, holding it expectantly. Merrill stared at him a long, pregnant moment and finally returned the honor. Riley wheeled smartly and strode out the door.

CHAPTER 2
FORT TEXAS
APRIL 12, 1846

Months later, Riley festered as a mere private. He felt agonizingly alone though encamped with four thousand fellow U.S. Army regulars in a muggy, smoky city of steaming hot canvas tents. They were pitched in lines by company for each regiment. The neat, perfectly aligned streets stretched more than a mile along the marshy banks of the lazy, muddy-brown Rio Grande. There was nothing "grand" about this river, Riley observed, other than how it grandly increased his consuming desire to leave. He felt like a boil ready to burst.

The adobe houses and church steeples of Matamoros seemed to taunt him from atop a high bluff, tantalizingly close on the other side of the river. The town overlooked the U.S. camp and its star-shaped, earthen fort that bristled with cannon. Riley's commander, newly promoted Major General Zachary Taylor, had dubbed the earthwork "Fort Texas," to announce U.S. authority over this stretch of land claimed by Mexico. Riley suspected that Taylor soon would have to assert that authority with more than a name. He felt a gnawing urgency to "go missing" before then. To do that and pay for ship's passage out of Matamoros, he desperately needed sergeant stripes with their extra pay.

No longer romantic, crisp, or clean, many of Taylor's soldiers now wore longer, matted hair and scruffy beards. Sweat-stained uniforms were faded and mud spattered. Horse dung and garbage littered the sprawling camp and floated in water-filled wagon ruts. Dung beetles thrived. Clouds of mosquitoes filled the heavy air, which smelled rancid from open latrines called "sinks."

Riley, however, maintained a well-brushed uniform and clean shaven face, per regulations and the example set by officers and sergeants. Though Riley had no stripes yet, he now stood in front of his company drilling them as if he did. And he knew that he must look the part. Riley had at last convinced Captain Merrill to display his martial prowess for their regimental commander. It was a hot, muggy Sunday, normally a soldier's day off. The hundred men stood two ranks deep and performed the drill with grudging precision. Many looked dazed and exhausted. Some wobbled on their feet with mild heat stroke.

Off to one side, Merrill watched in the shadow of Colonel McIntosh, astride his horse. On McIntosh's other side lurked a smug corporal whose appearance was slovenly compared to his own, Riley thought. As Riley shouted his last command, "In place, rest!," he saw McIntosh turn the page of a well-worn edition of "Scott's Infantry Tactics." McIntosh was forty-eight, with gray increasingly evident in his long sideburns and auburn hair. A few extra pounds pushed at the silver buttons of his dark-blue officer's frock. His drill demonstration finished, Riley strode over to face the officers. He executed a crisp "Present arms!"

"Well done, Private Riley," said McIntosh, saluting. "You have offered a truly professional display of the drillmaster's art." He tapped his book.

"Thank you kindly, sir," Riley said, shifting smartly to "Carry arms." "But 'tis the lads who deserve praise this hot day." McIntosh remained stoic.

"Duty for its own sake should be reward enough, Private," McIntosh replied, "unless, of course, you belong to a lower class."

Riley bridled at the familiar prejudice. The man could be British, he felt. He noticed that Captain Merrill looked embarrassed by McIntosh's slight.

The colonel stood in the stirrups and rose in his saddle. "Men of Company K, 5th Regiment!" McIntosh bellowed. "General Taylor will tolerate no further desertions to our barbarous yellowskin enemy across the river."

The ominous note in those ringing words struck young Private Henry Lamb, in the second rank. Fair, blond, and only nineteen, he skewed his face sideways to whisper earnestly to the man next to him.

"Parker, are the greasers now the 'enemy'?" Lamb asked in a thick Swedish accent. "Does that mean we are at war?"

"Only with our officers," the man whispered back in an Irish brogue. Private Richard Parker, red headed and the same age, nudged Lamb roughly. "Now hush afore that one fires a volley." Parker nodded at McIntosh.

"Yesterday, a Frenchman, Private Carl Gross of the 7th Regiment, tried to swim the river," McIntosh continued. "Provost guards shot and killed him." A murmur rippled through the ranks.

"At least he got out of this heat," whispered Lamb.

Parker frowned and nudged him again. He saw that McIntosh had become aware of the whispering in ranks, strictly forbidden.

"Per emergency general orders, all future deserters shall be shot!" McIntosh boomed. He glared directly at Lamb and Parker.

Riley stood at rigid attention, but his brow furrowed at this new wrinkle in his plan. Captured deserters were never shot except in times of war. Then he noticed Captain Merrill staring right at him. Riley quickly averted his eyes.

"Now, since it is the Sabbath," McIntosh concluded, "I am

granting you free time until evening retreat."

"For seven dollars a month, a man could consider all his time free," the irrepressible Lamb whispered.

Parker could not suppress a smile at this but managed to smother it when McIntosh fired a withering look. The colonel leaned down to Merrill and nodded sharply in their direction. Merrill sighed in resignation but nodded to agree. Both Lamb and Parker saw. Lamb turned white in wide-eyed fear.

"Dismiss the men, Captain," McIntosh said.

Merrill stepped to the front and drew his sword, tucking it up against his right shoulder. "Company!" he commanded solidly. The men snapped to attention as one. "Stack . . . arms!" Forming musket cones of four interlocked by bayonets, the men complied. Merrill ordered, "For the good of the service . . ."

"For the good of the service . . . ," they echoed in laconic reply.

"Break ranks!" Merrill snapped.

"Huzzah!" they shouted in unison with more relief than energy, most quickly removing their heavy cartridge boxes and white leather belts. They scattered at a walk in different directions. Many drifted down toward the nearby banks of the river, where a small crowd of other off duty troops milled about.

Merrill returned to McIntosh and exchanged a quick glance with Riley, waiting there beside the disheveled corporal. Merrill thought Riley fairly beamed with proud, expectant hope, except for that fleeting, worried wrinkle on his brow.

"At times, the merit of a good soldier such as Private Riley must supersede practice," Merrill suggested with respect. "I trust that now you appreciate my unorthodox recommendation for this display. But he has proven his worth."

"Considering your sergeant's recent death, what I appreciate is your immediate need," said McIntosh. He tossed Riley a condescending glance. "Private Riley does know the drill and commands respect," he said, "but with impending hostilities, we have other considerations. I feel more comfortable in giving one more stripe to a man born of this country, rather than three stripes to a man so newly arrived." McIntosh leaned down and handed the drill manual to the slovenly corporal, who saluted. He eyed Riley with a smirk.

Riley glowered, barely controlling his rage. Burning bile surged in his throat from an immediate, hot sense of betrayal. It seemed as if he had never left the despised British caste system at all.

"Thank you, sir!" Riley said to McIntosh as he solidly tucked his musket upright against his right shoulder. "The private will do his best to measure up to your every expectation." McIntosh blanched, taken aback but unsure if any disrespect was intended. Riley managed to suppress a look of disgust.

Barely controlling his own frustration, Merrill understood. He watched Riley closely as he turned, added his musket to a stack, and headed toward the river with a menacing swagger. This could turn into trouble, Merrill thought. But what could he do?

Riley heard the melodious sounds of a gaily uniformed Mexican military band drifting across the languid water, serenading American soldiers lining the muddy banks. The Yanks played cards, smoked pipes, wrote letters, and read newspapers to a soft brass rendition of the U.S. favorite, "Home Sweet Home."

The tune was unfamiliar to the sweating Mexican musicians. No wonder, Riley thought: they wore dark-blue, wool cutaway tailcoats called "coatees" with red trim. And their tall, black leather shakos only added to their misery. Riley had always found the military shako to be an impractical affectation, looking like a stovepipe hat gone mad with military braid and brass. But, he admitted, it did make the short Mexicans appear taller, more intimidating in a fight.

The musical performance sounded plodding and off key, but no one seemed to mind. This appeared to be a Sunday ritual, and the Americans looked expectantly to the other side for something more.

Riley walked the shoreline as he drank from his flask. Many of the troops he passed recognized him and shouted greetings, but he seemed oblivious, lost in dark thoughts. Parker suddenly trotted up beside him after running the length of the beach.

"Did you hear the news?!" Parker gasped breathlessly.

"What news?!" Riley snapped. "That I won't be seeing sixteen dollars a month as sergeant?!" His plan for returning to Ireland seemed to be hitting as many sour notes as the Mexican band, he thought. "This ain't no brothel. I'll not give them my body all night for the price of a quick poke."

"Henry Lamb's to be bucked and gagged!" Parker exclaimed, looking confused by Riley's curious response. Riley understood and felt a pang of guilt.

"And what could our Swiss angel do to deserve such hellish treatment?" Riley asked patiently, not overly concerned.

"Talkin' in ranks so's you'd think he was Irish, you would," said Parker.

"You keep missing their point, Parker," Riley said. " 'Tain't the talking in ranks nor the breaking of any damn rule. Soldiers break rules. It's what we're trained to do if you count 'thou shalt not kill,' " he quipped. Riley stared into Parker's eyes. " 'Tis them what are native born versus us what ain't."

"Faith we'd be a curious crew in a fight, though," Parker said. "An army of foreigners going to war in a foreign land to prove ourselves, so to speak, to native born Americans."

"Proving ourselves daft," Riley muttered. Parker looked hurt.

Riley relented, feeling he had just knocked himself off Parker's pedestal. "Nobody's going to war, Parker," he sighed wearily. He wondered how many times he would have to preach his gospel until taken on faith. Was he the only true believer?

"Then I'll never see the elephant," Parker whined, crestfallen.

"Once you taste battle, you'll dread seeing it again, lad," cautioned Riley, " 'til you find yourself somehow sadly missing that terrible thrill. Now, you'd best go find your lost Lamb," he added, "afore somebody skewers him for Sunday dinner!" Riley nodded at provost guards lurking atop the fort.

"I'll search downstream," Parker said. "He's probably hiding in the bushes so's not to miss those river girls!" Parker pointed toward the Matamoros shore with a lecherous yet somehow innocent grin. Riley nodded knowingly.

"You'd best stow your fixin's back in our tent first," Riley advised, "along with mine." He handed Parker his cartridge box, bayonet scabbard, and belting. "Won't be needing them no more."

Parker did not pick up on Riley's ominous tone. He merely nodded and strode away. Perhaps as tent mates, Riley admitted to himself, he had filled Parker's head with too many stories of his "glorious" military adventures, now all worthless, he thought. The Mexican band suddenly intruded on his brooding with a different tune, a romantic and wistful Spanish waltz called, "La Cachuca."

Riley recognized the addition of a fiddle playing along on the American shore. He followed the familiar sound around a large boulder on the bank and found a small gathering of infantry. The youngest, barely eighteen, was perched anxiously atop the boulder to keep an eye on the Mexican shore.

Playing at the base of the rock and hemmed in by the pressing crowd was a diminutive fiddler, Private Dennis Conahan. He was perhaps five feet tall. Beside him was Private Auguste

Morstadt, a towering, beefy German. Morstadt looked enraptured by the fiddle music. But he flinched at every sour note played by the Mexicans. Conahan recognized Riley as he nudged through the crowd.

"Make way over there!" Conahan blustered in his lilting brogue. "One of McIntosh's miserables seeks th'solace of fine music!"

"All less miserable we would be if greasers tuned instruments," said Morstadt in a thick accent. The group laughed except for Riley, who took a swig.

"You stalwarts of the 7th must know the bitter truth, Conahan," Riley said. " 'Tain't the greasers what are making this army miserable."

"Faith you know how to put a damper on a dyin'," moaned Conahan. "Carl Gross was a member of this company," he continued solemnly. "He was generous enough to get himself killed yesterday so his mates could forget their miseries at his wake today. And here you go and remind us all again."

Riley and Conahan wallowed in a bit of grim Celtic humor. One thing the Irish knew how best to handle was grief, it occurred to Riley. Perhaps it was because they were so accustomed to it. He marveled at how God mixed blessings with blessed curses.

"Here they come!" shouted the young lookout atop the rock. He pointed across the river excitedly. But no one looked alarmed, as if the Mexicans were attacking. Instead, every soldier stood and stared. Some removed their soft, dark-blue caps in almost religious reverence. They pushed to the water's edge.

"Up and at 'em, Morstadt!" Conahan shouted as he leaped onto the giant's back. Morstadt easily hefted Conahan up onto his shoulders, affording Conahan a look over the heads of the crowd. Riley stepped to the shore with them.

As the Mexican band played a syrupy American ballad entitled "Love Not," young, swarthy Mexican women filed down the bluff to the water with baskets of laundry. Two Mexican infantry guards in patched, dark-blue uniforms stopped a respectful distance away and sat down behind a veil of shrubs.

The women blithely disrobed. Full, light-tan breasts, taut upper bodies, and shapely thighs contrasted tantalizingly with sun bronzed faces, shoulders, and lower legs. They waded naked into the river to wash laundry and bathe, all the while very aware of the Yanks leering at them. Some tittered and laughed about it. Others flirted. A few mocked the Americans and flaunted themselves, beckoning at them with brazen sexuality to swim across.

"Greasers not fight fair," mumbled Morstadt, with a curious twenty-three-year-old sensitivity that belied his intimidating stature. The entire bank had fallen silent, as if the soldiers had stumbled into a church service.

"They look more than fair to these lonely eyes," admitted Riley. He recalled that the strumpets of distant Mackinac had more flesh on their bones, not that it mattered at the time. "Since this is all the 'fight' we're gonna get, I say Mexico wins!" he roared. But the group's raucous laugh was cut short.

"Deserter!" cried a sentry atop the fort as he pointed down river. Riley was shocked at the sight of Private Henry Lamb stripping off his sky-blue jacket and shedding his broghan shoes. He leaped into the river and started swimming for his life toward the other side.

"Stop, Lamb!" Riley bellowed, waving frantically from the bank. "You're a dead man!" He saw Parker running toward the spot.

"They've seen you sure!" yelled Parker. "Come back!" Lamb treaded water to turn and wave goodbye to his friend, then resumed swimming.

The parapet had grown crowded with soldiers. They joined those on the shore in waving and shouting. Some urged Lamb to keep going; most, to come back. It quickly became sport as soldiers exchanged bets in gold coin.

On the Mexican shore, the women laughed, teased, and urged him on in Spanish. More Mexican soldiers appeared on the banks and atop the bluff. They exchanged bets in silver coin as frantically as the Americans. The band played louder and struck up a discordant rendition of "Yankee Doodle."

Ten provost guards, distinguished by white armbands with black stars, formed a double rank atop the parapet. A grim sergeant looked at Lamb with regret as he reached the deepest part of the river, where the current slowed him down. The veteran knew it would be an easy shot at barely 50 yards.

"Ready! Aim!" the sergeant shouted. The men cocked and raised flintlocks to their shoulders. The sergeant took one last anxious look, to see if Lamb had turned back. He sighed reluctantly. "Fire!" he yelled. A solid volley crackled and spewed white smoke in a curling cloud out over the water.

Private Henry Lamb unleashed a surprised wail as he was riddled with .69 caliber musket balls. Misses churned the water around him. He sank from sight, and the swirling red stain of his blood vanished quickly in the current.

These Americans are too quick to kill their own, Riley thought angrily. He felt they made the bloody British look merciful.

The Mexican women screamed in horror. Thankfully, the out-of-tune band at last stopped playing. Suddenly ashamed of their nakedness, the women covered their breasts in embarrassment and scurried from the water. They snatched up their clothes and dressed as they clambered back up the bluff.

Stunned Americans milled about silently. Most began shuffling back to camp. Riley, Conahan, Morstadt, and the others traded bitter looks but said nothing. Words at times like these feel puny, Riley thought.

The gathering broke up as each soldier wandered off, consumed by his own shadowy anxieties. Parker stood alone at the spot where Lamb had leaped into the water. Tears traced down his cheeks as he stared helplessly at the relentless river. Could Lamb have made it had it been night? Should he himself try? Shocked by this shameful thought, Parker picked up Lamb's jacket and flung it angrily into the turbid, brown water. Still, he felt his loyalties shaken.

From a distance, Riley watched Parker knowingly, as if he could read the youngster's troubled mind. Suddenly, a U.S. fife and drum band atop the dirt rampart struck up the intricate, merry call to the midday meal, "Roast Beef." To Riley at this tragic moment it seemed insanely insensitive. But this was the army.

"Dinner?!" Riley asked incredulously. "Ain't we had our damn fill of salt pork and biscuit?!"

" 'Tis th'same at any cook's fire," said Conahan with a wry smile.

"Except the one you ain't yet been to," Riley quipped. A veteran at twenty-five and confidant of Riley's past, Conahan rolled his eyes knowingly. Riley changed the subject. "Dalton of the Second's corralled himself in 'Company Q,' again."

"Sure and he's feelin' crowded," Conahan sighed. "And hungry."

"I'll fetch him some Matamoros morsels," Riley replied. " 'Twill help us both stomach today's bad doings." He strode away heavily with his fists clenched. Conahan had seen that stride often, every time that Riley set out to pick a fight and clear his head.

Riley made his way through the bustling camp. He wondered how such orderly streets of tents could reek so of garbage. If this camp were British, he thought, flies would not be swarming everywhere. One thing the Brits knew well, he mused, was how to wage war cleanly. Here it seemed that scratching was the universal affliction as soldiers fought fleas and lice, even as they shopped.

Sunday was market day in Mexico, or Texas, or wherever the hell he was, Riley brooded. Native vendors squatted in the dirt with goods spread on blankets. Swarthy Mexican men touted souvenirs of hand carved wood burros and flutes.

More reticent women, wrapped in colorful rebosas, shyly offered woven shawls and scarves. Others cooked Mexican food over small charcoal fires. Farmers offered fresh vegetables and fruits.

As Riley navigated the maze, his simmering rage kept him blissfully ignorant of ominous signs. Batteries of the new horse artillery, in which every gunner rode for added speed, were rolling into camp. Mounted Dragoons charged "heads," melons atop poles, and slashed them with sabers to the squealing delight of admiring Mexican girls. Blue ordnance wagons heavily laden with ammunition rumbled into the livery park behind straining yokes of oxen. And on the fringes of the main camp, Riley saw a ragged column of arriving state volunteers, called up to bolster the numbers of Taylor's small army. Clad in jaunty, colorfully trimmed outfits mostly of gray, these undisciplined patriots were despised as amateurs by Riley and the regulars in sky blue. He paused to watch, joined soon by other regulars. They began shouting insults.

The rowdy, dusty infantry at first ignored the catcalls as they trudged into camp. They were being guided by mounted regulars of the 1st U.S. Dragoons, charged with controlling them. The Dragoons looked rakish with mustachios and dark-blue jackets trimmed in yellow. And by law they were all native born. Stern Colonel William Harney, forty-five, was their commander. He was red headed with the angular look of a martinet. Riley was reminded of British officers he had learned to despise.

"Give a cheer, lads!" Riley joined in, hoping to ease his rising bile with the usual remedy of a good fight. "Looks like the prisons are empty at last!" The regulars laughed and clapped.

Riley spotted a particularly gamy volunteer pick a louse from his beard and inspect it. "Is it a grayback or just another volunteer?!" Riley bellowed. More laughter erupted. Passing volunteers scowled.

Riley stepped to one side to buy fresh tortillas and beans from a Mexican woman and her husband, an old soldier. Wearing a tattered blue and red Mexican uniform ten years old from the Texas Revolution, he rolled tortillas. His wife tended the beans, simmering in shredded beef and savory spices. The soldado had no legs and sat on a blanket, his stumps protruding in front of his torso.

Riley and the old veteran stared at each other a long moment. Riley felt naked when the old man unleashed an enigmatic, knowing smile, as if he could read Riley's mind. Riley shook it off, chalking it up to his own growing sense of guilt and now doubt about his plan. He held up two fingers to the woman for his order. She handed him one taco. He took one bite and gestured at the surrounding Mexican vendors.

"Ain't it plain?" Riley said, overly loud so all could hear. "One taste of the food tells you whose land this is!" The regulars laughed. The woman smiled in compliant non-comprehension as she prepared his second taco. Riley continued to eat while watching the volunteer troops. They started singing the same waltz that Riley had heard back in Fort Mackinac:

Green grows the laurel, all covered with dew.
I'm lonely my darling, since parting with you.
But by our next meeting, I hope to prove true,

45

And change the green laurel for the red, white,
and blue.

As Riley took the taco, one of the Arkansas volunteers spied
the old Mexican in uniform. The scruffy private stopped and
stared, enraged.

"By God, I've walked a thousand miles t'kill greasers," he
drawled, "and there's one now!" He pulled a huge, gleaming
Bowie knife, leaped out of ranks, and slashed the helpless old
man's arm. The woman screamed.

"Hold!" Riley bellowed. But the heedless volunteer knocked
Riley's second taco into the dirt as he reared back, ready to slit
the Mexican's throat. Riley's huge fist stopped him solidly and
forced him to drop the knife by bending his arm behind his
back. He twisted it viciously and broke bone with a chilling
crunch. The volunteer yelped and fell moaning to the ground.

"And the disciplined regular bests the boastful volunteer!"
Riley fairly crowed, standing over him. Gathered regulars
cheered. Outraged Arkansas volunteers began to break ranks
and come at them. Pushing and shoving quickly gave way to fist
fights. A riot loomed. Harney and a squad of Dragoons arrived
at a dusty trot to restore peace. They pushed their horses into
the mob and used drawn sabers to bully the volunteers back
into ranks.

"Bind up the soldier's wounds!" Harney ordered his sergeant,
who dismounted and ran to the writhing volunteer. Harney
drew his saber, waded his horse through the crowd, and slapped
the kneeling sergeant on the butt with the broadside of his
blade. "I said the soldier!" he yelled. Harney's flaming glare
withered the sergeant, who gingerly moved to the quietly suffering old soldado. He tied a bandanna around the bleeding arm
as the woman watched in tears.

"Thank you kindly, Colonel Harney, sir," Riley said with a
salute. "There is no accounting for the rabble in ranks these

days." But at the sound of Riley's brogue, Harney's face hardened. He left Riley standing there, frozen in a salute per regulations until returned.

"Between Irish trash and disgraceful volunteers, we'll kill each other before we ever fight the damn greasers," Harney said to his amused aide. He returned Riley's salute offhandedly while turning his horse, an insult, and rode away smirking.

"Flaming arsehole," Riley cursed under his breath. "Should've known."

A trim but shapely Mexican girl discreetly watched Riley from the crowd as the woman gave him two new tacos in thanks, waving off Riley's offered coin.

He started making his way through camp again. The Mexican girl shadowed him. She wore her red rebosa draped like a hood over her long, raven hair and across her face, so that only her flashing black eyes showed. When the final unit of volunteers entered camp, a hush blanketed the Mexican crowd. Riley stopped to stare, and the Mexican girl sidled up to him. She pulled her rebosa more tightly around her. The sight of the Texas Mounted Volunteers, more commonly called Texas Rangers, gave her a chill.

Captain Jack Hays rode at the head of the column, flanked by U.S. and Texas flags. Wearing a brace of Sam Colt's new five-shot revolving pistols at his waist, he was leader by being the toughest in a tough bunch. They wore a flamboyant assortment of buckskins, tailcoats, and red flannel "battle shirts," crowned with broad-brim sombreros, caps, and even top hats.

Heavily armed, long haired, and bearded, these frontier fighters traded hard looks with sullen native Mexicans as they rode by silently except for the lyrical jingling of their large rowel spurs. Riley stared in fascinated, grudging admiration. He knew professionals when he saw them, almost like looking in a mirror, he thought with a smile.

"Los diablos Tejanos," the Mexican girl whispered, making a sign of the cross as the Rangers rode past.

Riley looked at her in curious, sublime non-comprehension. He was struck by the fire in her eyes. It flashed like the black flint in a musket hammer when it struck the steel lock. "I know you can't savvy a word, but as a rule volunteers be brag with no bite," he said to the girl. "In a fight, though, I'd wager on them quiet ones. They got sand."

"A man such as you should not have to endure insults," she purred, discreetly handing him a flyer. "There are those who will treat you with respect."

The flirtatious look in her eyes held the veiled promise of unspoken delights, it seemed to Riley, even as he stared aghast at her excellent English. She had dropped the rebosa from around her face.

He was stunned by her beauty: high cheekbones, a strong, delicate nose, and, best of all, a wide, sensual mouth with soft, inviting lips. But before words could come out of his gaping mouth, she slipped back into the surging crowd. Riley stared at the seductive sway of her full hips until she was gone. He was reminded of the gentle sway of a clock's rhythmic pendulum, marveling at how the right woman could make anything sexual. Even the color of her skin seemed inviting, like coffee with heavy cream.

Riley shrugged off the mysterious event and read the flyer. His eyes grew wide. "God is Irish after all," he muttered, believing he had been given a Divine solution to his dilemma. He cast his eyes heavenward. "Thank you kindly, Sir." He looked around nervously, stuffed the flyer inside his jacket, and resumed walking, but at a faster pace. He could hardly wait to tell Dalton.

Toward the back of camp were rows of open latrines, not much more than narrow, deep trenches. Plank boards perched over them like benches. A few soldiers sat bare ass on the boards as Riley strutted past in a hurry, grimacing at the stench. He waved off a swarm of flies. In the distance, he could hear rowdy singing as some prisoners dug more of these "sinks." Riley recognized the tune as an old English drinking song, "Derry Down," but with new "soldier words" to match their misery. And he recognized the lead singer's voice.

Riley found the prisoners securely shackled, each with a thirty-pound iron ball chained to one leg. He located Patrick Dalton, swinging a pick axe in shirtsleeves as he puffed his clay pipe. Dalton, beefy with solid muscles evident in his sweat-soaked shirt, was in his mid-forties. Since first meeting him, Riley had marveled at how fit he was for such an old soldier.

Riley grinned from behind a rope perimeter as Dalton led the singing:

> A poor soldier's tied up in the sun or the rain,
> With a gag in his mouth until he's tortured with
>   pain;
> Why I'm blessed if the eagle we wear on our flag,
> In its claws shouldn't carry a buck and a gag.

"How could such a grand baritone 'sink' so low, Patrick Dalton?" Riley chided as he clapped. Dalton shot him a glare that could fry bacon.

"Digging this sink ain't nearly so low as the shithouse adjutant what put me here," he growled in a thick brogue, clenching his billowing pipe.

"Brung you something to help you more quickly fill it up!" Riley laughed, holding up the tacos. Dalton eyed them hungrily, cursed under his breath, and resumed digging.

Riley strode toward the adjacent enclosed area identified with a whitewashed sign, Provost Compound. Someone had scrawled graffiti on the sign. It read "Company Q." The compound was little more than a barren plot of hard ground contained by rope strung between pecan trees, mesquite bushes, cactus, and blue army wagons. As he walked along the rope approaching the gate, Riley could see the inspiration for Dalton's impromptu "Soldier Song."

About a hundred prisoners, all regulars, languished in corporal punishment. Some sat with backs roped to wagon wheels, arms lashed up and behind them. Some were staked spread eagle in the blazing sun, gags in their mouths. Some sat gingerly astride tall, narrow, wooden horses with oversized wooden sabers resting on their shoulders. One stumbled along the perimeter with a knapsack full of rocks on his back. Two were tied to tree limbs by their thumbs with toes barely touching the ground.

And half a dozen sat baking "bucked and gagged," with wrists bound and slipped over drawn up knees, a musket jammed painfully behind the knees and over the arms. A cloth-wrapped bayonet was stuck as a gag in their mouths. Each prisoner wore a rough-cut board hung around his neck with his crime lettered on it, such as "Swearing," "Drunkenness," "Thief," and "Brawling."

A provost guard stood at the open entrance. He was an artilleryman under arms and looked like an infantryman in sky blue, except that his jacket was piped in yellow instead of white, like Riley's. But his trousers sported a red stripe for artillery. Riley tried to walk past by merely waving the tacos in his face with a cheerful smile, but the guard blocked him with his musket.

"Would you keep the succor of the angels from one of our own suffering lads," Riley said, "and on such a fine Sunday, too?"

"Sundays don't mean blazes to me," he said, scowling. He spit tobacco to one side. "No food for prisoners until after retreat. Them's the orders."

And yet another heathen, Riley surmised. He spied a potential ally inside the compound; fit and thin, an artillery corporal about Riley's age. He cursed in German at two other "red-leg infantry" until they meekly ladled water for two parched prisoners, lashed to wagon wheels. The corporal's bearing was martinet.

Sensing an opportunity, Riley immediately imitated by bracing himself. "Corporal of the guard!" he shouted, much to the consternation of the sentry. "Stand to!"

This British command grabbed the attention of the corporal, who marched briskly to the gate. He presented himself with a courtesy attention. "Corporal Henry Ockter," he said in a refined German accent, "Battery B, 4th Artillery." Ockter then added, almost apologetically, "Detailed as infantry to provost duty." He stared at the guard. "What is the trouble here?!"

"Him," the guard said, spitting tobacco juice. Ockter looked at Riley, who clicked his heels in a show of respect.

"Private John Riley, Company K, 5th Infantry," he said crisply, "and may I say it gladdens my heart to meet a fellow professional artilleryman." Ockter perked up. "You must chafe in an army what wastes good gunners like ourselves as mere infantry." Riley appealed to an age-old military rivalry.

"You are correct, sir, in both respects," said Ockter, pleasantly surprised. "I am late of his Prussian Majesty's Royal Heavy Artillery."

"And I am late of her British Majesty's Royal Artillery," Riley said, nodding as if he had guessed as much about Ockter.

Ockter looked impressed. He snapped to full attention and shifted smartly to, "In place, rest." "How may I accommodate you, Private Riley?" he asked.

"Permission to feed a friend, Corporal," Riley opined. "But Sergeant Dalton would only need one of these." Riley deftly offered one taco to Ockter as he held back the other, arching an eyebrow. Ockter took it. Dutchmen are quick to catch on, he thought, inwardly smiling at how American prejudice had transformed Germans from "Deutchland" into "Deutschmen" and, finally, "Dutchmen."

Minutes later, Dalton downed the taco hungrily. He had slipped his burning pipe into his cap at a spot where the dark-blue wool was shiny and singed from this well practiced maneuver. Riley sneaked a drink from his flask, eyed the area warily, and put his arm around Dalton's shoulders. He gently walked Dalton away from the others, who kept digging latrine trenches. Dalton looked suspicious, picked up his heavy iron ball and clanking chain, and shuffled along.

"The greaser priest'll be missing your sweet voice at evening Mass," suggested Riley. "And that of Private Lamb as well, permanently." Dalton frowned the question: Riley nodded sadly. "Shot to doll rags swimming th'river."

"Them are the wages of sin," Dalton said, exhaling deeply. "But I miss holy Mass through no fault of mine, and me keeping the slate clean six months among these half-bred Indians."

He suddenly dropped the ball with a clattering, dusty thud and pushed up his cap to scratch his head. A dung beetle fell to the ground. Dalton instantly stomped it. "I am surrounded by half -bred Indians and full-bred bugs," he opined. "Then today I face a crisis of conscience."

"Having a bit of a struggle myself, Patrick," Riley replied. He looked around nervously, wanting no one to overhear. "We need to have a little chat."

Dalton nodded with his mouth full, finishing the taco. "Our whorehouse pimp, Colonel Harney, orders me to stand guard tonight, he does," Dalton continued in a fury, "and him knowing I lead the choir at Mass. Bah! Horse soldiers!"

"Since the greasers have been kind enough to loan us one of

their priests," said Riley, "I say the least we can do is give him a good choir."

"I had to either kill the blaggard or curse him, and it was a terrible struggle to choose," Dalton said, nodding to agree.

"Just cursed the blaggard myself," Riley said, "but something tells me I did it more elegantly than some." He tapped Dalton on the chest.

Dalton pulled his pipe from his cap and scowled, noticing it had died. "For all to hear," Dalton said proudly, "I called him a damn white livered, tallow faced skunk I would see in hell first afore obeying his treacherous order."

Riley winced, then looked around again to make sure they were not being heard. " 'Tis a sad fact that under the cover of darkness, others might go missing at Mass," Riley whispered excitedly.

He pulled the flyer from his pocket and handed it to Dalton, who looked curious. But before he read it, Dalton picked up his jacket to rummage for his tobacco pouch. Riley paced impatiently. He noticed an imprint on the sleeve where Dalton's sergeant chevrons once were sewn. "I see you've lost your stripes," Riley ventured.

"In twelve years' hard service, I would be a poor soldier not to be busted at least once," Dalton admitted, stuffing tobacco into the bowl.

"And I have lost mine," Riley said suggestively.

"You cannot have lost what you never possessed," retorted Dalton, "at least, not in this army." His smile faded. "Remember, lad, officers are like whores: they will promise you anything but give less than you pay for."

"So I got me a new brilliant plan," Riley continued without missing a beat, nodding urgently at the flyer. Dalton opened it and started reading. "It looks to me that for the both of us it's time to change employers," Riley whispered.

"I have known the black plan held in your heart since first we shared a pint," Dalton said, his face twisting into a frown as he read. "And I might be tempted to desert, if only to shed this jewelry." Dalton rattled his leg iron for emphasis. "But I shall not join the other side," he said with finality, finished reading. He looked as if he had been insulted. Dalton fired up his pipe and exhaled a furious cloud. Riley glared at him toe to toe. "The taste of that word 'traitor' is too bitter even for this tainted mouth. And it is a sin best forgot by himself," Dalton said, jabbing Riley with his pipe.

Riley gulped a swig from his flask. He felt like O'Malley was again berating him. Was Dalton his new surrogate father?! He blustered in rebellion.

"For professionals like us there can be no 'side,' Patrick!" Riley avowed. "There is only the shilling and who offers the most." He looked around anxiously. "The greasers are offering fifty dollars cash, rank in their army, and three hundred-twenty acres of land!" Dalton merely stared at him stupidly, Riley thought. How could he be so blind?! "I'll go home a rich man," Riley purred. "And so could you."

"And if you sighted me down the barrel of your greaser musket, would you pull the trigger?!" Dalton asked, almost sweetly.

Riley stared stunned and speechless. It was the one possibility he had not considered. Damn! Riley thought, strangely at a momentary loss for words. "Ain't gonna be no damn war!" Riley managed, avoiding an answer. "For one blessed time, after the damn politicos settle and stash the booty we've bought 'em, you and I can have something to show for it!"

Dalton glared at him as much in pity as in anger, making Riley even more agitated. "No friend of mine asks me to so shame myself," Dalton said quietly.

"Then give me back my ticket home!" Riley demanded, ripping the flyer from Dalton's hands and stuffing it inside his jacket.

"If they catch you, 'twill be a ticket to hell," predicted Dalton. He crossed himself. "God Himself will not help you."

"The Lord helps those what help themselves," Riley retorted. "Stay shackled if you choose, but I'm helping myself to my own liberation." He turned and strode back toward camp. "If I can't get my stripes one way, I'll get'em another," he vowed.

"You will get more than you bargained for, boy-o!" Dalton shouted.

Grim faced as he puffed his pipe, Dalton sadly watched Riley leave. He could see the sun hanging low over the bluffs of Matamoros and bathing the U.S. camp in rich, golden light. The flag was being lowered as the bugles played "To the Color." Dalton thought it poetic in truly tragic Irish tradition.

Riley churned along the wide thoroughfare that separated the sea of small troop tents from Officers' Row, a line of large wall tents that stared down the company streets of the enlisted men. It was the supper hour.

As Riley walked, he saw on one side squads of soldiers crouched around their cooking fires eating the familiar salt pork and hard biscuits, softened by frying in the pork grease. On the other side, he saw officers seated comfortably at tables beneath large tent canopies. Black slaves in civilian attire served some of the tables; hired Mexican women, the remainder. On silver platters, they presented chicken, turkey, and wild boar to senior and junior officer staffs, seated on comfortable camp chairs. Their places were set with china dishes and silver candelabra that shimmered in the twilight.

At the tent complex serving as regimental headquarters, Riley found Captain Merrill seated at a small field desk. Near him, the dark-blue silk flag of the 5th U.S. Infantry gently wafted on a pole. Like all regular colors, it featured an eagle with outstretched wings, one talon grasping arrows for war; the other, laurel for victory, which was why Riley knew the regulars loved that song "Green Grows the Laurel." As officer of the day, Merrill was in charge.

Riley approached just as a tall, white-haired servant black as flint stepped to Merrill and poured coffee from a silver pot into Merrill's simple tin cup. A candle lantern burned on the desk as twilight darkened.

"Top of the evening, sir," said Riley, forcing a cheery tone with a salute. He knew this would be the trickiest part of his new brilliant plan.

"From my next top soldier?" replied Merrill ruefully.

Riley shrugged as if the lost promotion no longer mattered. He hoped his acting would prove skilful enough. He took courage from knowing it always had done so in the past. " 'Tis the eternal way of things, sir," Riley said philosophically. The slave produced an extra tin cup and poured Riley some coffee. "Seems somebody's always got to be on the bottom, so somebody else can perch on top."

Merrill saw the stoic slave take note of Riley's words. "What do you say to that, Sandy?" Merrill said to the slave, who looked surprised and a bit fearful. Slaves were seldom asked opinions about anything. If caught voicing one by a vengeful owner, they could be punished.

"It ain't my place t'pay no mind, sir, one way or t'other," Sandy said.

Riley looked at Merrill curiously. He felt an odd kinship with this capable officer who, like himself, dared to question the status quo.

Merrill pointed behind them at the long tent canopy beneath which Colonel McIntosh was hosting several senior officers for dinner. "Sandy is the sla—uh, 'servant' of Major Rains, a southern officer of the 7th Infantry," Merrill said, his clipped

56

New England twang rising more to the surface with his ire. He nodded toward a thin, affable officer with chin whiskers. "He's a fine officer," he added, staring at Rains a long moment, as if trying to understand something beyond his comprehension. "Somehow, Major Rains deems it more gracious to toss a bondaged cook into the mess pot instead of food," he said.

Merrill turned again to Sandy, who fidgeted. He kept casting a wary eye back toward his master at the table. "For once, Sandy, feel free enough to speak plainly," Merrill urged with a sympathetic smile.

"Like th'private say, it's th'way things is," Sandy ventured. "But I say, it's jest fer now." Sandy let a thin, patient smile escape. Riley stared in surprising respect as Sandy bowed and returned to the dinner. He recalled the look on the face of that captured runaway back in Mackinac. He had the same smoldering dark eyes.

"Our southern officers bring them along like so many pieces of extra baggage. And the rest of us must pretend not to notice," Merrill observed. "It is not gentlemanly to discuss their 'peculiar institution,' for now." He looked up at Riley. "Perhaps, at least, this gentleman and officer of the day can solve whatever problem you have, Private Riley." Merrill's tone was nevertheless wary.

"The private should like a pass, sir, to attend this evening's Mass down the river," Riley said with humility, managing an almost believable look of piety.

"Your religious zeal has previously escaped my notice, Riley," Merrill said, suppressing an urge to smile.

" 'Tain't that the private's mum didn't teach him proper, sir, but it seems he's never having the blessed time to practice his faith," Riley replied sheepishly, "unless he's desperately needing a miracle." This time, Merrill could not help but laugh. Riley unleashed his best sheepish grin.

"General Taylor insists that we grant all passes for Mass, as you well know," replied Merrill as he wrote the order. "He knows we would lose half the army otherwise. Tell me, what miracle do you pray for, Riley?" He looked up.

"For a change in good Colonel McIntosh's heart, sir," Riley lied with innocence. He snatched up the pass. Merrill looked unconvinced, and Riley could tell. He saluted, turned, and began to walk away at a measured pace. He ached to run, yearned to fly away quick as a puff of pipe smoke. But running would give him away. "Have faith, sir," Riley called out. "The private will be sewing on them sergeant stripes, sir, one way or t'other!"

Riley passed Sandy cooking at a field kitchen within earshot of Merrill. Sandy thought Riley looked nervous as he strode past. "I 'spects it'll be t'other," he said softly. "I knows a runaway nigger when I sees one."

Riley heard the barely audible whisper and felt a moment of panic, which must have showed on his face. Sandy merely put a finger of promised silence to his lips. Riley nodded thanks and kept walking. He soon approached the main entrance to the camp.

"Halt and be recognized!" bellowed a sergeant of the guard. Several sentries barred his path with muskets, bayonets fixed.

"I'll be attending Mass this fine evening, Sergeant," Riley said. He stepped up gingerly and presented his pass. "And I am behind my time."

The sergeant looked at the pass, eyed Riley, and nodded at the open road. It seemed to Riley that it had acquired an almost Divine glow in the dusk of a rising full moon; surely a sign, he thought. Riley blessed himself, strutted through the gate, and quickened his pace. Towering succulents and mesquite pressed him on either side. He opened his flask and felt smug. He had refilled it at one of the sutlers, licensed civilian purveyors of such off-duty "necessities." Now he took a long, satisfying swig: it tasted like impending freedom.

After high Mass two hours later, moonlight shimmered upon the black water of the Rio Grande in eerie likeness to that road out of camp. A small rowboat followed the course plotted by the moon across the river toward Matamoros. Two young Mexican altar boys worked the oars while an aging Franciscan priest in brown robes stood at the tiller. A pile of Catholic ritual accouterments lay at the priest's feet: vestments, candelabra, incense burners, communion utensils, and a staff crowned with a wood cross. Embossed with gold, it had an ornate carved image of a Hispanic crucified Christ.

The cross rested against a mound of altar cloths covered by an oilcloth tarp. When the boat thudded with a lurch sharply against the far shore, the cross slipped and smacked the top of the mound. The "mound" moaned. The altar boys burst into giggling. Frowning, the priest quickly ushered them out. He grabbed his chalice and the cross to follow.

Beside the boat, he paused to wave the cross above his head in a signal. A squad of lean Mexican soldiers trotted toward him down the bank. The priest pointed the cross at the tarp as he departed.

The soldiers looked sinister with sculpted, black mustaches and faces weathered like sun-bleached mahogany. Their aging, dark-blue coatees and trousers blended with the night but for garish, double-breasted green lapels. Though crossed with black equipment belts, the splash of green shined through in the moonglow. Most wore black shakos disfigured by hard frontier service; a few, dark-blue caps like the Americans but banded in green. They surrounded the boat and leveled their British Baker rifles, fixed sword bayonets gleaming.

Sergeant Enrique Mejia, twenty-eight, commanded silence with crisp hand signals. He ventured closer. His shako was battered and his mustache peppered with gray, but he had manicured both perfectly with professional pride. He leaned over the side of the boat and snapped the tarp away from the mound. Mejia frowned.

Riley was slumped over and looking pathetic. One hand held his head and the other his now empty flask. Embroidered altar cloths were half draped across his body. He stood slowly with arms raised. A few religious shrouds clung to him as he rose. Since the Mexican soldiers measured little more than five feet high, to them Riley appeared to grow to an overpowering size. They moved in closer and encircled Riley's swaggering bulk with rifles and glistening bayonets.

"May the saints protect you and sorrow neglect you," Riley pronounced solemnly, giving a blessing with his right hand in a shaky sign of the cross. "And bad luck to the one what doesn't respect you!"

Playfully, he pricked the nearest bayonet tip with a finger, then jerked it back. He sucked the punctured digit with a laugh. To Riley's surprise, the Mexicans were not amused and somehow seemed offended.

"Another one," said a grizzled corporal in Spanish. "It must be the moon making them crazy." He bared a toothy grin, teeth stained beyond his twenty years.

"This one is a giant!" exclaimed the youngest private, barely seventeen. He pushed back his floppy blue cap to stare in awe.

"You are merely small!" heckled the toothy corporal. He held out his thumb and forefinger to measure about two inches, pulling a few laughs from the others. But Sergeant Mejia remained grim. He scrutinized Riley, who swayed on his feet while frantically trying to read the situation.

Riley looked expectantly from swarthy face to face, not understanding a word. He squinted, trying to focus through his alcoholic haze. He could barely discern small, blurry figures wearing what looked to him like patched green coats and black top hats. Something suddenly struck him as funny. He began to laugh uncontrollably. The Mexican riflemen looked at one another in confusion.

"All my damn life been trying to catch me a leprechaun," Riley slobbered, weaving. "And now the 'little people' catch me!" He forced a harder laugh but saw the Mexicans remain mirthless with the blank stare of non-comprehension. Riley fumbled inside his jacket and pulled out the flyer. He waved it above his head in a glorious state of drunken delirium. Laughing, he bellowed, "Take me to your pot of gold!"

"It is an evil plot," Mejia snarled, glaring at Riley. "They only let their lunatics escape!"

"What should we do with this drunken fool?" asked the toothy corporal. "He is harmless."

"Then why waste a bullet?" said Mejia. "Put him with the others."

Riley appeared about ready to pass out. So, the young private poked him in the butt with his bayonet. "Yeeowch!" he yelled. Riley gingerly hopped out of the boat. He dropped the flyer, and it floated down to the waterline as the Mexicans erupted into laughter. "Leprechauns hell!" Riley yelled. "Such cruelty can only be the mark of the greaser!" The laughter ceased. Riley perceived anger on their faces. "Was it something I said?" he asked sweetly. Obviously, he thought, they understood at least that one word. We are making progress, he thought.

"I do not know his words," snarled the toothy corporal, "but I understand his insults."

"What do such rude assholes want over here?!" asked the young private.

"Your woman," snapped the toothy corporal. "She is afraid of a real man with a real mustache!" He twirled his glorious bush.

The squad laughed as the youngster frowned. He tugged at

his thin lip hair, so wispy as to be non-existent. Riley mustered a tentative half-smile, trying to join in, hoping to defuse what he now perceived as a deteriorating situation.

"Maybe they are not so crazy after all," said Mejia, "just drunk and horny." A few chuckled. Mejia gave Riley a rough shove to make him walk up the beach.

"Don't be getting pushy," Riley warned. "I'm going! Don't nobody here speak nothing but greaser?!"

"Keep poking him," the young private urged. "If he passes out, he would be too big to carry!" The squad moved into the silent darkness punctuated sporadically only by Riley's occasional yelps.

His desertion flyer lay in the sand. River water gently pulled at it in a repetitive, caressing, seductive motion until it was swept away into the black current that carried it helplessly out to the sea and an uncertain fate, much like Riley himself.

CHAPTER 3
MATAMOROS
LATE APRIL 1846

Riley stared vacantly out the rusty, iron-barred window of the crumbling adobe and stone cathedral. Nothing had gone right, he brooded, his sense of hopelessness and forlorn abandonment engulfing him in a wave of self pity. It seemed that Fate once again had robbed him of his rightful status among professional soldiers. Both attempts to improve himself and escape his lot had ended in disaster, through no fault of his own, of course. First, he deserted the British to the United States across Lake Huron; and now, the United States to Mexico, across the Rio Grande. It all proved fruitless. Perhaps, he thought, imprisonment in an old church was a warning to mend his wicked ways. On the other hand, he smiled sadly, maybe it merely meant he should avoid rowboats.

Behind him, lounging about the floor in varying degrees of boredom, were forty-one U.S. deserters, all regular infantry privates much younger than Riley. Rowdy harmonies soared and resonated among the ancient bricks as a few Irish songsters vocalized a familiar tune, "All for Me Grog." At least, he consoled himself, he was not alone in this hole. Riley had sung the tune himself in taverns on the Mackinac waterfront. The rowdy but melancholy seaman's drinking song bemoaned a tar whose evil ways kept him broke from gin, beer, and tobacco. Riley sympathized: his flask was again dry as a powder horn.

The narrow Matamoros street just outside was lined with wood and adobe buildings badly in need of repair. Mud and cracked adobe glared through chipped plaster barely covered with peeling whitewash. Aging women and farmers hawked wares under tattered canvas awnings. The few buyers were Mexican soldiers who haggled price and pleaded poverty. They wore threadbare uniforms, faded dark-blue specters of past glory. But Riley perceived an air of urgency.

Most civilians seemed to be leaving. Women with children in tow carried belongings in baskets on their heads or bundled on their backs. Men too old to be in uniform led small donkey carts piled with furniture. They rolled past in a steady exodus looking frightened, depressed, and achingly poor. They resembled every refugee Riley had seen in a dozen other war-torn nations. But to his knowledge there was no war here, yet.

"Matamoros shone grander from across the damn river," Riley admitted with a sad little laugh to young Parker, newest deserter among the prisoners. Back against the wall, Riley slid down to sit on the dirt floor beside him, scattering a nest of dung beetles. Parker looked glum. Both had heavy beard stubble. Skin grime glistened beneath sweat from lack of baths.

"I'm blessed if I know where them river girls went," Parker whined.

"Where everything's always been, Parker," said Riley. "Someplace else." He surveyed the dank old place of worship now serving as a jail. It reeked of dried sweat and urine. Scratching and louse picking were the only diversions other than singing.

As each lad traded off a new verse peculiarly suited to his plight, Riley marveled at how in every army of the world it seemed soldiers could rise above their miseries by croaking out a tune, no matter how badly. On each chorus, many of the despairing deserters joined in to bellow, "And it's all for me grog . . ."

Throughout the impromptu concert, three amused themselves around a small wood fire by roasting a skinned rat impaled on a stick. Others made sport at a charcoal fire by dropping cockroaches onto tin plates held over the coals. They bet on which bug might scurry off the hot plate first and escape. Riley thought every man here probably felt his own feet burning from a fire of his own making.

"Careful there!" Riley called out. "If they shed too much flesh, dinner'll be slim!" They hurled back curses. "Heathens," Riley muttered. The singing continued with what seemed endless verses, Riley thought.

" 'Tain't at all what I expected," sighed Parker.

"I expect nothing no more but what I can do for myself," Riley opined with a reassuring nod. "And so far, here, that's nothing." Parker flashed a rueful smile. "I was surprised, though," Riley said, "when the greasers tossed your shiny young face through that door and into this muck, just days after me."

"Couldn't stay on th'side what murdered my best friend," Parker said, "especially after you was gone," he added. "Then I found a flyer, blowin' 'round camp before th'damn provosts grabbed it. Figured it was a sign. So I followed it to you, as it were. Still, wish Lamb had made it."

Riley felt an uncomfortable twinge of guilt. He barely knew the late Private Lamb, but he identified with Parker's pained expression. It recalled his own pain and guilt from when his first comrade in arms had been killed.

An Afghan Muslim musket ball had torn off half his head, spattering Riley with the pink and red pudding of his brains. The ball would have hit Riley except he had ducked below the stacked meal bag parapet to steal a drink from his flask, the same vessel that was now empty.

"Sometimes in this profession, you can let friends get too close," Riley cautioned. "You can be blinded as to what's best for your own self." He thought of his argument with Dalton. Parker looked around and again at Riley, as if to question his opinion of what was best. Riley laughed and nodded toward the choral group. "They could use a good baritone."

"Dalton would do grand, he would," Parker said idly. Riley stared at Parker hard as the youngster watched the singing, blissfully unaware that he had rubbed salt into a fresh wound.

Suddenly the heavy wood doors opened wide on creaking, rusty hinges, and bright sunlight flooded the chapel. With rifles at the ready, six Mexican privates trotted in with a clatter. One of them was the youngster with the wispy mustache. Sergeant Mejia followed with the toothy corporal who carried a two-foot wood baton. Finally, a Mexican captain entered in a staff officer's uniform.

The singing abruptly stopped. The only sound was the scratching of scurrying rats. The prisoners were struck by the jarring contrast between their own filth and threadbare uniforms and this resplendent intruder.

Captain Francisco Moreno stood proudly before them in a dark-blue cutaway tailcoat with red bib lapels, all edged in gold embroidery. Gold bullion glistened on his pristine black shako, along the seams of his dark-blue trousers and on his swordbelt, which supported a fine French blade and flintlock pistol.

In his late thirties, Moreno presented a portrait of refined civility with a hard edge. His cultured mustache ended at a jagged scar on one cheek. With cool detachment, he studied the dejected deserters. Riley similarly took stock of Moreno. He had seen this type before, he thought, sensing an opportunity. He quickly grew more intrigued and sat up.

"Stand to, lad, in the presence of greaser gold!" he whispered urgently with a nudge to Parker's ribs. Slouching Parker pulled himself erect.

When Moreno looked satisfied that all deserter eyes were upon him, he struck a match, lit a Cuban cigar with suave flair, and nodded at Mejia.

"Hear me, you sons of whores!" Mejia bellowed in Spanish. The Americans looked at one another in non-comprehension. "You want to be soldiers of Mexico?!" he continued. "It is time to prove you are good enough!" With a cocky laugh, Mejia waved his corporal forward.

He waded into the scattered Americans, only a few of whom grasped that they were to stand and leave. The corporal freely swung his baton to hit the deserters on their backs, arms, and legs as he pointed toward the door. The Americans looked and saw only more riflemen with weapons leveled and bayonets pointed toward them. Moreno looked disappointed at the lethargic response.

Riley chose to seize the moment. "I'll form the lads on you," he whispered urgently to Parker. "Form over there, by his elegant self!" He jumped to his feet and yanked Parker up. "Now be quick!" Parker looked confused as Riley shoved him. He stumbled toward Moreno and stopped near the door. Moreno stared in bemused suspicion.

"Fall in on Parker, lads!" Riley yelled, striding into the startled deserters. "Double quick, now!" A few rose and obediently began to walk toward Parker. "Move out smart! You know the drill!" More responded to Riley's practiced air of command and voice of authority. They stood and walked more briskly to Parker, where they formed a tight, practiced column of twos.

"That's it!" Riley exulted. "Show them we're regulars, by God!"

Moreno looked mildly impressed. But his gaze was drawn back to three twenty-year-olds who refused to fall in. They continued cooking their rat while ignoring both Riley and the Mexican corporal, who headed toward them.

"Such a wee feast for a hearty hunger," grumbled one in a Scots accent. " 'Twould be wasteful to move afore we've ate the bonnie rat."

"Sure an' 'Paddy O'Lordship' there can eat this," snapped another in an Irish brogue. He spat a glob of tobacco juice. The others grunted.

"I ain't in no army now," growled a beefy, bearded Britisher in thick Cockney. "And what soldier would take orders from the oldest bloody private on parade?!" They chuckled. Riley heard and looked their way. He cast a glance at Moreno watching with a doubtful frown. Riley scowled as yet another brilliant plan teetered on the brink of failure.

"Get into ranks you filthy cockroaches!" yelled the toothy corporal. He strode to the cook fire and loomed behind the obstinate, bearded Britisher, who remained squatting in non-comprehension and continued turning the rat.

When the corporal pulled back his baton to beat the man, Riley stepped between the two and booted the deserter hard in the butt. He sprawled forward with his face in the dirt. Furious, he rolled over and glared up at Riley, who shrugged innocently. "Better my boot than his baton!" Riley exclaimed, nodding at the startled Mexican corporal. "Now fall in on Parker, you slovenly soldier!"

Moreno perked up. He stared at Riley along with everyone else in the deathly quiet room as the bearded man slowly rose with fists clenched.

"And who the hell promoted you t'bloody general?!" he growled.

"God hisself when he made me Irish," Riley quipped. The bearded Britisher sneered as laughter passed through the Hibernian ranks. Even the Irish tobacco chewer chuckled, rose, and walked toward Parker. But the Cockney malcontent looked ready to fight. He reconsidered when transfixed by Riley's steely glare, stood, and walked sullenly with the Scot to the now-formed column. Moreno nodded questioningly at Sergeant Mejia, who looked skeptical.

" 'Tain't finished 'tween us," the Britisher warned over his shoulder.

"And we've long wanted to give the boot to Great Britain!" Riley roared. The Irish majority erupted in hoots, howls, and laughter. "At the route step! Forward, march!" Riley commanded. Like regulars, they obeyed to follow the Mexican guards out the doors as Riley counted cadence. "One! One! One-Two-One!" he sang out, exchanging a look with stoic Moreno as he swung past. Moreno watched them leave, then fell in behind.

The deserters tramped down the church steps and onto the main plaza. Long, single-story adobe buildings defined a rough rectangle of dirt surrounding a covered well.

They filed past various assembled companies of the frontier army of Mexico at drill. Hard service had faded their outdated uniforms, single-breasted, dark-blue coatees with red facings. Their sky-blue trousers were patched and torn. And they sported a variety of military headgear, from battered leather shakos to jaunty wool caps. Most wore broghan shoes; some, sandals with trouser legs rolled.

"Close it up, lads!" Riley thundered. He already had formed a low opinion. "Amateurs on parade! Won't be hard to best this motley bunch! For the professional soldier, Hip! Hip! . . ."

". . . Huzzah!" the deserters responded in weak unison. Most lacked Riley's sudden burst of enthusiasm. Parker, however, managed a mighty yell and unleashed a shy smile at appreciative Riley, who felt he had been given another chance; perhaps to rise above, perhaps to escape. Right now, either would do.

Moreno had been watching Riley while keeping up at a distance. When the deserters cheered, they were shuffling past an assembled company of hard-core Mexican veterans. Moreno smiled slightly and removed his cigar.

"Long live the Republic of Mexico!" he cried in Spanish,

waving his cigar grandiosely at the troops.

"Viva!" they shouted in a perfectly chilling, deafening roar that resembled a battle cry. Riley and the deserters were overwhelmed and slightly unnerved. Moreno looked smug and resumed smoking his cigar. He had made his point.

"Patriots, bah!" Riley grumbled to Parker, marching beside him. "Nobody gets you killed quicker."

Many of the swarthy Mexican soldiers sneered, scowled, and frowned in contempt as the Americans marched past. One private could not contain himself.

"You bray like jackasses!" he yelled. "Why should we pay jackasses?!" He spat at them. "We need no one to fight for us!" The irate corporal attacked the enraged private and beat him mercilessly into silence with his baton. The man dropped to his knees, hands covering his head. The Americans stared anxiously as they passed. Not one understood the Spanish.

"An Irishman could talk hisself to death, he could," whispered Parker.

"A good Irishman would talk the good corporal out of his 'shillelagh,' " Riley cracked. Parker forced a little laugh, still unconvinced.

"*Silencio!*" roared Sergeant Mejia practically in Riley's ear. He cringed, whirled a glare at the stone-faced Mejia, then grit his teeth in grudging subservience. He followed Mejia and guided the Americans toward a row of wagons and oxcarts across the plaza.

Riley watched Moreno pause to look back at the beaten Mexican soldado. He stood looking wobbly in ranks but was being congratulated by his comrades. Moreno looked somewhat surprised at first, then sagged. Whatever his plan was, Riley thought, it was not working out as well as Moreno had hoped.

At the wagons, obviously disgruntled civilian men of Matamoros waited in a ragged line under guard. The men ranged in age from teens through late forties. Soldiers in the wagons forced them to take uniforms, weapons, and leather accouterments. Others urged them to dress quickly and showed them how to put on the unfamiliar equipment. Then they were shoved roughly into ranks and drilled in the Mexican manual of arms to a cacophony of Spanish commands.

"Ain't possible this bunch means to fight," Riley whispered to Parker as they marched past. "Conscripts the likes of these would harm themselves more than the Yanks." Parker choked back a laugh. "We'll bolster their bluster, pocket their gold, and then go missing," Riley advised.

"But go where?" Parker asked, sincerely confused.

Riley had no answer. He had become aware of Moreno marching behind his left shoulder and within earshot. Riley looked at him, but Moreno gave no hint that he understood a word. He merely acknowledged Riley with a polite nod.

Riley halted the deserters behind the row of wagons and between two lines of assembled Mexican troops facing one another. Several tables near the wagons were piled high with old Mexican uniforms, dark-blue, tattered coatees trimmed in red. A dozen runaway slaves already were wearing shakos and sky-blue trousers. They stood at the tables fitting themselves. One of them was Sandy, the cook for Major Rains. He alone remained in civilian clothing. The blacks were laughing and joking with one another until the American soldiers marched in. At the sight of whites in sky-blue U.S. uniforms, the stunned blacks fell silent. Some looked scared; others, angry and defiant.

"They come t'git us!" cried one teenager to Sandy, the elder of the group. "Massa's sent sojers t'take us back!"

A more militant runaway overheard and stepped up, grabbing the teenager by the shoulder. "Dumb nigger! Ain't no slav'ry here!" he shouted. "An' if they try, we be sojers now." He grinned. "We kin fight 'em." Both looked to Sandy, leader by being the elder. He patiently smiled as he watched the deserters.

"If th'white sojers come over here, they g'wan after them 'fore us," Sandy said softly. The two looked at him surprised. "Ain't nothin' so fierce as slavers chasin' runaway white niggers." They all laughed.

Riley looked toward the laughter and recognized Sandy, who nodded at him slightly. But Riley overheard grumbling among his men. He turned to look behind him. Many appeared angry at the sight of blacks in uniform.

"There's shame enough soldierin' with greasers," warned the Irish tobacco chewer.

The bearded Britisher grunted next to him. "The shame's on our bloody 'general' here who'd lower us to such," he growled, eyeing Riley. Others around him mumbled in agreement.

"Quiet in the damn ranks!" Riley bellowed.

Mejia drew his short sword and swept it across the front of the deserter column with its point toward the ground. *"Formar en batalla!"* he commanded.

Riley did not understand. He stared at Mejia and shook his head helplessly. "Don't savvy greaser," he whispered with a respectful smile. Moreno walked up to Mejia with an amused look.

"Perhaps you must draw this 'professional soldier' a picture, Sergeant," Moreno said in Spanish. Mejia rolled his eyes in frustration.

"Formar en batalla!" Mejia yelled again. He stepped off the entire width between the two Mexican companies as he angrily scraped a line into the dirt with his sword. Some soldados muffled laughter as they watched at attention in line two ranks deep.

"Company, front!" Riley bellowed proudly, at last understanding. The column deployed smartly onto the line two ranks deep.

They faced the row of wagons and tables of uniforms. The opposed lines of Mexican troops stood at each end, enclosing a rough sided square. Riley saw that one company was uniformed like Mejia and his guards, with green lapels, and carried British Baker flintlock rifles. The other company, like the troops on the plaza, sported simple red facings and carried British Brown Bess flintlock muskets. A few blacks other than the runaways already were under arms in the Mexican ranks.

"Have them remove their jackets and put on ours," Moreno said to Mejia.

"Our small coats will not fit these fat pigs," Mejia replied.

"It may no longer matter," Moreno said with a sad, resigned smile.

Mejia looked confused but marched to Riley. "Strip off these offensive rags!" he commanded. He tugged at Riley's buttoned jacket, trying to bridge the language gap. "Put on the uniform of Mexico!" He pointed at the tables.

Riley got it, nodded, and unbuttoned. "Company, dis-robe!" he sang out.

"Are we joinin' the wenches at the river?!" Parker joked. He threw down his coat and ground it with his boot heel. "That's for Lamb," he mumbled.

"Canno' we keep it a spare?" asked the Scotsman. He carefully folded his U.S. jacket and laid it on the ground. "It is such bonnie wool." A glob of tobacco juice suddenly plopped onto the jacket. The Scot glared at the offender.

"When you get your land, raise 'bonnie' sheep!" quipped the tobacco chewer, wiping his chin. More laughed when the Scotsman shrugged to agree.

But most deserters struggled quietly with mixed emotions. They unbuttoned and removed their sky-blue jackets, yet hesitated before dropping them. Others let loose quickly but stared at them lying in the dirt, suddenly remorseful. Riley saw, understood, and eyed Moreno, who was watching intently.

" 'Tis plain Scotty knows a shrewd deal," Riley said for all to hear. The torn men looked at him. "You're trading one ratty old coat, grown small from pain and sweat, for a new one with three hundred-twenty acres stuffed in its pocket!" He managed a wry smile. "The greasers are shortchanging themselves!"

Laughter lightened the mood. Riley pulled his empty flask from his jacket and tucked it into his trouser pocket, aching for a stiff drink. "Now, slip into something what fits!" Riley yelled, flinging his old jacket without a care. "Break ranks!"

"Huzzah!" Parker alone shouted as he led the herd. Most trampled their U.S. coats. A few stepped around them carefully, as they would an old friend fallen on a battlefield. Some tossed a poignant glance and merely walked toward the tables. The anxious blacks stood aside, watching. Riley walked to Sandy.

"Major Rains might go missing supper tonight," Riley said.

"I 'spected t'see you here," Sandy replied. "Remember, I knows a runaway nigger when I sees one."

Riley laughed and nodded toward Moreno, who stood apart, watching. "So does he, I'll wager," said Riley.

"Like yo cap'n on th'other side?" Sandy asked. "He lost a bet with hisself that you'd stay."

"Merrill's too smart to bet against a sure thing," Riley said. "Your good major lost a bundle on you, though," he joked. "Suppose that one's a betting man?" Riley nodded toward Moreno.

"Back when I's a field hand," Sandy said, "we had us a black overseer, one o' us set apart an' a little 'above.' He knew what nigger'd be runnin' into th'swamp afore th'nigger knew hisself. He'd catch 'em an' whup 'em harder than th'white man."

"I suppose all niggers ain't black," Riley mused. Sandy merely smiled.

Mejia's guards nudged the newly uniformed black runaways

at bayonet point into the rear rank. Mexican and black veterans accepted them lustily with a few cries of "Viva!" and slaps on the back. Sandy looked quietly proud.

"You soldiering with them others?" Riley asked, a bit in awe at the unusual sight of blacks in ranks. Those he had fought with the British were savage tribesmen with no knowledge of tactical formation, no uniforms.

"You might say I's just bein' born again at nigh on fifty years," Sandy said, shaking "no." "What time I gots left, I ain't cuttin' shorter for ten pesos a month."

" 'Tis a safe bet since there ain't gonna be no war," Riley opined.

Sandy looked at him incredulously. "I s'pects I'll jus' bet on me an' make my way t'Mexico City," he replied. Sandy picked up a small bundle of belongings wrapped in a tied tablecloth and nodded at passing refugees.

"And I'll just make my way back home," Riley said, adding in a whisper, "to Ireland." Distracted by Parker waving at him with a large Mexican coatee, Riley did not see Sandy's look of concern.

"I'm blessed if this ain't the last what might fit the likes of you!" Parker yelled to the general laughter of the deserters, most of whom now wore Mexican coatees. The one worn by Parker fit perfectly. Others looked too tight with sleeves too short. The beefy, bearded Britisher had no choice but to leave his hanging open, unbuttoned except for one at the collar.

"Time to take my next step," Riley said, nodding at the uniform table.

"Don't trip," Sandy said dryly, turning to walk toward the refugees.

"May the road rise to meet you and the wind be at your back," Riley offered with as much sincerity as he ever mustered.

Sandy stared after Riley as he walked toward Parker. He felt sorry for the big Irishman like he did for his few kindly masters over the years. He knew that someday the enormity of their sins would overwhelm them, and it would come as a tragic surprise. Sandy sighed in finality and fell in with the river of refugees.

Moments later, Riley fidgeted in a tight, dark-blue, single-breasted coatee faced in red with sleeves too short. He stood at attention beside the others, formed into a line two ranks deep. Moreno and Mejia slowly walked the line and inspected the men, still wearing their sky-blue U.S. trousers and dark-blue caps.

"It is just enough Mexican uniform to keep our soldiers from killing them by accident," Moreno said in Spanish.

"In the smoke of battle," Mejia said almost wistfully, "unfortunate accidents can happen."

Moreno frowned. "For Mexico, such a battle itself would be a most unfortunate accident," he replied. Mejia looked doubtful. Moreno smiled with a sigh. "But no matter. We shall all do our duty, eh, Sergeant?"

Mejia bowed his head as they reached the end of the line and faced Riley, who stared rigidly straight ahead as Moreno scrutinized him. "Have him put them into our ranks," said Moreno. He stepped out of the way to watch. Mejia turned to Riley.

"March your stinking carcasses into our lines!" Mejia snapped. He pointed to the red-trimmed infantry, now standing with three feet between each man. The entire front rank of swarthy Mexican faces looked hostile.

"Attention, company!" Riley shouted, stepping out to face the deserters. Riley surveyed their faces. The bearded Britisher looked surly. Anxiety and fear were evident on many others. Parker alone looked eager. "My best guess at all this greaser lingo," Riley said, "is that it's time to step into their ranks." More looked apprehensive. "Think of yourselves as soldiering whores," he advised, "and this is the brothel what's paying the most." A few chuckled, easing tension.

"I say it's time to vote ourselves a bloomin' real officer!" shouted the bearded Britisher. Riley fired a glare at him.

Sensing trouble, Mejia signaled a few guards forward. Moreno stopped them with a casual wave of his hand. He beckoned Mejia to watch.

"Do you have a name," Riley asked kindly, adding with an edge, "or is your father known?" Laughter rippled through the ranks.

"John Price, Second Infantry, or so's I was," he said.

"And standing for election to officer, are you?" Riley said. Price nodded.

Riley gestured him out of ranks to stand before him. "I give you John Price!" Riley shouted, implanting his right broghan shoe sharply into Price's groin.

Price dropped to his knees holding his testicles and trying to scream, but only a squeak came out. Riley threw a right uppercut to Price's jaw, which lifted him off his knees and bent him back. He toppled flat onto his behind, writhing.

"Price ain't standing no more!" Riley bellowed. He squared off to face the entire wide-eyed group. "Will another 'candidate' present hisself?!" He glared directly at Price's two pals. The Scotsman and tobacco chewer averted his eyes. "Now that we've shown the greasers the rules of Irish democracy," Riley said, "let's show them soldiering!"

"Ready your men, Sergeant," Moreno said, watching closely.

Mejia looked at Moreno in confusion but nodded and turned, crossing to the infantry with green lapels. *"Preparen!"* Mejia shouted. With crisp precision and the solid crack of hands slapping wood stocks and leather slings, the guards leveled their rifles waist high, ready for anything.

To the deserters, it looked as if they were about to be fired upon. They looked at one another nervously and then fixed on Riley. "Damn impatient they are!" he quipped, offering Price a hand up. Price hesitated a moment, then took it with a nod of embarrassed thanks. He sheepishly limped to his place in ranks. "Moving targets are tougher to hit, lads," Riley advised ruefully. "So it's step lively and into their ranks you go. Break ranks!" He waved them toward the line of red-trimmed Mexican infantry.

But as each deserter tried to step into the open space between every two Mexicans, they barred his entry with their muskets. At first, the deserters reacted with confusion. The Mexicans screamed insults and jeers at them in Spanish. Many spat in contempt and made rude hand gestures.

"We do not serve with braying jackasses!" cried one soldado.

"You do not love Mexico!" cried another. "You only love what we pay!"

"You are not Mexican!" shouted another. "You will only desert again!"

The deserters grew angry as they tried to bully their way into the abusive Mexican ranks. One hot-headed young soldado barred Riley and spat in his face. Riley deftly grabbed his musket, twisted it easily out of his hands, and flipped it over. He now held the surprised soldado's own bayonet at his throat.

"Little boys what play with knives can get cut," Riley snarled. Though frightened, the young soldado mustered his courage.

"Kill me!" he cried. "Better to die like a man than serve with your kind!" Other Mexicans near him shouted "Viva!" over and over at his bravery. Riley looked about in surprise and non-comprehension at the Spanish insults.

"If they don't want us," Parker hollered in frustration, "why'd they sweet talk us over here?!" He was staring down two scowling Mexican veterans. Other deserters echoed his frustration in angry shouts.

"This must be a test, lads!" Riley yelled, pleased with himself at figuring it out. " 'Tis a brilliant greaser plan to see how truly bad we wants in!"

"I don't wants 'in' with their kind," growled Price, staring past two hostile Mexicans at runaway blacks in the rear rank. "But I do wants 'out' with a parcel of greaser land!" He and some others laughed.

"Massa 'fraid 'cause we free?!" taunted a black teenager.

"Free is one thing, boy," snapped the Britisher. "Standin' bloody equal in ranks is another." Many grumbled to agree. "And I ain't no 'massa'!"

"Sinners can't be choosers!" spouted the tobacco chewer as he grappled with the musket of a surly Mexican. "Leastwise th'yellowskins and us share the same church!" He spat. "We'll be forgiven for crossin' God's lines of race."

"Price an' me are proud Protestants," argued the Scotsman. "We canno' be changin' our faith like takin' off old clothes!"

"Sure and you must be stupid then!" hollered Parker, drawing peals of laughter from the Irish.

The Mexicans and deserters pushed and shoved each other in stalemate as insults escalated up and down the ranks. Riley seethed with frustration until he determined the only way to break the impasse. His own brilliance, he thought, could blind a lesser man. "If you can't pass the test square," shouted Riley, "cheat!" He gave the young soldado a brutal stroke to the chest with the butt of his own musket. It knocked his breath out and buckled him to his knees.

With yells, screams, and curses, the deserters pitched into the Mexicans in a bloody, vicious, raucous release of stifled hostility. Some Mexicans dropped their muskets in a "macho" gesture to even the odds. One on one, the deserters bested the smaller Mexicans. But the Mexicans soon ganged up on them.

Riley laughingly flattened several soldados before he was brought down by teamwork. Two Mexicans came at him from the front while another tackled him from behind. When he toppled over backwards, four more soldados jumped on him and pinned him down. He roared and flailed like a penned lion.

Moreno stared at Riley in grim disappointment. He turned to Mejia beside him near the waiting guards. Mejia looked anxious to join the fight.

"We force a leader to rise among them, and now it looks futile," Moreno said. He nodded toward the line of green-trimmed infantry. Mejia understood, saluted, and waved the line toward the melee with his sword.

"*Frente!*" Mejia commanded.

"Viva!" they shouted back furiously.

The riflemen marched forward, waded into the mob, and began clubbing deserters and Mexicans alike with rifle butts. Corporals swung their hard batons with glee, putting an end to the fight.

Moreno watched in dismal disappointment. "Put them back in the church," he said. "Let them bathe. Serve them a hearty meal tonight."

"Their last meal?" Mejia asked hopefully.

"Bring their leader to me," Moreno replied. Mejia saluted, turned, and marched toward the dejected deserters, now encircled by guards. "Sergeant Mejia!" Moreno called out. Mejia turned. "Bring him after he has bathed."

Later that night, Riley sat alone in the spartan adobe office of Captain Moreno. A Spanish colonial desk, two chairs, a cot, and a campaign chest comprised the furnishings. A wall map of Mexico resembled that which he had seen in the office of Captain Merrill back in Mackinac. But in this version, Texas ended at the Nueces River with no land marked "disputed." In the candlelight, Riley's face showed a few cuts and bruises. But he looked clean with hair washed, still wet and slicked back under his cap. An incessant hum from night insects floated in through the open window and door. The air was hot and muggy.

Riley watched a few soldiers cross the empty plaza to a small fire for the guards. A lone soldado with a guitar tended a coffee pot there as he strummed a haunting, melancholy melody. Restive, Riley watched a few roaches cross the floor and bet to himself which would climb the wall first. He sweat profusely in his tight wool coat and tugged at his high collar. His gaze fixed on an engraved crystal decanter full of what he hoped was whiskey atop the desk with glasses. Beside it rested a stack of the familiar desertion flyers. He grunted.

Riley tossed a furtive glance at the empty doorway. An elbow and trouser leg of a guard standing just outside was all he could see. No one was at the window. Riley uncorked the decanter and inhaled a deep whiff. He was thrilled by the exotic, alcoholic aroma. He pulled out his flask, grabbed the decanter, and quickly filled the flask to overflowing. Some spilled on the desktop. He pocketed the flask, carefully replaced the decanter, and wiped the desk dry with a sweep of his sleeve. He had barely sat back when Moreno stepped into the open doorway, his silhouette backlit by the bonfire outside.

"On such a warm night, Private Riley," he said in perfect English, "you must help yourself to a drink." He had an aristocratic Spanish accent.

"Thank you kindly, sir," Riley said, looking dumbstruck as he stood to attention, shocked at hearing English. He suspected Moreno knew of his "raid" on the decanter but was unsure. Moreno looked bemused. He forged ahead and poured himself a stiff shot into a glass as Moreno walked behind his desk.

"I am Captain Francisco Moreno," he said, "aide to his excellency, General Arista, commander of Mexico's Army of the North."

"We both know who I am, sir," Riley said, more suspicious than impressed. "But why his worship would bother with the likes of me, one of us don't know." He offered to pour a drink for Moreno, who waved it away. Riley downed his in one gulp. His eyes grew wide as what felt like liquid fire burned its way down his parched throat. It burned good, he thought.

"We call it 'aguardiente,' " Moreno said politely. "It means 'burning water.' " He unbuckled his sword belt and looped it over the back of his chair.

"I call it the succor of the angels," gasped Riley, pouring himself another. " 'Tis been a long dry spell, sir."

"You are discomforted by our heat," said Moreno, taking note of Riley's sweat and his soaking sleeve. "You may remove your coat."

"It appears easier over here to take a coat off, sir, than to be putting one on," Riley replied, his tone sweetly sarcastic.

"Already, you appreciate my problem," said Moreno, a little surprised.

Riley removed his coat and draped it across his chair back. He sat down and tugged at his wet, clinging shirt for air. "I know now that for weeks you been hearing 'damn yellowbellies' this and 'stinking yellowskins' that," Riley said blithely. "The lads are grand soldiers but possessed of foul mouths."

Moreno stared stunned, amazed at Riley's lack of self-awareness and even civility. Oblivious, Riley poured another drink and downed it.

"I'd have muzzled 'em myself," Riley continued, brandishing a fist, "had I thought any greaser could understand the Queen's English, sir."

"This 'greaser' was born and reared in Spanish Florida, Private," Moreno said. His eyes flashed anger, but he managed a thin smile of genteel patience. "I was taught English by Jesuits so I could better understand my enemy." Moreno stared unflinchingly at Riley.

"If that is the case, sir," countered Riley with a twinkle, "the good sisters should teach Irish waifs every tongue in the book!" Moreno ignored the jest. Riley began to feel uncomfortable, even threatened, from his icy, steady stare.

"Thank you for making my task less difficult," Moreno said with sinister self-control. "Today confirmed my darkest fears." Riley looked at him in surprise. "You must understand," Moreno continued, "my men see norteamericanos as morally bankrupt, a race that would buy or sell anything." He picked up his decanter to admire its fine engraving. "And what they cannot buy, they steal." Riley shifted uneasily in his chair.

"When necessities are scarce, as it were," Riley replied, " 'tis the instinct of wolves and soldiers to forage, sir."

"Just so," Moreno said brightly, as if to thank Riley for helping him make his point. "If left to freely roam our countryside," Moreno said, "men like you would prey on our poor population like so many wolves without a pack."

"Men like you and me," Riley corrected, "we keep the wolves penned, we do." Moreno lit a cigar thoughtfully. "Like we done today," he added in smug confidence. "The general, he noticed, did he?"

"Wolves from different packs never hunt together," Moreno replied sadly.

" 'Tis all a waste then," Riley sighed. Riley thought he got Moreno's point and stood, taking his coatee from the chairback, gently folding and placing it on Moreno's desk. " 'Twas a tight fit anyway," he grumbled. Then he brightened. "Afore you send me on my way, do I got any wages coming?" he asked with naïve sincerity. With money, he could always "go missing" again.

Moreno stared unblinking. "In Mexico City, they design new uniforms," Moreno said, fingering the worn wool of Riley's coatee. "On the frontier, we can still get use from these old ones. Nothing in Mexico is discarded so long as it can have a purpose," he added, pointedly.

Riley frowned at his foreboding tone. He did not like where this was heading. "You made our purpose plain enough," Riley said bitterly. He picked up a desertion flyer from the desk and read loudly, " 'Abandon your desperate and unholy cause,' you wrote. 'Throw away your arms and run to us, and we will embrace you as true friends and Christians!' " Riley glared.

Moreno merely blew a casual smoke ring. "The Christian act of mercy now would be to save everyone so much suffering and trouble," Moreno said flatly, "and kill you all."

Riley stared in openmouthed shock. " 'Tain't like we weren't invited!" Riley recovered, standing and thrusting the flyer at Moreno. " 'Here you will find land to cultivate,' you said! Just for traipsing across as a private, you offered three hundred-twenty acres!"

"When I wrote that," Moreno said, "I had not considered this distasteful prejudice. My problem, Private Riley, is that my men will not open their ranks to 'inferiors.' " He feigned helplessness.

Riley looked momentarily surprised before his face clouded in rage. " 'Inferiors', is it?!" he growled, clenching his fists. "There ain't nothing in your greaser ranks but inferiors!" Moreno braced at the slur, but Riley remained oblivious. "We are regulars, by God!"

"You are nothing!" Moreno snapped. Riley stared. "You are deserters in the uniform of an army that detests you!" Riley was confused by this lethal turnaround in his plans. He sat back down and slumped. "If we throw you into prison with norteamericanos captured in battle, they will kill you as traitors."

"Damn us one sin at a time, if you please," Riley seethed. "Deserters we are, right and proper," he admitted. "But we are traitors only if we fire on the old flag, so to speak. 'Tain't like there's gonna be no battle."

Moreno looked at Riley almost in pity. "If we send you back, the norteamericanos will shoot you," Moreno continued, "just as we shoot our own despicable deserters."

Riley glared at his choice of words. "They hang you," Riley corrected, "and then only in time of war, in which we ain't." He mustered a sardonic smile. "In these blessed times of peace, they mercifully flog your back to butchered meat and brand a red hot *D* into your face." He put a finger to his right cheek, then stared curiously at Moreno.

Moreno idly touched the scar on his own cheek. "Revolutionaries in '36," he said thoughtfully, "the Alamo."

Riley recognized the name of the battle with a respectful nod. Then he yanked his shirtsleeve up and bared his right arm. He fingered a jagged, sunken, purplish scar in his upper arm. "Wogs in '42," he touted, "Afghanistan."

Moreno nodded in respect but seemed more interested in a blue tattoo emblazoned on Riley's forearm. The crossed cannon crest of the Royal Artillery Regiment floated above a scroll inscribed with the title "Master Gunner." "A sergeant, I suspected," Moreno said, "but of artillery was too much to hope for." Riley looked at him curiously. "It is our most glaring weakness," Moreno said.

"My previous, previous employer," Riley said proudly. "If you don't murder me," he added in grim humor, "you'd get a professional, tried and true."

" 'Tried,' yes," Moreno said, "but 'true' only to your greed." Riley shrugged. "This army of poor patriots does not trust any not native born."

"I see some prejudices respect no national boundaries, sir," Riley said bitterly. Moreno suddenly slammed his hand onto the map, startling Riley.

"No more than some soldiers!" Moreno snapped. Riley sat erect. "We face a *norteAmericano* army fortified on our own soil!" Moreno calmed himself by taking a long puff on his cigar.

Riley poured himself another drink, downing it in one gulp. " 'Tis nothing but a Yank bluff in a game of brag, sir," insisted Riley, "and the pot is that land what stretches between where each of you thinks their country's dirt starts."

"Not to mention all our state of California, Private Riley. I fear this border dispute is merely a ruse for the war, since they offered to buy California, and we refused to sell our birthright. We have a saying," Moreno lamented, staring at the map. "Poor Mexico. So far from God, so near the United States."

Riley eyed Moreno. "I can help you bluff them back, as it were," said Riley with forced bravado. "We just need to overlook each other's faults 'til we end this little game of brag. You get your land"—he smiled—"I get my land."

"If you survive," Moreno cautioned as he paced a slow circle around Riley, who scoffed. "I had hoped to lessen the number of invaders," Moreno said, indicating the flyers, "and then mix better trained *norteAmericano* soldiers with our recruits."

"Don't you mean 'conscripts,' sir?" asked Riley with disdain.

"Certain classes must be forced to do their duty," Moreno replied. "Even for professionals, some duty is distasteful."

"For the price promised, this professional can soldier with any damn distasteful 'inferior,' " Riley asserted. "Greaser, darky, or even British."

"And the others?" Moreno asked, glaring.

"They'll do what I tell them," he said casually. "Just give me the chance I come looking for." Riley nodded toward the flyer on Moreno's desk.

Moreno shook his head. "To admit that my idea has failed is embarrassing for me," Moreno sighed, "but it is fatally unfortunate for you."

"Begging the captain's pardon, sir," Riley persisted, "but 'tis working so well that General Taylor's plugging the flow to your side with bodies."

"It is a sad fact," said Moreno, "that in our business, bodies solve most problems."

"Bad luck to me, then," Riley surmised, pouring himself another drink. "I'll be killed not even doing what I do best." Riley gulped down his drink. As a soldier, he had long ago accepted death as an ever-present possibility. What he could not accept, he realized, was the possibility of dying for nothing as a failure.

"Mexico needs the peculiar talent of your kind," Moreno suggested, "more than she is willing to admit." Riley stared at him. "In the manner of our Aztec ancestors, she would sooner stack bodies in a temple built to the god of pride." Moreno paced. "But how can I not kill you? I cannot free you," he added, "and this stubborn arrogance serves only to keep you out of our ranks."

"And why shouldn't it do just that!" Riley exclaimed, perking up. Moreno looked at him while hiding a small, rising hope. "Let your lads 'stand to' in their bigoted ranks," Riley said, "while we 'stand to' in our bigoted ranks!" Moreno was intrigued yet somehow did not look very surprised.

"And who would officer this company of deserters?" Moreno asked, already knowing the answer.

"It should be the most professional deserter of the bunch, sir," Riley said matter of factly, then gesturing at Moreno, "under himself, of course, as captain."

"You will remain here tonight under guard," Moreno cautioned, pointing at the cot. "I must obtain certain approvals, arrange details." Riley eyed the decanter, cheerfully nodded, and walked to the cot.

"Mightn't one of those details be my rate of pay as your new lieutenant?" Riley asked. Moreno picked up Riley's coat from the desk and tossed it to him.

"A teniente earns fifty-seven pesos a month," he said,

"roughly equal in dollars."

"And to think," Riley mused, his blue eyes twinkling as he folded the coat into a pillow, "the Yanks could've hung onto my hide for three stripes and sixteen dollars a month." Riley laughed. He flopped grinning onto the cot, clasping his hands behind his head. Moreno stepped to the doorway and looked at Riley.

"We shall see who struck the better bargain," Moreno said and then left.

Riley took several more swigs of the fine whisky, comforted by the thought that he could "go missing" after just one month's wages and gain passage on a ship. He drifted off quickly and enjoyed his deepest sleep in months.

At dawn, massed Mexican drummers and buglers played "Assembly." Riley staggered out of the office to find the young guard with the wispy mustache.

"*Alto!*" he commanded, raising his rifle.

Riley gave him a groggy, hungover look of contempt as he buttoned his coatee. "Soon enough, you'll be saluting me," he muttered.

Sleepy Mexican soldiers stumbled into ranks throughout the plaza as the drumming and bugle blowing continued incessantly. Corporals wielded batons to flay those moving too slowly. The soldados looked encumbered by bulky cowhide backpacks and blanket rolls. Riley nodded toward them as Moreno marched up with Sergeant Mejia, the toothy corporal, and a squad of riflemen.

"Full marching order?" Riley chided. "Ain't we pulling back from the river?" he asked.

Moreno gave him a blank stare and waved him into ranks beside him. The detail kept marching with the young private falling in behind. "General Arista is waiting to meet you," Moreno said. The detail continued briskly across the plaza.

More troops emerged from barracks and tents to fall into ranks as they struggled to pull on their heavy packs.

Riley stared at quite a few who itched and scratched while standing at attention. "I see the fleas are the same on both sides of the river," he joked.

"Of course," Moreno snapped, all business. "They are Mexican fleas."

The detail halted in front of a two-story Spanish Colonial house. General Arista emerged buckling on his gold embroidered sword belt. He was radiant in a blue and red uniform like Moreno's but with more gold embroidery. Rather than a shako, he wore a fore and aft hat ablaze with red, white, and green cock feathers.

And to the obvious surprise of Riley, Arista was a tall, white-skinned Mexican with red hair and freckles.

"Excellency, may I present Teniente John Riley," Moreno announced.

Riley stepped forward smartly and held a salute in rigid British style.

Arista looked amused and merely nodded with a casual wave of his hand. "Our military protocol is not yet that developed, Teniente," Arista said in English with only a trace of Spanish accent. Riley looked even more shocked as he lowered his hand. "A mere nod of respect is all we demand, not a 'salute.' "

"You look as though you'd spout Gaelic, your worship," Riley said. "You're not at all what I expected."

"I was educated in Cincinnati, Ohio, Teniente," Arista replied, smiling. "And you are everything Capitan Moreno warned me about." Arista held out his hand. Moreno laid a shining gold epaulette in his palm. As Riley stood at attention, Arista slipped the epaulette beneath the fabric loop on Riley's right shoulder.

"Excellency, he believes we would have killed them," Moreno said in Spanish. Arista chuckled.

"Well done," Arista replied. He fastened the epaulette to Riley's shoulder button. "Through him, we will control them." Riley remained rigid at attention.

"He thinks it was his idea," Moreno added. Again, Arista smiled. He stepped back from Riley, who did not understand a word. He barely contained his pride at becoming an officer.

"Teniente Riley, you will train the *norteamericano* deserters into artillerymen under command of *Capitan* Moreno," Arista said to Riley's joy.

"Thank you kindly, sir," Riley replied, twitching his shoulder. "But I always thought these things weighed more."

"Give it time, Teniente," Moreno whispered.

"Today, you must prove the worth of your tattoo," Arista said more gravely. Riley looked puzzled as he watched Arista stride to his horse, held by an aide. He put one foot in the stirrup and turned to Riley. "And today we must prove the worth of our manhood." He mounted, wheeled his horse to face his waiting troops, and drew his sword. "Soldiers of Mexico!" he bellowed in Spanish. He trotted expertly to the center of the plaza. "Meet the barbarian invaders!" He pointed his sword.

A mounted officer in a well-worn, double-breasted red coatee and lancer helmet gave a sword salute, wheeled his horse, and yelled crisp orders. His company of Jalisco Lancers emerged from a narrow alley behind him. Clad in rakish but aging coatees of deep red with green facings, they trotted out proudly with eight-foot lances tipped with flashing, razor sharp blades and fluttering red pennons. Some lowered their lances to prod the group on foot and held captive in the center of their column.

Riley gaped in shock when he saw that the battered prisoners were 1st U.S. Dragoons, Colonel Harney's own. Mexican ranks hurled hoots, howls, and Spanish insults at them. The Americans obviously had been captured in battle. Uniforms were ripped and torn. Faces and hands were cut, bruised, and powder blackened. They mustered nervous looks of defiance as they navigated the abusive gauntlet. Riley counted more than sixty of them, all ranks.

"I never bartered for no shooting fight," Riley said ominously.

"Our cavalry forded the river eight days ago," Moreno explained, unconcerned by Riley's outrage. "They killed sixteen Dragoons, captured the rest."

Riley scowled as the lancers herded the dejected Dragoons across the plaza, roughly pushing them out another alley. " 'Tis a sin not to pity the native-born bastards," Riley growled bitterly as the Mexicans continued their catcalls. "But I'm the one at the little end of the horn, ain't I?! I never bargained for this." Riley bristled, realizing he had been duped.

"For reasons known but to you," Moreno snapped, "you chose not to believe your own eyes!"

" 'Tis my Irish birthright to swallow my own blarney and spit up anyone else's!" Riley replied, though sounding a bit deflated.

"Today, you join the main body of our army," Arista resumed in Spanish to his troops. "At this historic moment, our army is crossing our river to drive the rest of these pirates from our soil! Viva Mexico!" Soldados echoed his cry with a vengeance. *"Marcha regular!"* Arista commanded, pointing his sword. *"Frente, marchen!"*

Company officers and sergeants shouted more commands. Troops formed a column and began tramping out of the plaza. Fifers and drummers struck up a light, jaunty Mexican marching tune. Arista walked his horse back to Moreno.

Arista smiled arrogantly at glowering Riley. "Deception proved necessary, Teniente," Arista said, "when I was ordered to commence hostilities. Some among you might have warned the norteamericanos."

" 'Tis plain you can trust us now, sir," Riley replied through his teeth. "We're in greaser blue, as it were, up to our necks."

Arista gave him a cold stare. "Take him to the guns," Arista said to Moreno in Spanish. "They have one hour."

"I will need the rest of Manzano's company of riflemen," Moreno suggested. "There may be unpleasant consequences. Mejia's squad is too few." Arista knew exactly what he meant. He nodded approval.

"Lieutenant Manzano will hate to miss the battle," Arista warned.

"There will be others," Moreno replied laconically, "unfortunately."

"This war shall be short," Arista scoffed, not liking Moreno's negativity.

"Excellency, that is our best hope," Moreno replied.

Arista grunted. "If these dogs refuse to obey," Arista snapped in English as he looked down upon Riley, "make your previous threat a reality." Arista turned and urged his horse to the front of his column.

Riley blanched at Arista's English words. For the first time, he realized that Dalton could prove right, that Riley could find himself sighting Dalton down the barrel of his "greaser musket." It was kill old friends or be killed yourself. His stomach suddenly felt queasy, like after eating under-cooked pork.

Arista led his long, tramping column out of the dusty plaza. Mexican musicians struck up the "La Cachuca March," a joyous if monotonous little ditty. Somehow, music always made impending death and mayhem seem less real, Riley thought. But to him at this moment, it felt very real indeed.

A few minutes later, while Riley's deserters followed Mejia and the guards down a different path, Moreno and Riley walked together past fortified cannons on a bluff that overlooked the Rio Grande. Star-shaped Fort Texas lay just across the water on the far bank. It looked so close; Riley felt he could lob a rock at it.

The garrison-size U.S. flag, almost forty feet long on the fly and twenty feet on the hoist, rippled mightily in a stiff breeze atop the fort's massive earthen walls. The flag flew from a white ship's mast carted inland from the anchored fleet as the only "flagpole" strong enough to hold it. Taylor was making a point, Riley mused. Some U.S. troops could be seen inside the fort, but, strangely, the adjacent tent city appeared empty. Where did they go? Riley wondered.

He and Moreno paused to let Mexican artillerymen cross their path and man six old, iron guns of British manufacture; large, they could fire nine-pound solid cannonballs, shells, and cannister. The gunners picked up implements and waited at their posts. They looked eager, anxious.

"I earned my British stripes working nine-pounders like them," Riley said almost in a reverie, nodding at the cannon. " 'Twas too long ago."

"Indeed, Teniente," Moreno said bemused, "perhaps it was one of these very guns. They are Napoleonic surplus."

"Not that long ago," Riley countered, "though it feels like it."

"Now you must earn more than mere stripes," Moreno warned. Riley frowned when he saw Mexican gunners begin to ram powder bags and cannonballs down the gun muzzles, all to shouted Spanish commands by artillery officers. "In less than an hour, we bombard that fort," Moreno said as he gazed across the river. "You and your men must fire the first shots."

"We got friends on the other side!" Riley managed, staring stunned at Moreno. His mind again flashed back to Dalton's grim words.

"Your 'friends' are enemies of Mexico," Moreno snapped. "And you are now Mexican soldiers. You must do your duty."

Riley realized he was trapped. He pulled out his flask and downed a heavy swig as he stared across the river. The morning sun was higher now and bathed the fort in rich light. The heavy bronze U.S. guns glistened.

"No soldier ought to know who he's got sighted down the barrel of his gun," Riley muttered, feeling a pang of guilt. He could almost see Dalton's face.

"What you aim at is your choice," Moreno said, sounding sympathetic. "What you might actually hit is the choice of God."

"Captain, you're right about one thing sure," Riley sighed. He flicked the gold fringe on his epaulette with a finger. "This trinket's already grown heavy."

Thirty minutes later, in a fortified battery, Riley stood atop the double-trailed wooden carriage of a small iron cannon, one of four tiny guns that fired three-pound solid shot. Looking sullen, his deserters stood as crews at each gun. Many sported black eyes, facial cuts, and bandaged heads from yesterday's fight. They looked angry, trapped, and betrayed. And Riley knew they all blamed him. But he alone knew that their lives depended on what he did next.

"Some say war 'elevates' us all," Riley pleaded. "Seems it has 'promoted' us." He took a hit at his flask.

"To bloody greaser patriots?!" taunted Price. A few chuckled. Some swore amid general grumbling.

"To fools playin' with tiny toy guns! Three-pounders yet!" shouted the tobacco chewer. He spat a glob onto the barrel of his dwarfish cannon.

"No, you lout," snapped Riley. "I mean this damn war's upped us from being flogged to being hanged!" A hush fell on the group. " 'Tis as walking dead men we are cursed." Eyes stared hard at Riley. "If you're captured or daft enough to go traipsing back, with no benefit of last rites they'll hoist your arse up by your neck." Mutters of resentment rippled through the Irish majority. "If you stay, you'll do your duty or they'll do theirs."

Riley pointed behind them. A full company of guards with

green lapels stood in double ranks, rifles at the ready. Among them were the toothy corporal and the youngster with the wispy mustache. Moreno watched with Sergeant Mejia and Lieutenant Camillo Manzano, a young, smug, aristocratic officer. His blue uniform sported double-breasted green lapels with gold embroidery.

"Faith I come t'soldier for greaser land," said the tobacco chewer, spitting for emphasis, "not to shoot at my old mates." Many echoed his sentiments.

Riley looked across the river. "We all got friends over there," he said more bitterly. " 'Twas their choice to stay." He took another swig, silently cursing Dalton for his stubbornness.

" 'Twas my choice t'leave, and I'm damn proud of it!" shouted Parker, who stepped up on the trail of his gun to be seen. "I curse that striped banner what killed my friend Lamb, and for what?!" He shook his fist at the U.S. flag. Some muttered in agreement.

"Like me, most of you are immigrant 'Poper scum'," taunted Riley, pausing to see the effect. Most cringed at the familiar insult. He pointed across the river. "They deem you good enough only for the dirty jobs they can't stomach themselves, and that includes soldiering!" Some shouted to agree. Riley inexplicably felt a tiny thrill of encouragement. He eyed Moreno, who offered him just a hint of approval with a discreet, slight nod. "Their shithouse adjutant officers say, 'Thank you very much,' with the sting of the lash!" More shouted in angry agreement. "At least greasers are gracious enough to offer some of the land you're soldiering for!" Riley was gratified by a unanimous rousing cheer.

"Aye to that but for one thing," scowled the Scot. "My mother reared no bonnie son to be a branded traitor." A hush fell. Some mumbled to agree.

"Traitor to what?!" Riley demanded, feeling desperate now

not to lose them after coming so close. Thankfully, none could answer.

Suddenly, the melodic vocal music of Latin chanting drew near as a priest and altar boys approached in what seemed to Riley as an odd intrusion. The cleric was walking the line of the adjacent Mexican battery to bless the guns and kneeling artillerymen. Riley hastened to capitalize on the image.

"Would you pledge loyalty to a land what curses your faith?!" Riley shouted. Many crossed themselves and yelled angry disavowals. The priest passed through the deserters, Riley crossing himself. The priest walked on down the line, and Riley resumed, pointing across the river. "It should be painted on that flag, 'No Irish need apply!' " More deserters shouted in angry agreement. Riley held the smoking match aloft so all his men could see it. "Patriotism cannot be native born," Riley yelled, "but only earned by them what expects it!"

With a unanimous shout, the deserters agreed. Many punched the air with clenched fists while others upraised their artillery rammers. Riley knew the pivotal moment was at hand. He hopped down from the gun and stepped to its breech. He held the smoking match just above the vent. "Now," Riley commanded quietly, almost reverently and as much to himself as his men, "fire and be damned."

Riley touched the match to the vent. The gun belched orange flame and white smoke with a cracking boom. As it recoiled and rolled back six feet, Parker touched off his gun. Almost immediately, the other two guns followed. Then the entire line of larger Mexican guns erupted with a louder roar as the bombardment commenced in earnest, filling the air with the hissing shrieks of shells. The deserters stood frozen, staring at one another almost in disbelief at what they had just done. Riley took note and determined not to lose them.

"Load!" Riley bellowed, shaking them out of their momentary

panic. "Take your time, like I showed you!" Price rushed in confusion to shove a powder bag down a still smoking barrel.

Riley smacked him in the butt with a sponge staff, then thrust the dripping implement into his hands. "Sponge first!" he roared, then added sweetly, "else you'll blow your dumb arse clear back to Bristol!" Price nodded sheepishly.

Riley walked his line of guns and corrected the clumsy movements of the former infantrymen, all new to artillery. It showed, he thought. But they managed to load and roll the recoiled guns back into position. He felt a glimmer of pride in what he had created. He bellowed, "Fire!"

"Relax the men, Sergeant," Moreno told Mejia in Spanish as the guns roared again.

"Yes, my captain," Mejia replied in undisguised disappointment. He walked toward his men and yelled terse commands. The guards lowered rifles.

"They have signed their own death warrants," Moreno said as he watched the deserters. He looked across the river and added, more to himself, "Much like our country." Beside him, Manzano overheard and scowled. Heavy white smoke drifted across the battery in the brisk morning breeze.

"Captain, we cannot let norteamericanos remain on our land," he said almost as a matter of fact.

Moreno eyed him patiently. He is so young, he thought. "We cannot win this war," Moreno said quietly. Before Manzano could protest, Riley strode up.

"These tiny guns are too damn light for the job!" Riley complained, adrenaline pumping. "Shot's falling short! We need more powder!"

"It is not important," Moreno said. "This is only a diversion."

"You're only diverting fleas and bugs!" Riley said. "The damn camps are empty!"

"They have gone to meet our army," Moreno replied almost casually, lighting a cigar. "But may I present one who bridles at being left behind, Lieutenant Camillo Manzano of the rifle company from the 11th Infantry Regiment, our support?" Riley smiled thinly at the choice of words. He thought "guards" would be more honest. He snapped to attention and bowed in respect, as did Manzano, though with more reserve. "He speaks English," Moreno added.

"Wouldn't a grand officer such as yourself rather be firing volleys than playing watchdog to the likes of us?" Riley said, testing the waters.

"Any opportunity to kill norteamericanos would be welcome," Manzano replied cooly.

Riley straightened as if slapped: He got his answer.

"Teniente Riley, to sound so convincing to your men, must you believe what you told them?" Moreno inquired.

"Does it matter?" Riley said, looking incredulous. He nodded at the sweating deserters now working the guns more smoothly, firing round after booming round. "Got the damn job done, didn't I?!"

Riley turned and strode back to his men. Moreno stared after him curiously; Manzano, in utter contempt. The two officers walked to the edge of the bluff. They saw small bursts of Mexican shells explode above and beneath the thick earthen walls of Fort Texas. Only a few hit inside, scattering American gun crews as they finally began running to their posts. Many shots fell short and sent spouts of water up from the river. Moreno looked resigned. Manzano bristled.

"Right shall make might," Manzano asserted in Spanish. He turned to a Mexican gun crew near them. He drew his sword and thrust it high toward the U.S. fort. "Viva Mexico!" he shouted.

The gunners echoed his cry and fired the gun with a cracking roar. They loaded with enthusiasm and more patriotic shouting. Manzano looked at Moreno proudly, as if he had made his point. Moreno turned and looked across the river.

In the American fort, well-drilled professional gun crews deftly loaded and sighted their larger cannons with precision. In rapid succession, each gun fired followed by the next in line across the entire parapet. They began to re-load. Heavy shells exploded with metallic clangs and thumping booms amidst all the Mexican guns. Some Mexican gunners screamed and staggered away, wounded with savage, bloody slashes from shrapnel. Others dove for cover.

Parker and other younger deserters looked shaken. Riley noticed. "Stand to your guns, lads!" Riley roared. " 'Tis better to give than receive!" He walked the line calmly. " 'Tain't possible to hide," he yelled. "If you hear their guns, you're still alive! If you don't, there's no use in worrying no more!" His grim, veteran humor steadied them.

"Viva la Republica Mexicana!" Manzano yelled at the Mexican gun crew just as the gun received a direct hit. With a horrific dull clang, the cannon barrel shattered in the explosion into dozens of jagged pieces of flying iron. The gunners disintegrated amid anguished cries. Arms, legs, and heads flew like leaves tossed in a hot wind across the battery. Manzano stood in silent horror, splattered in blood and brains. Moreno stepped up, stared sadly at the stunned young officer. Moreno calmly offered his handkerchief.

One week later, the rooftops and church steeples of Matamoros glistened in the setting sun behind the retreating Mexican army. A U.S. flag hung limp from a staff lashed to the tallest church steeple, the cathedral in which Riley and his deserters had been held. Tattered, powder blackened, and tired Mexican soldiers trudging along the roadside could hear victorious Americans in the distance lustily singing "Green Grows the Laurel."

As the first verse of the American song was repeated, one grizzled Mexican private cringed. He turned to the soldado marching beside him. "*No mas* 'green-gross,' " he moaned and held his ears in disgust.

" 'Green-gross,' " growled his friend, who spat and jerked a thumb toward the deserters, walking sullenly near them down the center of the road. The two Mexican veterans grunted with bitter, weary smiles.

Following the four small guns pulled by mule teams, the deserters shuffled along wearing rolled Mexican army blankets like horse collars over one shoulder and under the opposite arm. Soiled, greasy canvas haversacks were slung over their other shoulder, riding on their left hip. The salty Mexican teamsters in rough civilian clothing wielded whips effortlessly above the heads of the mules to drive them. They spewed Spanish profanity with each crack of the whip. Mejia and a few wary guards hovered on the flanks of the column, rifles ready. Price walked with the tobacco chewer and glared first at the teamsters, then at the guards. Another whip cracked.

"Same bloody difference, the mules or us," Price grumbled.

"Sure an' there's our muleteer," the tobacco chewer said, spitting. He nodded toward Riley up ahead, walking with Parker.

"They fear us more than the Yanks, lads!" Riley shouted, trying to make a joke and pointing at the guards. Deserters roundly cursed him.

"That's why they're hidin' the river girls!" Parker shouted cheerily.

Riley gave him a pat on the back. He saw Moreno watching from the roadside astride his horse, in the shade of a mesquite tree. Riley trotted to him. "Arista would've done more damage with them mule drivers," he said.

"Had we more soldados like those, we would have won," Moreno replied, nodding toward the road. Imperious Manzano was bringing up the rear of the column with the rest of his company. They marched past smartly, looking proud.

"But you don't have many like that," Riley said, "and you won't."

"And so our long retreat begins," Moreno said wearily, "as I feared." His worst nightmare had been realized. But he would continue to do his duty.

" 'Twill be but a brisk walk the few hundred miles to Monterey," Riley joked, missing Moreno's nuance entirely. "But why fall back at all? 'Tis just begging them to invade and cut out your heart. End it now, for us all! Talk truce!" Riley knew that formal surrender would mean capture, court martial, and the hangman's noose.

"We cannot give them that satisfaction!" Moreno snapped, pointing toward the Americans. He quickly recovered his composure. Riley looked confused. "Mexico would rather fight and lose," Moreno explained in a steady gaze, "than accept insult."

"There ain't no point in fighting," Riley asserted, "with no hope of winning." He stared defiantly at Moreno.

"So to you now it may seem," Moreno said calmly.

"You're playing the losing game of the patriot," Riley warned. "This professional won't bask in no glory from the end of a rope." He knew his men would mutiny if they felt there was no hope.

"Understand, Teniente," Moreno warned, "we do not waste trials on deserters. On sight, we shoot them."

"Then to save your lead for the Yanks, I alone tell my 'gallant deserters' whatever I think they need to know. Me and only me!" Riley glared.

"Teniente, I would not want it any other way," Moreno replied.

An old ore wagon pulled by two yokes of oxen rumbled into view. The wagon was crammed with dejected U.S. prisoners from all branches of service. Riley brightened when he recognized Artillery Corporal Ockter, the Prussian who had let him visit Dalton in the provost compound for the price of a taco.

"Mightn't I have a little chat with one of them prisoners, sir?" Riley asked sweetly. Moreno eyed him suspiciously. "To survive long enough until peace, we'll need more gunners what truly know the craft." Moreno understood and nodded. Riley strode quickly toward the wagon, waving his arms to stop.

Shortly, the wagon rumbled away and Ockter stood beside the road facing Riley. The shattered debris of the Mexican army continued to flow past. The Prussian stared in confusion at Riley's shining gold epaulette.

"You don't know whether to salute or to shit," Riley observed.

"I have no choice," Ockter replied stiffly in his German accent. "I have not been fed enough." He snapped a crisp salute, but Riley waved it off. Ockter looked insulted.

" 'Twill be hard for the likes of you," Riley explained, "but this bunch ain't long on military formality."

Ockter held his salute, insisting on a return. Riley rolled his eyes and saluted with a thin smile.

"Speaking of stubborn," Riley observed, "whatever happened to that solid son of Erin, Sergeant Dalton, the one I fed you for to visit in the provost jail?"

"I saw him fighting cactus and greasers with the 2nd Infantry at the Palo Alto fight," said Ockter. He slowly braced himself with the stiff bearing of a proud soldier. "If you had not heard, we won," he added, barely hiding a smile.

"So, Dalton weren't in the fort at all," Riley said, relieved and ignoring Ockter's comment. "And would the greasers have nabbed himself if you'd been serving a gun?" Riley asked.

Ockter shook his head *no.* "I was stumbling through smoke and cactus as red-leg infantry," Ockter said in disgust. "A dozen lancers seemed to rise out of the ground from a ditch." He shrugged. "I do not think they killed me because I cursed at them in German. They just laughed."

"If nothing else, greasers recognize talent when they see it!" Riley laughed. He flicked the dangling gold fringe of his epaulette. "So do I."

"I would rather eat rats in their prison than serve again as infantry," the artilleryman asserted with Germanic arrogance. He looked suspicious.

Riley nodded in sympathetic understanding. "I can offer you promotion quick as my wink and four enormous guns!" he lied, slipping his arm around Ockter's shoulder.

The Prussian looked intrigued as Riley walked him toward Moreno, watching within earshot. "And when this little fracas is over in just a few weeks," Riley soothed, "the greasers'll thank your Prussian arse with three hundred-twenty acres." Ockter's eyes grew wide. Riley sensed he had caught the dream.

Moreno frowned but resigned himself to be party to another Riley deception. And yet, had he not himself deceived Riley? Moreno questioned if he had not somehow become merely the flip side of Riley's tarnished coin. He felt unclean. But was it not his duty, right or wrong? More and more, this duty was proving to be as distasteful as it was necessary.

Chapter 4

MONTEREY: THE TRENCHES
LATE SEPTEMBER 1846

Quaint and ethereal, the old Spanish stone and adobe buildings of Monterey trembled along the banks of the Santa Catarina River as if recoiling from the encroaching ugly scars of American siege lines. Entrenched U.S. artillery peppered orange shell bursts throughout the city's streets as well as its surrounding Mexican fortifications. Explosions reverberated across the cultivated, high desert plateau and resonated in the mountains. The booming cacophony rolled across the valley like peals of crackling thunder, reminding Riley of the approaching storm clouds of Mackinac. Perhaps, he idled, old Judge Maloney had been right: His dream was that of a madman.

He hunkered down behind an earth and sandbag gun embrasure as a throbbing explosion showered rock, adobe, and dirt clods. Crouched beside him was Ockter, now in a dusty Mexican coatee emblazoned with two red-fringed epaulettes. Coughing, Ockter angrily flicked the fringe of one.

"In three months, you only have been right about the promotion!" he snapped. Riley pertly dusted off Ockter's other epaulette.

"Give it time, Sergeant," he replied dryly. Riley cocked his head at a sudden silence. "Ain't that loud?" he said. The barrage had ended. At last, Riley thought, maybe now we can show off a bit. " 'Tis time to tweak the eagle's beak," Riley announced. Ockter looked doubtful.

They rose and faced their battery. Earthworks in front of a

solid row of one-story adobe houses dwarfed the four tiny guns. The deserters huddled behind sandbags or lay curled up inside blanket lean-tos dug into the clay near their guns. Tin plates, cups, candles, and refuse lay everywhere. An empty trench with firing steps for infantry stretched off to one side. Looming above on the flat rooftops were Manzano's guards, their rifles poking over piled sandbags. Riley knew that their barrels were aimed as much at his men as the Yanks. He had to prove loyalty somehow, if only to stay alive long enough to escape this self-made prison. His brilliant plan had become tattered, but he clung to it now like a battle-torn flag more than ever, to rally himself.

"Counter battery fire, by section, three hundred yards!" Riley bellowed. Hostile glares shot back at him as his men walked sullenly to their guns. Riley eyed Moreno and Manzano, approaching briskly through the empty infantry trench. They bounded up onto a sandbagged observation platform. Riley nodded to Ockter, who took command as Riley trotted to them.

"Load!" Ockter ordered. The bedraggled deserters were filthy with weeks of beard growth and looked parched and weary. They rammed bags of black powder and solid copper cannonballs down the barrels, inserted cut fuses into vent holes on the barrel breeches and sighted the guns. They showed improved precision since Matamoros but lacked spirit. Riley clambered up beside Moreno and Manzano and held a spyglass to one eye. "Ready!" Ockter yelled.

"Fire!" Riley commanded. The four guns boomed one at a time and rolled back in recoil. The men instantly pushed the guns back into their starting positions and stood ready to load again.

On a low hill opposite Riley's battery across a slopng plain, four dusty puffs of dirt spit up about twenty yards in front of an entrenched U.S. battery of larger, gleaming bronze field guns. One tall cactus toppled over. The U.S. regular artillerymen hooted and howled scornfully, shaking their fists and bellowing curses. They loaded their guns, looking to Riley to be sturdy six-pounders.

"O'Brien's battery, luck of the Irish," Riley muttered, recognizing their unit flag and knowing they ranked among the best of Taylor's army. "Maximum elevation! Load!" he yelled.

"Our men have no enthusiasm, Teniente," Moreno observed wryly.

"Like the eunuch with the slut, sir, what they got is no firepower," Riley shot back. "And precious little water, sir," he added, "except for to swab the damn guns."

"Ready!" Ockter hollered after the guns had been loaded.

"Fire by battery! Fire!" Riley commanded. The guns roared again, but this time all four at once, followed by four more spurts of dirt short of the target. Moreno and Riley frowned as more peals of derisive laughter floated back to them across the plain. "Stand them down, Ockter," Riley sighed, suffering professional embarrassment. For morale, he hid his anxiety.

Hot and dehydrated, the men sought shade and collapsed in near exhaustion. Price tried his gourd canteen, peculiar to the Mexican army . . . empty.

"Bloody well right!" Price exclaimed, smashing it against an adobe wall.

"When the water finally gets here, lads," Riley shouted, "Price'll have to donate his share to those of us what still got canteens!" Parker led a few mocking cheers. Most, too spent, remained silent.

"Our wells were captured three days ago," Manzano informed Riley. Riley looked at Moreno, who nodded to affirm. Riley yanked out his flask.

"And that's the cork in the bottle, for those what needs water," Riley snapped. He took a drink and offered it to Manzano, who eyed him with disdain. Moreno turned away to hide a smile. Suddenly, the bugle call "Attention" sounded from the far end of the adjacent empty trench.

Mejia led a squad of guards to make way for General Ampudia and his staff, resplendent in red bib uniforms like that of Moreno but heavier with gold embroidery. Ampudia, like all the high-ranking Mexican officers that Riley had seen, was very light skinned. He sported a thick mustache and a graying goatee. Behind them trudged a company of nervous recruits. Clad in simple white canvas uniforms with red facings, their dark-mahogany Indian skin stood in stark contrast. Veteran corporals and sergeants, with lighter brown skin like Mejia and his elite company, beat them mercilessly, forcing them atop the firing steps.

"Our new commander, General Ampudia," whispered Moreno as he snapped to attention. "He commanded artillery at the Alamo," he added, idly touching the scar on his cheek.

"Attention, company!" Riley bellowed. The deserters stood erect. "His worship must find things here a bit backward," he whispered, "being on the inside of the fort this time."

Ampudia stepped onto the parapet and eyed the deserters and their gun emplacements. He gave a surprised nod of approval. *"Bueno . . . bueno,"* he muttered.

"Excellency, may I present the architect of these works," Moreno said in Spanish, "Teniente . . ." But the general cut him off.

"Do not waste formalities, Captain, on those who cannot appreciate them," he said in cultured English. "I have heard of Teniente Riley."

"I am flattered, sir," Riley said, unsure of Ampudia's meaning.

"I brought you infantry to help protect the guns," Ampudia said, gesturing at the Indian levies. They looked nervous, ill-trained, and confused.

"We'll rest easier now, sir," Riley said with caustic sweetness.

Ampudia could not miss the sarcasm. He turned to Manzano and pointed to the empty rooftop behind the conscripts. "Extend your rifle company to cover both the deserters and these Indians," said Ampudia. "We must hold all lower classes to their duty."

"Yes, my general," Manzano replied, nodding sharply.

"Kill any who try to leave," Ampudia concluded, staring at Riley.

"Been here weeks now, sir," Riley ventured carefully. "All we've seen of lovely Monterey is these damn ditches what you had us dig."

"It is as far as any dare yet trust you, Teniente," Ampudia replied. He looked again at Manzano. "Also, I suppose, I must allow these Indians to have their camp women," he added, his tone rife with condescension.

Riley cocked his head at this and looked curiously at Moreno, who almost smiled. Ampudia addressed his staff.

"Our feminine baggage is costly and cumbersome," he said in Spanish, "but without it, half this miserable frontier army would go home!" His staff of aristocratic officers joined him in a patronizing chuckle.

Moreno bridled at the insult as he translated quietly for Riley, watching the general and staff leave. Mejia and his squad stayed behind.

" 'Tis lords of high degree like himself what's made me contrary," Riley muttered to Moreno, who fell silent, brooding.

"It is his right," Manzano asserted with his usual arrogance.

Moreno gave him a reprimanding look, then turned to Riley. "With a mere nod of his head, he could have curbed your insolent tongue eternally," Moreno said. He nodded at a narrow alley between the buildings. A grizzled squad of veteran infantry, his guards, lowered their muskets and trotted to catch up with the general. Manzano glared at Riley, then led Mejia and his men back to the alley, where they climbed a ladder to join their company on the roof.

That night, Riley and Moreno warmed themselves at a small campfire on the parapet. Like all high deserts, Riley recalled, the Monterey plain sizzled during the day and froze at night. He eyed Mejia's riflemen pacing on the roof. His deserters huddled looking pitiful around their tiny cook fires behind the guns. Cornmeal was being fried in bacon grease. Parker, Price, and the others were silent and glum. They stared enviously at the infantry trench beside them.

Barefoot Indian women in simple peasant skirts, blouses, and rebosas were cooking tortillas and beans for their soldados. One balanced a plump, giggling senorita on his lap as he played a lively Mexican polka on a concertina. Occasionally, one hand would slip from the concertina to squeeze a soft breast. Although some women were matronly, all were seductive in their peculiar, sultry fashion, Riley thought. Or perhaps, he admitted, he had been alone far too long. Many flirted outrageously, passing earthenware jugs of spirits freely.

"Them ain't the likely girls we saw at the river," lamented Parker, licking his cracked lips as he watched. "Sure an' these look a bit rode hard."

"This sailor says any port in a bloody storm," growled Price, tending the cornmeal cakes.

The Irish tobacco chewer grimaced as he tasted the result. "Faith 'tis time t'jump ship," he mumbled. He sniffed longingly at the aroma carried on the breeze. "Them greasers got more than enough to go 'round," he suggested. Others groused in agreement, staring.

On the parapet, Riley and Moreno gazed out at the encircling U.S. campfires. Heavy guns boomed intermittently merely to harass the Mexicans. Riley watched the burning fuse of a shell arc across the sky and explode in the air harmlessly, like a firework.

"Each night, they move closer," Moreno observed. "They tighten the noose." Riley scowled at his choice of words. "Our spies say they tire of this siege. They will attack at dawn tomorrow or the next day."

"At that Alamo fight ten years ago," Riley said carefully, " 'tain't like you left them a back door. Maybe they'd have used it if they could."

"We are not yet trapped, Teniente. We still hold the road south from Monterey," Moreno asserted, sounding perhaps overly hopeful.

Riley looked relieved, though suspicious. Ockter climbed up and gave a smart salute. Riley rolled his eyes. "I keep telling you, Ockter, this army ain't that long on the blessed formalities," he said.

"I beg to report, we have only thirty-three rounds of solid shot left and no cannister," Ockter said, emphasizing the last. Riley looked at Moreno.

"You can't stop good infantry," warned Riley, "without a scattergun blast of cannister." He knew the tin cans filled with one-inch iron balls never failed.

"Corruption," Moreno said. "It was paid for, but it exists only on paper."

"Don't fret, Ockter," Riley joked. "If it don't get here soon, we'll reach over these breastworks and lift some from the Yanks just on the other side."

"They are cooking up trouble down there," Ockter warned, ignoring the sarcasm and pointing below.

Parker, Price, the Scot, the tobacco chewer, and a few others had ambled en masse across to the Mexican cook fires in the infantry trench. They carried their empty tin plates and tentatively approached the nearest fire, where sat the concertina player. The swarthy young woman on his lap deftly slipped one breast back beneath her camisa. The musician stopped playing and glared at them. Other soldados and the women stared in hostility, slowly gathering.

"Would you have somethin' in an Irish stew?" asked Parker innocently. He held out his plate to another woman tending the pot of beans. She hesitated at first, then smiled flirtatiously and started to ladle some of the simmering pintos onto his plate. With a sudden flash of gleaming blades in the firelight, nearby soldados jerked out Spanish dirks and daggers. The deserters recoiled, confused.

"Get your own women!" growled the concertina player in Spanish. The deserters did not understand but wisely backed away, grumbling and hungry. They heard laughter from above and looked up.

Manzano, Mejia, and his guards found it all very amusing, looking down on them, rifles ready, as if daring the deserters to start something. Rooftop campfires revealed backlit silhouettes of more women serving them food, as well.

"Are we part o'this stinkin' army or ain't we?!" yelled the tobacco chewer, shaking his fist up at the guards. They only laughed more.

"Seems 'army issue' don't include good food," Riley observed, "except what comes with army issue women." He tossed a questioning look at Moreno.

"Soldaderas attach themselves at their own whim," Moreno smiled, "like all women. The army must tolerate them, but we cannot control them."

"We're not likely to find them while stuck in these ditches," Riley said.

"In their own time, they will find you," Moreno replied.

"Hope there's time enough," Riley replied, "afore it runs out."

At first light of a crisp, chilly dawn, O'Brien's battery fired six successive booms to rake the Mexican defenses, enshrouded in early morning ground fog. The battered adobes behind the deserters took more hits, the rock and adobe adding a dull crunching sound to the cracking thumps of the shell bursts. Flying rock struck a few guards and deserters. A few shells burst among the Indian infantry, maiming some. Wounded soon cried out for water through lips cracked, parched, and bleeding. As the deserters hunkered down behind their guns, Ockter trotted to Riley, on the parapet with Moreno and Manzano.

"They still are beyond range of these popguns!" Ockter said. "But we should return fire anyway, if only for morale . . . and pride!"

"All the water we got is in the sponge buckets," said Riley, shaking his head. "Save it 'til we can hit something!"

An explosion ignited a wood awning on the adobe behind the infantry. Wounded Mexicans lying in the shade beneath it found themselves threatened by flames. Black smoke permeated the trenches. The bombardment ended, and the only sounds were crackling flames and the pitiful coughing of the wounded.

"Give them a hand!" urged Riley, who leaped from the parapet with Ockter. They joined Mexican infantry in moving the severely wounded into shade away from the flames. Coughing from the smoke, Riley and Ockter picked up an aging soldado with a sucking chest wound. They carried him into the shade of the observation parapet and gently laid him down in the dirt.

Moreno watched from above as they shooed swarming flies away from his clotted wound. He looked pleasantly surprised by the gesture. Manzano glowered as if such an act would be beneath him.

Suddenly, Riley saw something wondrous at the far end of the trench. "Am I dead, dreamin', or gone daft?!" he asked, punching Ockter to look. Twenty or so captivating young Mexican women emerged from the thick smoke and filed into the trench. Each carried three or four full, dripping U.S. wood and Mexican gourd canteens. They were clad in colorful, calf-length cotton skirts that swayed seductively with each step; thin, white, cotton camisa blouses, damp with water and sweat and clinging to their breasts; and bits and pieces of castoff Mexican military headgear. Barracks caps and shakos perched atop their flowing hair at rakish, sexy angles. Unlike the Indian women, they did not cover their heads with rebosas but tied them around their waists to accentuate their full, inviting hips. Their long hair hung free, caressing bare shoulders. Inviting smiles abounded. Riley thought they could pass for a theatrical troupe.

Cheers erupted among the soldados. The deserters stood and gawked in silent disbelief. They slowly drifted toward the trench as if in a daze.

" 'Tain't like no white women I ever seen," observed the leering tobacco chewer. He spat sloppily and wiped the dribble from his mouth.

"Not afore removing wee mountains o'clothing," added the grinning Scot.

"I can see their bloomin' pink titties!" exclaimed Price aghast, drawing rowdy laughter.

The women began to hand out full canteens to soldados and deserters alike, some dispensing water to the grateful wounded.

Parker took a canteen from a swarthy teenage girl of about sixteen who offered a flirtatious smile, her laughing brown eyes promising more before she moved on.

Ockter noticed Parker staring after her. "Now these are looking more like your frauleins from the river, Parker!" Ockter said loudly with a rare grin.

"Sure and I didn't recognize 'em with their clothes on," said

Parker in naïve wonder to guffaws of laughter. Parker flushed red.

Even Moreno looked amused. But Manzano glowered at this crossing of what he considered insurmountable racial and ethnic lines.

"They should show more respect," he said in Spanish, "even if these are mere camp followers."

"More than anyone, Lieutenant," sighed Moreno, tired of an attitude that he saw as a pervasive Mexican flaw, "a soldier needs a sense of humor." Manzano bowed at the reprimand, but Moreno knew he did so only out of courtesy, not understanding.

One stunning woman of around nineteen caught the eye of Riley. Strikingly lovely with strong, sculpted features, she had silken skin the color of creamy chocolate. She seemed animated by an innocent sparkle lacking in the others. She paused, weighed down by canteens, to brush sweat and matted hair from her forehead. Riley found something familiar about the fire in her flashing black eyes.

"That one's both shapely and handsome," Riley said in lusty praise.

"She could most easily be your daughter," Ockter scolded with prim Prussian propriety.

"Ain't as old as I look, Ockter," Riley asserted with an edge. " 'Tain't the miles, 'tis the damn road." He could not take his eyes off her. "Besides," Riley laughed, "either way, she's somebody else's daughter!"

"*Agua!*" cried the wounded soldado just laid down by Riley and Ockter. "*Agua por favor!*"

The young woman started to walk toward him. She momentarily stared up at Riley, who looked captivated by her. She gave Riley a shy but knowing smile, then knelt beside the wounded man. Thinking he was seeing a heavenly vision, the soldado reached out weakly, as if to touch her and confirm her reality. As she bent over him, her long, raven hair cascaded onto her sweating bosom.

Riley stared unabashedly down her low-cut camisa at full young breasts. He marveled at how their soft, tan flesh contrasted invitingly with her sun-bronzed face, shoulders, and arms. The wounded soldado looked up and into her eyes.

"Am I dead and seeing an angel?" he muttered in Spanish, drinking.

"No, you are still alive," she said. "And I am still Luzero, certainly no angel."

"If I am alive," replied the thirsty soldado, shaking his head, "I was saved by the angel of Monterey." Others nearby took up the cry as the women gave out more water.

"Angels of Monterey!" cried the grateful soldiers. Many crossed themselves as if the obviously fallen women were heaven sent.

Luzero rose to go to the next wounded man and caught Riley leering down her blouse. Inexplicably, she blushed and tossed him an embarrassed smile, tugged up her blouse, and walked away. Riley stared after her completely captivated. He found something familiar in the sway of her full hips.

Moreno noticed Riley's interest as Luzero passed beneath him on the observation platform. "Young woman!" he called down in Spanish. Luzero looked up. Riley stood as Moreno waved her up to the parapet. As she climbed the ladder, Riley could not contain himself. He bounded up after her, leaving Ockter shaking his head in disapproval.

"Where did you and your friends find water?" Moreno asked in Spanish.

"At the captured city wells guarded by norteamericanos," she replied. Some of the girls gathered below to listen. "They 'bribed' them."

115

The girls giggled but looked more proud than embarrassed, seeing themselves as patriots. Riley looked curious, not understanding a word but ready to burst. He cleared his throat, drawing Moreno's attention.

"A few of our soldaderas, soldier women who some call camp followers, sell more comfort than merely clean clothes and food," Moreno explained.

Riley certainly understood now, he thought. He looked at Luzero with even more interest, her tantalizing possibilities skipping across his mind.

"In a patriotic gesture, today they 'comforted' norteamericanos in exchange for this water," Moreno concluded.

"We were so-o-o good," bragged Parker's swarthy teenage girl in Spanish, "they even gave us their canteens!" The other girls laughed as she held one up and danced around with it like a trophy. The concertina player struck up a tune. Her calf-length skirt flared out as she twirled like a top and revealed her taut, stark tan thighs and the bottom of her shapely bare buttocks. Parker stared wide eyed as other deserters cheered.

"Faith I don't savvy a word," Parker mumbled, "but she makes her point plain, she does."

While deserters laughed, the young guard with the wispy mustache glared down at Parker from an adobe rooftop. He stood beside the toothy corporal.

"Your woman makes a fool of you," said the grinning corporal in Spanish.

"It does not matter," the youngster pouted. "They are the women of anyone who has the money."

On the parapet, Luzero teasingly thrust a sky-blue wood canteen marked *U.S.* at Riley. He took her hand, bowed graciously, and kissed it, to her surprise.

"For the first time in my life, 'tis a pleasure to meet a patriot," Riley said.

She tossed back her mane of hair with an infectious laugh. "But we have met before, Teniente Riley, leader of our Irish soldados," she replied saucily in a delicate Spanish accent. She deftly untied her rebosa from her slender waist, drew it over her head and across her face, and assumed a demure attitude. At last, Riley recognized her as the young woman who had given him the desertion flyer at Fort Texas. His jaw dropped open. She laughed and made a perfect curtsy.

"You have all been the object of much discussion," she added flirtatiously, barely hiding a smile. She said it again in Spanish as she climbed back down the ladder. Agreeing enthusiastically, the young women laughed, giggled, and chattered as they hurried to leave the trenches. The deserters stared in lusty hunger after them. Some removed their caps as they passed. Riley looked longingly after Luzero, drawing an unseen, jealous glare from Manzano.

"You are an officer now, Teniente," Moreno said deadpan. Riley turned to face him. "Compose yourself and close your jaw."

Gathered deserters at the base of the platform overheard and broke into laughter. Suddenly six shells whistled and slammed near the trenches with ear shattering explosions, forcing everyone to dive for cover.

After dark, each gun crew of deserters huddled around its own campfire as soldaderas cooked and served healthy portions of beans, beef, and tortillas. The Indian women did likewise with their men in the adjacent trench. Yet more women served Mejia's guards on the rooftop. The Indian concertina player serenaded with a lonely tune. A few guards stood at the deserter campfires.

Riley walked from campfire to campfire, checking on the mood. All night, he had eyed Luzero as she tended a central pot of beans and beef. He wanted to wait until she was alone. Right now, only the young guard with the wispy mustache was stationed with her.

The swarthy teenage girl sashayed up and presented a warm tortilla as she eyed the young guard. He looked hopeful as Luzero ladled beans into the tortilla and the girl deftly folded it into a burrito. Then she tossed him a haughty look, turned, and flitted to the adjacent campfire, where Parker sat.

The hurt guard looked at Luzero, who urged him to follow the girl with a nod. He took off.

"You should not grow close to such scoundrels," the young guard warned in Spanish as he stepped up to "his" girl while Parker devoured the burrito.

The girl ignored the guard and brushed back Parker's hair. Parker loved the gentle touch but looked confused. He stared first at the girl, then the young, glowering guard, not understanding a word.

"You have not come around for months," she pouted. The young soldado looked at her in disbelief.

"I have been busy!" he exclaimed. He wildly flung his arms out toward the surrounding debris of war.

"So have I," she purred. With a sexy grin at Parker, she whirled and left.

Parker and the young guard stared at each other in jealousy and confusion across a language barrier. Both looked frustrated. But Parker continued to eat.

"You soldaderas take no prisoners," Riley said amused as the swarthy girl brushed past him toward yet another campfire.

Luzero laughed as she wrapped meat and beans in a tortilla for him.

"The more men my friends conquer, the better they feel about themselves," she replied. Riley looked at her and arched an eyebrow. She smiled seductively. "With me, it is the more men I refuse," she added. Riley let out a burst of laughter as she handed him the burrito. He took a swig from his flask. She noticed the engraving as it glittered in the firelight.

"Got only a dim memory of being like them," Riley admitted. " 'Twas time wondrously wasted, happily enslaved to my bestial manly urges, charging 'round like a bull." Riley paused, sighing. "Then I got myself married," he blurted, quickly adding, "to my profession, as it were."

Luzero stared into his distant eyes. She reached slowly for his hand but only brushed it as she clasped the flask. He started at her touch as if suddenly burned, then let it go. She stared at the engraved Irish harp. It featured a naked winged woman as the front of the harp with her wings forming the top. Her bare bosom comprised ponderous, exaggerated breasts. "Do Irish women look like this?!" she asked innocently. "She is so . . . abundant!"

"Ireland is a lush and lovely land whose only 'abundance' is legends," Riley said, smiling. Luzero fingered the inscription, "Erin Go Bragh." "It says, 'Ireland the Brave,' in Gaelic, our native tongue," he explained.

"You speak a different sounding English," Luzero said, making him laugh.

"Forced on us long ago, when they invaded," Riley said. "They outlawed Gaelic. But its flavor still survives."

"Our native Aztec tongue was Nahuatl," Luzero replied, "suppressed by the Spanish, when they invaded." She fingered the Gaelic words again. "Few remember it now." She stared at him. "Yet you served in their English army."

"When the potatoes you sow rise from the ground already rotten," Riley explained bitterly, "you do what you must to survive."

"No wonder you Irish have come to help us!" Luzero said brightly. Riley smiled at her naivete. "Our peoples are much the same." She untied and pulled her rebosa around her shoulders. "*Buenos noches*, Teniente Riley," she whispered, her black eyes flashing in the firelight. Enjoying his favorite view, Riley watched her walk away. She disappeared into the alley.

Luzero scurried through the narrow walkway. Her path was suddenly blocked by Manzano, who stepped down from the roof ladder. At first startled, she recovered only to glare at him.

"Get out of my way, Camillo," she demanded in Spanish.

"Not so long ago, you welcomed any chance to embrace in the dark," he said tenderly.

She backed away as he reached for her. "I have changed my mind," she declared.

"I would make you do so again," he whispered. She pushed him off.

"Someday, I intend to marry, Camillo," Luzero asserted. "But I will only wed one who thinks of me at night instead of this military 'mistress.' " She flicked the gold fringe of his epaulette.

"Then why do you spend time with that old soldier?!" he demanded. Manzano tossed a contemptuous look toward Riley, now at Parker's cookfire.

"He is not as old as he looks," she replied. "His rough life shows on the outside." She flashed an impish smile. "I think I like you better this way, acting like an overly protective 'brother.' "

"But you know I cannot marry you," Manzano whined, instantly deflated. She had confronted this ancient, tiresome prejudice before.

"Neither can he, I think," she suspected. "But if ever he could, at least he would not care from what class I came."

"He could not know the importance of such things," Manzano bridled.

"Deliciously so," she smiled, pushing him out of her way as she left, tossing Riley a look over her shoulder.

"Today they were just sharpenin' their flints, lads," Riley

observed at Parker's cookfire, happily refilling his empty flask from an earthen jug of aguardiente. "They'll be at us on the morrow." Ockter and the rest of Parker's gun crew huddled there passing another jug and smoking. "We got no doctors. But we are at least well supplied with these medicinal necessities."

"First good meal since we been here," groused Price.

"The last was that night afore the Matamoros bombardment," said the Scot. They exchanged remorseful looks now swollen with anxiety.

"Leave it t'greasers to get it backwards," mused the tobacco chewer. "Holdin' the wake afore they dress out the corpse."

They all laughed except Parker, lost in dark thought. Ockter nudged Riley and nodded at him. Riley had calmed many a "fresh fish" before being tossed into the frying pan of combat. He stepped to Parker and kicked his broghan. Parker looked up. "Once you've seen that elephant," Riley said, sounding almost fatherly, "there ain't nothing more of him left to see, boy-o."

Parker managed a tenuous smile. "But back in Matamoros, he weren't chargin' right at me," he said. "He was across the river."

"Don't worry. You'll stand to, lad," said Riley. "Once you feel that fever rushing through your blood, it's like opium: addictive and deadens the fear. That's why I've drilled all of you so hard, so's you fall back on your training without no thought." He pointed at the swarthy teenage soldadera, dishing out food further down the line. " 'Tis like the first time you plow a 'fertile field,' as it were," he whispered. The others snickered at Parker's blush.

"All I can do is try, I suppose," he said. He looked at the group. "Back in Pennsylvania, my mum scrubs th'floors in the company town where pa digs th'coal. Th'floors never get clean from the dust in the very air. But she says there is honor in the noble effort tried."

"Faith I give up tryin' to raise potatoes back home," said the tobacco chewer. " 'Twas take a boat to America or starve."

"I quit diggin' the coal and come over after buryin' my own pa," said Price. "I watched him puke up his bloomin' lungs in the bloody mines."

"Just remember, the noble effort tried can get you killed," Riley warned. "Don't fall into that deadly trap of being the hero patriot."

"Worse fates there are," mused Ockter. Riley frowned at such folly.

"Aye to that!" snapped the Scot, toasting with the jug.

"If they get this far, remember, we got nothin' to fight with," Riley quipped, "except your feet." Riley looked at Parker with a reassuring nod. "Ain't no shame in using them." Parker nodded, relieved.

Moreno was watching from the observation platform. He fumbled for a match, cigar in his mouth. Sergeant Mejia struck one and stepped up to light it.

"Are your men ready for tomorrow, Sergeant?" Moreno asked in Spanish.

"They only ask who to shoot first," Mejia joked, "the norteamericanos out there or the ones in here."

"The ones in here are now Mexican, Sergeant," Moreno replied.

"And if drunks had wings," said Mejia, "the sky would always be cloudy."

Moreno laughed and waved him away. The sergeant climbed down the ladder. Moreno turned and stared at the flickering ribbon of U.S. campfires. He wondered if the Texans inside the Alamo felt as he did now, staring out from surrounded, crumbling walls at hundreds of enemy campfires, helpless, even impotent, and hoping that what was to come would count for something.

Dawn arrived with O'Brien's six guns firing their usual morning greeting. The crews loaded quickly as other U.S. batteries encircling Monterey opened fire in earnest. Thundering drums joined the roar of continual bombardment as sky-blue regulars and dusty, gray volunteers formed ranks amid fruit orchards, visible from the Mexican lines. Many grabbed apples and oranges on the run.

Shells burst across the face of Riley's earthworks. Riley lifted himself out of the muck beside one of the guns and brushed chunks of clay from his face. Ockter lay beside him, equally flattened by the barrage. He spat out dirt as the roar of the guns swelled to a thumping, continual, metallic din.

"Damn! O'Brien's good!" exclaimed Riley, as if somehow refreshed by the near miss. "We could best him, though," he bragged.

"With time and bigger guns, yes!" agreed Ockter, brushing dirt off.

"Got neither," Riley said. "Come on!" They ran for the parapet. A second salvo slammed into the earthworks. The deserters stayed huddled. Moreno was hunkered down behind sandbags on the platform. They bounded up.

"It is time," Moreno said, handing Riley a spyglass. Moreno loaded the flintlock pistol he wore on his black sword belt, cross-stitched in red with gold bullion accents. Riley stared. He always had wanted such a fine accoutrement but never had achieved the necessary rank. Give it time, he thought.

Riley looked through the spyglass. He saw the fields and orchards surrounding Monterey wriggling with the worm-like movements of troop columns. Colorful flags floated above them like flitting butterflies. On the far left, sky-blue legions moved forward looking irresistible. "The regulars are flanking the city," Riley said. In front, lines of dull-gray infantry formed near O'Brien's battery. "We're facing just the damn volunteers."

"We have not much better ourselves," worried Ockter. He looked down pointedly at the untested, nervous Mexican infantry beside them.

A shell slammed into the infantry trench. One Indian soldado was blown to pieces and the two beside him horribly mangled. Engulfed by the gore, some started to run. Fierce corporals wielding batons shoved them back.

"The Yanks make your point elegantly," said Riley. He stared at Moreno. "We'll be needing that road south." Moreno merely nodded up at the roof.

Manzano and Mejia were forming their company in double ranks on the forward edge. They stood shoulder to shoulder with looks of defiance. Their Mexican tricolor flag whipped above them in the morning breeze. Shells exploded all around and streaked overhead, but they held.

"They will do their duty," said Moreno.

"Against the Yanks or us?" Riley half joked to Ockter, who saw no humor in the situation.

"That is entirely up to you, Teniente," Moreno replied. He looked to the front. "They prepare to advance." He nodded to Riley.

"Stand to your guns, lads!" Riley bellowed. The deserters hesitantly left shelter to take up their implements and go to their crew positions. "Hurry them along, Ockter!" Riley urged. Ockter clambered down and ran back to the guns.

"You will run to your guns!" he bellowed, kicking one laggard in the butt. "You have no time to take!" Ockter strode down the line, pushing and shoving them into place. "If they reach this wall, you have nothing to stop them!" More shells whistled and burst nearby. "You keep them out there or in here you die!"

Adrenaline and fear were evident on their faces as they waited at their posts. Suddenly, the cannonade stopped. For a moment, all that could be heard was the snapping of the Mexican flag in the dry, hot wind.

"Shit if that ain't loud!" blurted Parker, who glared nervously up at the flapping banner. A nervous chuckle rippled through the crews. The jarring sound of massed drumming erupted, rolling like a wave toward them across the plain.

Jaunty gray-clad infantry churned forward through clouds of drifting smoke from the cannonade. Illinois and Indiana volunteers advanced to the drum cadence in ragged lines. Boyish, eager looks illuminated their young faces. State and national flags flew high. Fifers began to pipe "Green Grows the Laurel." Officers bawled commands and dressed the lines with gleaming swords.

"Load!" Riley bellowed. "Counter infantry fire, two hundred yards!"

Ockter echoed the command, and the crews loaded the guns feverishly. As some rammed powder bags and cannonballs down the barrels, others cut lengths of instantaneous primer fuses, jammed into barrel vents.

"For those what care," Riley announced, "we're not facing our old regular regiments. They're attacking cross town. Since no regular worthy of the name would have a friend among the disgraceful volunteers," Riley scoffed to a few anxious laughs, "send 'em to hell with no guilt!" he yelled. "Fire!"

The four guns belched orange flame and white smoke with a cracking boom. They each lifted off the ground and rolled back quickly in recoil.

Seemingly harmless, bouncing little balls of copper ripped gaps in the gray lines. Amid moans and screams of terror,

untested volunteers saw comrades dismembered, disemboweled, or beheaded. Pockets of the ill-disciplined troops hesitated.
Some froze as others tried to march forward. Officers rallied
them by ordering the battalion to fire. The entire line let loose a
ragged, sputtering musket volley with a smoky, rattling roar.

"They're firing short, lads, out of fear!" Riley yelled, seeing
musket balls kick up a jagged line of dust twenty yards in front
of the breastworks. "Let 'em close ranks, then break them like
pins in an alley with more solid shot!" To Riley's chagrin, Ockter saluted before executing the command.

The hollow thunk of sponge staffs yanked from gun barrels;
the scraping of powder bags rammed home; the cold rattle of
cannonballs rolling down barrels: In Riley's mind, it joined with
the clatter of advancing troops marching closer to compose
what he saw as a first movement in the symphony of battle.

Riley looked at the nervous Mexican infantry in the trench.
They hugged the walls of the breastworks. Their sergeants and
corporals flailed and swore at them to stand and fight, but it
may be to no avail, he thought. "Faith their mothers would be
proud," Riley sneered.

"They can fight well when inspired," Moreno insisted.
"Remember the Alamo? They demand more than mere money."
Riley grunted in doubt. Moreno strode into the trench with a
cocky air. The disgruntled Indians ignored him.

"These pale jackasses think you have no balls!" Moreno bellowed in Spanish. This grabbed their attention. Some cursed at
the deserters. "Can you stand and fight like men?!" he asked.
"Or will you die whimpering in these ditches like scared dogs?!"
Moreno gestured for them to rise. Sergeants yelled orders. They
stood and aimed muskets over the breastworks. "Wait for my
command!" Moreno folded his arms and stared at Riley defiantly.

"Fire by battery!" Riley yelled. Four gunners stepped to the breech of their guns and held the smoking slow match above the touch hole. Riley looked at the approaching lines of gray infantry drawing nearer, nearer; fifes and drums pounding closer. But not yet time for the second movement, Riley thought.

"The music's bloody loud enough!" growled Price. "Do we fire or join the bloomin' parade?!" He wiped sweat from his powder blackened forehead. The deserters grew more nervous.

"Fire or swing from some bonnie gallows!" snapped the Scot.

"Wait for the command!" Ockter bellowed, pacing behind the line of guns.

"They're nearly on us, you Prussian prig!" hollered the tobacco chewer.

The shrill, thundering screech of the fifes and drums was nearly ear splitting now. Ockter stepped to the Irishman. "Prussian I am proud to be," he said firmly, "as you must be proud to wait for the command!"

"Proud as spit," the Irishman growled. He let fly a glob of tobacco juice over the embrasure toward the Americans. Parker laughed nervously.

"Hold! Hold!" Riley bellowed from the parapet, peering through his spyglass. "Hold 'til even the damn greasers can't miss!" Moreno heard and glared up at him. Riley was oblivious, waiting for his "symphony" to reach fever pitch.

The entire line of U.S. volunteers fired a second volley barely fifty yards in front. Musket balls splattered into the adobe buildings and spewed up dirt across the earthworks. Two deserters spun and fell with cries of anguish. One had a shattered arm; the other, several fingers of one hand blown off by the .69-caliber lead balls. Parker looked pale as Ockter pulled the wounded into the alley.

Riley saw Moreno calmly lighting a cigar even as the balls whizzed and thudded all around him. Well, he thought, at least his commander showed the calm nerve of a veteran, reassuring the shaky Mexican infantry. Riley nodded and raised his flask like the baton of a conductor. "Fire!" he bellowed.

"Fuego!" Moreno yelled at the same time.

All four guns, the Mexican infantry in the trench, and Manzano's double ranks on the rooftop erupted in a thunderous volley of flame and smoke. U.S. volunteers fell in clusters amid a chorus of pitiful wails and terrified screams. The .75-caliber Mexican musket balls ripped and tore ugly, gaping red holes in the prim, gray uniforms. The solid shot of the cannon decapitated and disemboweled volunteers one behind the other, as if toppling dominoes.

The entire battalion lurched to a stop when volunteers gaped in shock at the gore, some slipping on slithery pink intestines lying on the hard dirt. They refused to take another step. Officers cursed and cajoled, but panic prevailed.

The entire Indiana regiment broke and ran headlong for the rear, many Illinois men following. A few rallied to back bravely off the field as a rear guard.

"Viva!" shouted the elated Mexican infantry over and over, as much in surprise as joy. Manzano's guards cheered from the rooftops and waved their flag. Manzano and Mejia exchanged a manly embrace.

"Mexico is proud of you today!" Moreno shouted to the infantry in Spanish. He strutted to the parapet and re-joined Riley.

"Huzzah! Huzzah!" the deserters cheered as they waited for the next command from Riley. Many waved their caps. A few danced little jigs.

"Jesus, Mary, an' Joseph . . . I'm still breathin'!" Parker said elatedly. He patted his own chest, then gave the Scot a bear hug.

"Aye to breathing long an' deep, laddie," the Scot grinned, relieved. "The worst is over!" But the roar of battle continued unabated across the city.

Riley frowned as he looked to their front through his spyglass, then handing it to Moreno with a troubled look.

Moreno peered through it. *"Los diablos Tejanos,"* Moreno muttered, then looked at quizzical Riley. "Devil Texians."

The sinister Texas Rangers rode their horses at a walk past O'Brien's guns and through the shattered volunteers, scowling in contempt at them. They formed a solid line of a hundred horsemen across the front of Riley's sector.

"They won't be so quick to turn tail," said Riley, remembering them.

"Texians embrace this war," Moreno said bitterly, giving the spyglass back to Riley. "It makes legal for them the killing of Mexicans."

"Load!" Riley yelled. "Counter cavalry fire, reduce range to one hundred yards!"

"That is too close!" Ockter shouted, worried.

"They'll ride right into it when they go from the trot to the gallop," Riley asserted, familiar with the pace of standard cavalry charges. Still looking doubtful, Ockter started lowering the muzzle on Parker's gun.

Across the plain, Captain Jack Hays drew his Colt Paterson revolver. The entire line of anxious horsemen pulled similar pistols, each containing five shots triggered by percussion caps on a revolving cylinder. Hays galloped down his line with pistol held high, long hair flying behind him, hazel-blue eyes afire. "Give 'em hell, boys!" Hays shouted. With a blood curdling yell, the Texans broke into a full run, an uncontrolled horse race. Whooping and hollering, they thundered across the open ground straight at the Mexican infantry trench.

"Would you look at that!" Riley roared to Moreno. "Them pony whores are charging th'whole damn way!" Riley pointed at Ockter. "Now!"

"Fire!" Ockter commanded. All four guns roared and recoiled. The whizzing copper cannonballs left a faint trail of greenish smoke as they overshot the fast-charging horsemen and thudded harmlessly behind them. The Texans rolled and foamed closer like an oncoming whirling dust storm.

"Depress the damn muzzles!" Riley yelled. "Point-blank range!"

Moreno looked at the infantry in the trench. They fired a ragged and sputtering volley too soon, triggered by fear. The balls fell woefully short.

The fast-riding Texans quickly covered the open ground and rode right up, onto, and over the earthworks. As the infantry frantically struggled to re-load their single shot flintlocks, they were decimated by the five-shot repeating pistols.

Some Texans jumped their horses into the trench. Desperate, visceral fighting erupted as Bowie knives confronted Spanish dirks and repeating pistols faced clubbed muskets and bayonets. Manzano's infantry fired rifles from the roof and emptied some saddles, but the soldados in the trench were hopelessly outgunned. Those not killed or wounded ran from certain death. Their only escape was through the deserters and into the alley.

"Turn this gun!" Ockter directed, pointing toward the trench now being overrun. Parker and his crew turned their four-pounder, but fleeing Mexican infantry blocked their field of fire. Ockter looked up at Riley in frustration. The other deserters started to roll their guns toward the alley, but it was clogged with Mexican infantry. Riley looked at Moreno, who nodded in resignation.

"Use your feet lads!" Riley yelled, pointing at the alley. "Take the wounded! Leave th'damn guns!" The unarmed deserters joined the soldados in running for their lives, carrying their half-dozen wounded.

Ockter stood still, looking outraged. He picked up the heavy wood trail of Parker's cannon. "A Prussian does not leave his gun!" he shouted up at Riley as he struggled alone to pull it barely inches. Parker and the others stared as if beholding a lunatic, torn whether to run or help manic Ockter.

"A Prussian follows orders!" Riley bellowed, drawing a look from Ockter as if he had been slapped. "Now get the hell out of there!"

Ockter tossed Riley a grudging salute and shooed Parker and his crew into the panicked throng escaping into the alley, leaving the gun.

"We had best join them!" Moreno urged, pointing to the front.

"Sweet Jesus! The native-born bastards are on us!" Riley gasped.

Volunteer troops had rallied to follow the Texans in a surging, irresistible mob. They approached the rise to the breastworks cheering, rolling like a dusty, gray wave crested with glistening bayonets and billowing flags.

Riley and Moreno leaped from the parapet and ran gracelessly toward the crowded alleyway. At the last, Moreno whirled and fired his single-shot pistol, killing a close Texan charging them with a Bowie knife.

A dozen volunteers stormed up and stood atop the earthworks. They took aim at Riley, Moreno, Ockter, Parker, and the fleeing gun crew, last to enter the alleyway. Riley turned just in time to see them cock their muskets. "Brace yourselves, lads!" he yelled, crossing himself, ready for the worst.

"Fuego!" shouted Manzano from the rooftop. His entire company of Mexican riflemen fired a crisp, booming volley, blasting the volunteers off the earthworks and buying some precious time.

Riley looked up and saw Manzano, Mejia, and the others cheer as they re-loaded. He gave a quick nod of thanks and doffed his cap before disappearing into the alley, but not before seeing Mejia laugh at him. "Damn!" he growled.

"Retiren!" Manzano shouted. The guards backed up warily to descend ladders at the rear. Mejia fired a parting shot. They filed down onto a narrow dirt street with stone sidewalks, crowded with fleeing Mexican infantry and deserters.

CHAPTER 5
MONTEREY: THE STREETS
SEPTEMBER 22, 1846

Riley emerged with Moreno last from the short alley and hurried onto the street. They glanced over their shoulders, expecting to see volunteers and Texans charging after them at any moment. Strangely, there was nobody. An eerie silence engulfed them other than the monotonous, distant roar of ongoing battle from the far side of Monterey.

"Looks like Mejia's lads bought us some breathing room," said Riley, catching his breath.

"We should not waste it," Moreno replied. "We have nothing left with which to fight. We must quickly reach the staging area for our reserves."

"The more space between us and them Yanks, the better," Riley said, striding quickly now to keep up with Moreno, already heading up the narrow street. It was lined with one- and two-story adobe and stone buildings, many damaged from the artillery bombardment. Chunks of adobe, brick, and stone littered the ground.

Further ahead, Parker's gun crew approached a grisly tableau. The stiff and bloated, bloodied limbs of a lovely but dead young woman protruded from beneath the heavy wood timbers of a fallen balcony. Her hands still clutched a tin watering can. Broken clay flowerpots from her garden lay everywhere with red rose blossoms sprinkled throughout the debris.

Parker slowed to stare, visibly shaken. Feeling a peculiar chill in the muggy air, he crossed himself. His comrades understood his sudden discomfort.

"You canno' dwell on such things, laddie," said the Scot. "Innocents always die in war; there's nothin' for it."

"Least she weren't one of your river girls," teased the tobacco chewer.

"Too many bloomin' clothes!" joked Price, evoking his black British humor. Parker shook off his doldrums with a short, stifled laugh.

"Keep moving!" Ockter urged, stepping up to hurry them along. "We must have someplace to be, so let us get there!" Ockter watched Parker and the others hustle off. He needed orders. Without them, Ockter felt he would become part of the chaos engulfing him. He paused to wait for Riley, approaching from the rear of the disorganized column with Moreno, Manzano, and the guards. "How far must we retreat?!" Ockter asked, clearly irritated. "All we have done is dig ditches and play with tiny toy guns. Now we do not even have those!"

" 'Tis all we been trusted to do, Ockter," Riley grumbled. "Just keep the lads moving 'til we get somewhere safe."

Ockter grunted, saluted, and trotted to catch up with the others. Riley turned to Moreno, sweeping his hand toward the retreating mass of soldados and deserters.

"Monterey is lost and so are we, unless we get to that road south," he said, downing a swig.

"Form a rear guard!" Moreno commanded, ignoring Riley.

"*Si, mi capitan!*" Manzano replied crisply. He eyed Riley. "It is better to die fighting," Manzano said.

" 'Tis better not to die," Riley insisted.

Manzano waved Mejia to him. They issued orders in Spanish. Their guards formed ranks to face any oncoming Americans. Then they began backing up slowly, following other Mexican infantry and Riley's deserters.

Mejia found the nervous young soldado and the toothy

corporal huddling in an alcove, sharing a canteen while the distant roar of battle continued. The young soldado watched Parker shuffling past and glowered at him.

"All they want is our women," the young soldado said in Spanish.

"All they want is your woman!" replied the toothy corporal with a laugh.

"If we keep retreating, the green-gross will take all our women and more," grumbled Mejia, shoving them into the street. "Now fall in and keep moving!"

Moreno and Riley stopped beside the fallen balcony and stared reverently. Riley had seen Parker's stunned reaction, understood his revulsion at the sight of something to which Riley had grown numb over the years. But, somehow, Riley's hardened heart felt moved. Perhaps it was the tragedy of seeing a woman lying dead among her dead dreams, most of her obviously treasured roses now wilted and mutilated. But Riley spied one still healthy in its potted soil. He stooped and picked up the red rose, snapping its stem. Moreno looked at him.

"Roses and shamrocks," Riley mused aloud. "They growed wild in our hills back home." To Moreno's astonishment, Riley wistfully breathed in its aroma as they resumed walking and stuck the rose in his cap. "Home is such a damn hard road to travel," he said.

"Teniente, soon that road will get harder," admitted Moreno. "Our only road south fell to the norteamericanos early yesterday morning." Riley glared at Moreno, who casually lit a cigar. "The deception was sadly necessary."

"Captain," Riley sighed, "your black heart has got itself a touch of the blarney." Riley understood perfectly. He just hated being on the receiving end of the deception. It may have served Moreno's purpose, but for Riley it served only to spur a greater desire to leave, to find that road home and take it.

Suddenly, Riley's battle-tuned ears detected the terrifying whoosh of incoming shells sounding much closer than the distant ongoing battle. "Take cover!" he yelled, echoed in Spanish by the shouting Moreno. They both flattened themselves, covering their heads with their arms.

With breathtaking rapidity, six large explosions shattered the narrow street with blinding orange flame, choking white smoke, and ear-splitting, crackling booms. The deafening roar fell off quickly, replaced by screams, moans, and the clatter of falling adobe, rocks, and shrapnel, sounding to Riley like metallic rain. When the deadly downpour ended, Riley slowly pushed himself up, coughing in the smoke. He helped Moreno to his feet.

"My God!" Riley exclaimed looking. "Ain't there nobody left?"

Broken, mangled bodies of deserters and soldados carpeted the street in a ghastly mosaic. But as the heavy smoke dissipated, more and more survivors appeared, stumbling out of alcoves and doorways, trying to regain their senses. Riley and Moreno worked their way slowly up the street to assess the damage.

Mejia stumbled out of an alcove, brushing plaster off his uniform. Moreno walked up, and Mejia braced to attention. "I will reform the column," Mejia said hoarsely, choking on dust. "These two will no longer be with us," he added, gesturing deeper into the alcove. Moreno saw the toothy corporal and the young soldado, lying broken and bloody, together in death and debris.

"Where is Manzano?" Moreno asked.

"In a daze, wandering up the street," Mejia replied. "He looks lost."

"I will gather him up," Moreno said, relieved. "His spirit will uplift us."

Riley found Ockter seated against an adobe wall. He was calmly tying a bloody bandanna around his head and now empty left eye socket, the eyeball itself lying on the ground next to him. Amazed at Ockter's demeanor, Riley knelt beside him, putting an arm around his shoulder and offering a swig from his flask.

"Do not worry," Ockter said, downing a stiff shot. "I only need one eye to sight a gun. Tend to the others." He nodded across the street.

Riley walked to Price, tying a stick and rag tourniquet to his bleeding thigh. Beside him, the tobacco chewer was lying atop the broken body of the Scot. The tobacco chewer's forehead was gushing blood from a shrapnel gash. Riley poured whiskey on it.

"Yee-owch!" the tobacco chewer roared. "Pile on th'agony why don'tcha!"

"Wrap this 'round your thick skull," Riley said, pulling a filthy gun cleaning rag from his haversack. He looked down at the Scot, killed instantly with a metal shard through his heart. "At least Scottie went up quick," Riley said.

"He will miss stretchin' hemp with the rest of us, he will," said the tobacco chewer, crossing himself.

"Don't make me sorry I wasted that whiskey," Riley glared. "Where's young Parker?"

"Gone up," said Price, sounding glum. He nodded up the street.

Heart sinking, Riley walked fearfully toward a pile of wood beams and bricks. He found Parker leaning against the other side. Riley thought he looked like he had just fallen asleep, with eyes wide open. Riley stared in choked emotion at Parker, who seemed to be staring right back at him but in wide-eyed, sightless wonder, a disturbing look of peacefulness now gracing his cherubic face.

"We must move on, Teniente," Moreno said, stepping up to Riley.

"Them sightless eyes . . ." Riley said, paying no attention to Moreno. He brushed welling tears from his face, feeling an odd sensation of guilt. It unnerved him as something alien to his nature. "Them eyes come with the damn job," he said. "Would they had first seen something better of life."

"Manzano and Mejia are re-forming the column," Moreno pressed. "If the rest of us are to see more of that life, we must move on."

Riley shook off his stupor, took a swig, and managed a few steps toward the column with Moreno. The monotonous cannonade and musketry that had droned like an endless death rattle across Monterey for days suddenly stopped.

"What's that?!" Riley snapped, cocking his head at a sepulchral silence. Then a lone Mexican bugle began blaring a mournful, unfamiliar melody, joined by more and more bugles until it sounded like a brass dirge resounding throughout the shattered city. Riley looked at Moreno. "What's it mean?!"

"It means your salvation, Teniente," Moreno replied in tired resignation, letting a long sigh escape. "There is a truce," he said. "It means you and your men will not be made prisoners of the norteamericanos."

Riley stared in stunned disbelief. Conflicting feelings of joy, relief, and remorse battled within him. Poor young Parker, the Scot, and the others may not have died in vain, he thought, feeling cautiously elated. With a truce, the army would not be surrendered. He and his Mexicanized deserters would not be hanged and might yet get their bounty of land. Perhaps, he marveled, he could find and follow that elusive road home after all, and even in good conscience.

CHAPTER 6
MONTEREY: THE PLAZA
SEPTEMBER 26, 1846

General Zachary Taylor looked like a disreputable snake oil salesman. He wore a rumpled, soiled linen duster draped limply over his simple dark-blue uniform. With arms folded, he stared hard as flint from beneath his crumpled straw sombrero at General Ampudia, who seemed to glow in the brilliant sunlight. He was resplendent in a glittering blue and red full-dress Mexican uniform enriched with gold bullion embroidery. He stared at Taylor with stiff, proper arrogance, a flagpole between them. Two Mexican staff officers finished folding the tricolor. They walked to Ampudia, who barely nodded at Taylor, turned, and mounted his horse.

The Mexican officers left as a color guard of U.S. regulars carried the folded U.S. flag to the pole. A bugler played "To the Color" as the banner was raised reverently to fly above the main plaza of Monterey.

The rectangle of adobe and stone buildings dominated by a domed cathedral was crowded with parked U.S. artillery, limbers, wagons, and ceremonial troop formations. Three companies of sky-blue U.S. regulars stood at attention along one side of the plaza. Three dull-gray volunteer companies faced them across the plaza as they stacked arms. On the flat rooftop above lounged Jack Hays and his Texas Rangers, bored and baking in buckskins beneath the hot sun. They amused themselves by peeling oranges with Bowie knives.

As the flag was raised, Ampudia nodded at his own color

guard, waiting at the head of the disheveled Mexican troop column that comprised the battered survivors of his army. They began marching forward to pass in front of the U.S. regulars and out the other side of the plaza as they left Monterey. Mexican drummers beat a slow, steady cadence as sullen and weary soldados trudged past.

"Present arms!" commanded Captain Merrill of Riley's old Company K. As senior captain, all three companies obeyed his order and executed this display of military respect. Ampudia himself gratefully acknowledged the gesture with a deep nod as he rode past. Merrill gave him a sword salute, kissing the hilt of his blade and sweeping it down to one side.

The regulars held their salute as Mexican infantry continued to march past. The only sounds were the funereal drum cadence and the steady tramp of feet.

Taylor had mounted Old Whitey to watch. Colonel Harney rode up with a Dragoon escort and saluted. Taylor cast a quick glance at the volunteers. They stood restively in ranks looking surly behind their now-stacked arms.

"Good work," Taylor said in his Southern twang. "If we'd left th'damn volunteers armed, they'd have shot down th'greasers like dogs," he observed. Harney looked as if that was not such a bad idea.

In a column of twos, Riley's surviving deserters approached the plaza. They marched with the artillery train. In front of them, a bronze nine-pounder gun was pulled by a limber and six mules. Behind them, in a separate formation, marched the surviving riflemen guards with Manzano and Mejia. Moreno rode his horse beside them. Bringing up the rear was a wagon pulled by oxen.

Riley marched at the front beside Ockter, who now sported a rakish leather eye patch. Riley's eyes grew wide when he saw the formation of U.S. regulars ahead at present arms. "Prepare to receive honors!" he bellowed. "Dress ranks!"

The deserters aligned themselves, closed the interval between sets of two, and entered the plaza marching proudly despite dressed wounds. Price limped on a carved wood crutch. The tobacco chewer beside him had a bandaged head. None carried weapons, just haversacks, canteens, and blanket rolls.

"One!" snapped Ockter to set the step. "One! One-two-one!" he barked, and the men tramped left-right-left with solid precision in a lock step.

Merrill was the first man Riley saw. His heart sank with a surprising sense of shame. "Damn!" he muttered. He avoided Merrill's eyes by turning to check on the formation. Riley hoped Merrill would not recognize him.

"My God, Riley?!" gasped Merrill when he did the very thing. Merrill could not believe his eyes. He stared in dismay that quickly turned to disgust. Then he realized that his battalion was showing military respect at "present arms."

"Shoulder arms!" he commanded angrily. "Order arms! In place, rest!" The ranks obeyed quickly with practiced snap and speed, the clatter of equipment and muskets sounding like that of one man instead of three hundred.

Riley jerked around to see the entire line assume a casual attitude with faces showing contempt, though still holding ranks. He glared back at Merrill, then stared straight ahead. Merrill tossed Riley a look of profound pity.

Now allowed to talk in ranks, first one, then two, then a dozen of the regulars recognized and pointed at old comrades in Mexican uniforms. Singular cries of "Traitor!" and "Deserter!" swelled to a chorus.

"Paddy O'Greaser, for shame!" taunted one Irish regular.

"Poper scum or greaser, same diff'rence!" yelled one regular.

"Hey, Riley!" bellowed another. "Fill your yellowbelly with this!" The private had pulled a soft tomato from his greasy haversack. He threw it.

The tomato hit Riley hard and splattered his back. He whirled in a rage, only to see the nearest regulars burst out laughing in ridicule. A barrage of fruit and vegetables followed, pelting all the deserters.

"Stay in ranks!" bellowed Merrill, stepping out front and holding his sword above his head with both hands, as if to push back the surging line. "Otherwise, you may do as you please," he added sadly. A cheer resounded, and another barrage of fruit and vegetables was unleashed. Apples and tomatoes pelted Price, the tobacco chewer, and others near them in ranks. Curses and insults reached a crescendo of abuse.

"I'll bloody well ram this cripple stick up your arse!" Price threatened, thrusting his crutch into the air. Boos and guffaws drowned him out as smashed tomatoes nearly made him slip and fall.

The tobacco chewer picked up a bruised whole tomato from the ground. "Fond of solid shot?!" he yelled, hurling it back and hitting a surprised regular hard in the face. A return barrage of apples forced him to cover his head.

"Quiet in the damn ranks!" Riley bellowed. "Regulars stay steady under fire!"

"Not regular greasers!" taunted a nearby U.S. corporal to the guffaws of his mates. "Stinkin' Mick yellowbellies!" He spat in Riley's face.

Riley trembled in rage, clenching his fists. But he steeled himself to look straight ahead and continue marching. Keep them moving out, he thought. If they broke ranks and started a brawl, they would be made prisoners and hanged. The deserters dutifully imitated him and marched through the barrage.

Casually eating an apple, Taylor watched astride his horse. Beside him was Harney, his squad of Dragoons in line behind looking bemused.

"With respect, General Taylor," Harney said, "I'd be hanging Riley and his Irish pukes right now, if we'd not settled for this truce."

"I took th'goddamn town, didn't I?!," Taylor snapped. He knew President Polk wanted quick, cheap victories. He had just handed him a dandy. "The price would've been too high with too many more American lives."

"Yes, sir, but greasers have no honor," Harney pleaded. "We parole this horde with their arms, and we'll just have to fight them again."

"Well, then, Harney, we'll just have to whip 'em again," Taylor replied.

"My apologies, sir," Harney blanched, though still unconvinced.

Taylor hated reprimands and instantly looked remorseful. Harney was a good soldier, Taylor understood, if perhaps a bit hard. "Don't make any damn war personal, Harney," Taylor said more softly. "It'll bind your guts." He bit into his apple. "And it's a shameful waste of good fruit." Secretly, Taylor hoped this display of venom would squelch future desertions.

Watching from the rooftop behind the volunteers, Texans with peeled oranges sheathed their Bowie knives. They squished the bare fruit and began lobbing the dripping result across the plaza in a long range "bombardment."

One peeled orange splattered onto Ockter's face. He stiffened in rigid Prussian style and continued to march straight ahead, not even wiping his face.

"So shamed I have never been," Ockter said, trembling in a controlled rage. Tears rimmed his eyes, tracing down his stubble-covered cheeks.

"Better shamed in truce than hanged in surrender," snarled Riley. Ockter looked doubtful. "With this truce, we give 'em the damn town but keep our weapons—and our necks. This way we'll live, even if it's only to get even," Riley vowed. Somehow, he found himself hoping Luzero was not witness to his shame. He could hardly wait to break free of this losing army, hopefully with her by his side. He would put all this behind him, quickly.

The volunteers across the plaza began to sing "Green Grows the Laurel," in rowdy, discordant voices to taunt the departing deserters. Their derisive disharmony joined with more howls from the regulars and fruit from the Texans to chase the last of Riley's column from the plaza under a perfect maelstrom.

As the deserters trudged down the empty streets leading out from Monterey, the cacophony reverberated among the narrow adobe and stone walls. To Riley, it sounded even louder within his own ringing, throbbing head, as if the shameful noise echoed inside his mental footlocker. He wondered if there was enough aguardiente in all of Mexico ever to drown its memory.

Chapter 7
RINCONADA PASS
SEPTEMBER 26, 1846

Twilight bathed rocky Rinconada Pass in stark, eerie shadows as the artillery train labored up the steep desert grade west of Monterey. Battered infantry units and the Jalisco Lancers accompanied the ponderously slow artillery. The soldados wore glum, depressed faces. To Riley, they conjured an image of ragged desperation as they trudged through the dust. Some fell beside the road to drink from a spring-fed pond nestled among towering succulents. The lancers prodded stragglers to rejoin their ranks. Occasionally, a gunshot resounded with finality among the overhanging cliffs as the last testament of a Mexican deserter.

An overburdened artillery wagon pulled by a yoke of tired oxen became mired in a mud hole near the pond. Riley, Ockter, and the disheartened deserters broke ranks to pull on ropes and push wheels.

Moreno watched astride his horse from the roadside trees, Manzano standing beside him. The tired guard company waited nearby in formation.

"Pitch camp here," Moreno said softly in Spanish. Manzano nodded at Mejia, who bellowed orders. Guards stacked arms and broke ranks. They began unrolling blankets and gathering firewood

"Look how Riley joins his men like another ox," Manzano said with a smirk. He watched Riley sweating with the others at the wagon. "He lowers himself to their level."

"Remember, he came from their ranks," Moreno replied. "He still thinks like one of them, no matter what he may say. He will learn."

"They are too different from us," Manzano continued. "They deserted their own kind. Why should they stay with 'stinking yellowskin greasers'?!"

"It is our duty to Mexico to help them find their own reasons," Moreno cautioned. "And, however distasteful, we will do our duty, eh, Manzano?"

"Yes, my captain," Manzano replied apologetically. He looked down the pass. Like a snake wriggling across sand, remnants of the Mexican army stretched for miles strung out on the narrow, dry road. Canvas wagon tops and fluttering, colorful flags were all that could be seen above swirling dust in the fading evening light. "The wagons of wounded and the women with food should catch up soon," he said. "Our men are starved."

"We do not wait only for them," Moreno said. Manzano looked at him curiously. As usual, he found Moreno difficult to fathom.

With a half-hearted shout, the deserters at last freed the stuck wagon. The civilian teamster, a wiry Mexican with a large mustache, cracked his whip above the heads of the oxen. Creaking and groaning, the wagon lurched forward.

"Gracias!" the grinning teamster shouted. *"Muchos gracias mi 'green-gross'!"* he added, again cracking his whip.

Riley, sweating and out of breath, gave him a quizzical look. He had heard that expression frequently of late.

Ockter stepped up breathing heavily as the wagon lumbered away. "The greasers pitch camp," he gasped, sweeping his arm.

Riley nodded as Ockter faced the deserters, now gathering around them. They looked exhausted, defeated, depressed, and angry. And Riley knew they all blamed him.

"You've stuck us in a bloody mire deep as them poor dumb

beasts!" growled Price. "What's going t'free us?!"

"Sure an' winnin' this grand war!" taunted the tobacco chewer. A few laughed bitterly. " 'Tis at the end of a rope we'll be findin' our freedom." Many groused in agreement.

"Beasts dumb enough to get captured get the only land they deserve," Riley snapped, "six feet under!" A sullen glare replaced the grumbling. "Bed 'em down," he said to Ockter. He slipped off his blanket roll and slammed it to the ground beneath a large tree. "Got to wash off the stink of this damn day." Ockter snapped a salute. Riley ignored it and strode across the road to the pond.

Night had fallen by the time Riley made his way to Moreno, standing at a small fire. The Mexican guards lounged around several large bonfires. The deserters were encamped just beyond them. Feeling refreshed, Riley had shaved, and his wet, dark-brown hair was slicked back beneath his cap.

"Two fights and two retreats, sir," he observed to Moreno. "Seems I've finally found something this so-called army's good at." Moreno ignored the sarcasm, handing him a steaming tin cup of coffee. He sipped it and spat it out. "My own taste runs toward something stronger." Riley tossed down the cup.

"Taste for anything may be acquired through necessity," Moreno replied calmly, "and duty."

"Hanging ain't high on my list," Riley replied. "You stuck us in a brawl brought on by your own selves and leaving us no back door. Losing means capture, and capture for us means hanging!" Riley had never felt the sense of near panic that he now was fighting to suppress. It seemed to swell inside his chest and rise in his throat. The worst of it was that he had done it all himself.

"For the price agreed upon, you take the chance of any soldier," Moreno stressed.

"Got no chance to take!" Riley shouted, causing heads to

turn around the Mexican campfires. " 'Tis a losing fight. And I think himself knew it afore the first punch was throwed." Moreno looked impassive. "I say you owe us a back door. This ain't no Alamo!" Moreno glared at him as Manzano, Mejia, and four guards arrived at a brisk pace.

"We have posted guards on the deserters," Manzano said in Spanish. Moreno nodded in approval.

As usual, Riley bided his time impatiently while Spanish was exchanged. He did notice though that now he occasionally understood a word here and there.

"Post more men down the road," Moreno said to Mejia. "When the prisoner column catches up, hold them for me."

"Yes, my captain. Are we at last to rid ourselves of these green-gross cockroaches?!" Mejia asked, looking cautiously hopeful.

Moreno merely waved him off to lead his men away, Manzano staying. Riley stared after Mejia thoughtfully, then skewed an eye toward Moreno.

"Savvy damn little of your lingo," Riley said. "But I knows a bit of English when I hear it stirred in. What the hell is a 'green-gross'?!"

" 'Green grows the laurel . . .' " sang Moreno in a melodic baritone voice. "As in laurel given to the victor?" he added bitterly.

"Shit and I'm sick of that damn song," Riley growled. Since he first heard it so innocently a lifetime ago in Mackinac, its nagging melody and words now reflected his desperate situation and seemed nothing to Riley but an evil omen.

"Just so, Teniente," said Moreno, "our simple people are sick of seeing fierce white men invade their towns singing that song. They have no Spanish name for such pirates, so they call them by what they hear as its first two words."

"But why'd Mejia and that bullwhacker lay it on us then?"

frowned Riley.

"Some still can see no difference!" Manzano interjected. Riley glared at him. "Some find 'green-gross' awkward, so they massage it into what they think is a new Spanish word. It rolls off the tongue easily, like spit," he sneered, spitting and just missing Riley's broghan. " 'Gringos.' "

"Our less educated people do not understand where that word first came from," Moreno added, hoping to calm the situation. "It rises within them . . . as if a distant memory surfacing in their blood, suddenly recalled by that song. In Spain in the 1700s, 'gringo' described foreigners who could not speak Spanish," he continued. "Curiously, it often referred to immigrant Irish."

"Got us a darlin' word, too," Riley fairly snarled, staring at his shoe. "It describes cocksure brown braggarts what can't shoot straight." He glared at Manzano. " 'Greasers.' "

Manzano reared up straight and took a step toward Riley, exactly as Riley had hoped. He needed a good fight to clear his mind, as it always had in the past.

"It is my distasteful task," Moreno said solemnly, stepping between them, "to make this crude experiment work." He looked grimly at Riley. "Or end it with unfortunate, fatal consequences."

"Where I ain't wanted, never been one to stay," warned Riley. Moreno cooly lit a cigar and stared at Riley, who returned his gaze steadily. Musket shots resounded again up the canyon, distracting Riley.

"Regrettably, some of our soldados tire of the struggle," Moreno said. "They decide not to stay. Our guards shoot them where they find them." He exhaled smoke, arching an eyebrow.

"Do they hit anything, sir?" asked caustic Riley. He straightened to attention, turned, and strode into the darkness.

"Someone should slap the jowels of that jackass," Manzano

said in Spanish. Moreno shook his head, though amused by the thought.

"Like any wild jackass once corralled," Moreno replied, "his braying means nothing. He nevertheless remains corralled."

Riley walked through the encampment of glum deserters. Hostile eyes tracked his every step. What little talk there was fell quiet as he approached. A few were smoking. Some were shaving. Many were scrubbing their uniform coats with canteen water and drying them by the fires. Price brushed furiously at one stubborn spot of tomato juice.

The tobacco chewer returned from bathing in the pond. He chuckled at Price as Riley passed. "Don't bother," he said loud enough for Riley to hear. "Some stains don't never come clean."

Riley had stopped to frown at him when Ockter suddenly walked up out of the surrounding gloom.

"The men have nothing to eat, sir," he reported with a salute. Riley returned the salute halfheartedly, more as a joke.

"We've had our fill of fruit," growled Price, drawing a few chuckles. He resumed brushing the stain.

"The greasers are waiting here for something," Riley opined. "I'll wager it's the generous ladies with some food." To himself, he hoped that Luzero would be among them. He felt his heart beat faster at just the thought of her. He had not felt like this since he was a teenager back in Ireland and chasing his first lass.

"And if it is not?" asked Ockter, pushing for a reserve plan.

"Then we'll do what we're getting so damn good at," chimed Riley, glaring at Price and the tobacco chewer. "Chew on our pride." He walked to the tree and began unrolling his blanket. He eased down and rested against the trunk.

Later, six primitive oxcarts and wagons, many with solid wheels, creaked to a jolting stop in the road beside the pond. Pitiful moans, groans, and Spanish prayers could be heard from wounded soldados crowded into the rickety vehicles. Six tired soldaderas climbed down and carried canteens to the pond. Several women crossed the road with baskets and filtered into the encampment.

One of them was Luzero, her dusty clothes smeared with blood from the wounded. She felt worn down and heavy, overwhelmed with what seemed futility and waste. She looked around for Riley, hoping she did not look as bad as she felt. She did not quite know why yet, but for him she wanted to look good.

From the edge of camp, Moreno watched the women distribute food to the thankful Mexican guards. He saw Luzero pause and look about in the darkness until Ockter approached her. Moreno knew for whom she was looking. She left with Ockter to head for the deserter campfires. Moreno puffed his cigar, mulling over what he believed were growing possibilities.

"Perhaps a doctor in San Luis Potosi can do more for your eye," Luzero said, fussing with Ockter's eye patch. He shrugged, knowing it was hopeless.

"I need but one eye to see a pretty fraulein with food," Ockter said, doffing his cap to her as they walked.

She smiled. "I only have tortillas and some hard cheese," she said at the edge of the deserter camp.

"That will be fine for most of us," Ockter said pointedly. He nodded toward Riley, seated with his back against the tree trunk and staring transfixed into the blazing fire. He did not see them, appearing distant and depressed.

"What he needs, I must bring from the wagon," Luzero said, handing Ockter the basket of food. She headed back toward the vehicles as Ockter stared after her a moment, then walked toward the deserters at the fire.

Looking forlorn and lonely, Riley sat holding his empty flask in his lap. He was running a finger idly over its inscription.

" 'Ireland the brave,' " said Luzero out of the darkness.

Riley looked up to see her infectious smile. She held out a wicker-wrapped, earthenware jug of aguardiente.

"Viva darlin' Mexico!" Riley grinned. "You truly are an angel," he added, eagerly taking the jug. He patted the blanket beside him. "Now don't make me drink alone," he teased. She looked over her shoulder toward the road.

"We wait only long enough to water the wounded," Luzero said.

"Not all the wounded are shot," Riley replied, again patting the ground.

She shrugged and plopped down. Luzero held out a carved wooden cup she carried on a cord about her waist. Riley filled it, seeing her eye the red rose in his cap as he poured. She saw and smiled in embarrassment. He instantly pulled out the rose and stuck it in her thick, wild mane of raven hair.

"Thank you for such a beautiful rose!" she effused. "I could not help staring at it," she continued. "I have grown up with the army since I was sixteen and never saw any soldado wearing such an ornament!" She laughed lightly.

" 'Tis in its more rightful place now," Riley replied. "Was lately reminded of the wild roses that growed back home, in Ireland . . ." His voice trailed off.

"Is that where you are right now, remembering your old home?" she asked innocently. "Is that what helps you in your mind to survive this horror?"

"Thank you kindly, for caring enough to ask," Riley said. "But it's the afterwards feeling of alone what I can't stomach after any fight, win or lose." She considered his eyes as he stared at the deserters eating at the campfire. "And here I got no veteran mates who know what I mean, 'cept for Ockter, of course, but he's a Prussian." He doubted if Prussian military ever felt anything after a fight except whether they executed their plan perfectly. He shrugged a tired laugh.

"Well, you are not alone now. We must have a toast!" Luzero said sprightly, holding out her cup, trying to pull Riley up from his Celtic gloom.

He managed a weary smile. "To roses what don't wilt," he said, "and friends what don't fade!" Riley touched her cup with the entire demijon, flipped it for support to rest on his forearm and drank with a mighty thirst.

From Riley's position behind the tree, he could not see the road. Just as well, Moreno thought, as he watched the arrival of a squad of Jalisco Lancers. They had brought eighteen dejected U.S. prisoners, barely recognizable in the flickering, distant firelight. The lancers easily kept them bunched with expert horsemanship and prodding, as if herding cattle or sheep. They were the finest cavalry in the Mexican army. A lancer lieutenant trotted nearer the cookfire where Moreno, Manzano, and Mejia stood eating tortillas and cheese. The lieutenant dismounted, walked up, and braced to attention. Moreno nodded, his mouth full.

"I bring the gringo prisoners, Captain," he said in Spanish, "per your order." He dusted off his jaunty red jacket.

"Have them build a separate fire in that clearing," Moreno said, pointing. "Let them rest and give them water." The lieutenant looked confused.

"With respect, Captain, is not water too precious to waste?" he ventured. Manzano and Mejia exchanged knowing looks of foreboding. Moreno waved him away as if shooing a fly.

"See that he does as I command," he said to Mejia, who nodded and followed the lieutenant.

"Will they even reach the prison at Mexico City?" asked Manzano.

"The misfortunes of this war are unpredictable," Moreno replied. "But we need recruits." Manzano looked disgusted.

"We will do our duty."

In the deserter camp, Luzero knelt in rapt attention facing Riley. She waited breathlessly for the next morsel of Irish blarney to be fed to her. He had managed to shed his pall of depression.

"And so, the poor potato farmer, he couldn't believe his Irish luck," crooned Riley at his most charming, telling a story. "He'd nabbed his own self a leprechaun, and the roguish elf squealed like a tiny banshee, he did!"

He lifted the demijon to down some more aguardiente as Luzero laughed in delight, clapping her hands in innocent, child-like glee. As Riley drank, he flashed a lusty look usually reserved for a fallen woman. Oddly, he felt guilty.

"I love a happy ending!" Luzero said. "The little people takes the farmer to his pot of gold!"

Riley wagged a finger at her. "Mind what I said, the little people are impish rascals, they are," he warned, drawing a look of worry from Luzero. "That elfin cobbler, he took the man to the very bush beneath which his pot of gold was buried. The man tied his red bandanna to the bush, so's he'd know it again, and he run home to fetch a shovel for to dig it up."

"He left that little people alone?!" Luzero whined aghast.

Riley's eyes twinkled in delight at her charming butchery of English. "And when he come back," Riley concluded breathlessly, "red bandannas fluttered in the breeze from every bush as far as his eyes could see."

Luzero looked as if she could cry. "Oh-h-h," she moaned, "I want him to find the gold!"

"So do I, darlin'," Riley whispered. He drank again. "So do I."

"But how can he ever find it?" she whimpered.

" 'Tain't possible to know, having never caught me a leprechaun," Riley replied. " 'Til then, I'll be lookin' under every damn bush I can find." She punched him playfully in the chest and burst into laughter. He offered to fill her cup, but she shook her head and stood, though somewhat shakily.

"Your stories they are like magic, like religion and dreams," Luzero said. "And dreams they are everything."

"Only dream I got left was to go home again," Riley sighed, his smile fading as he glanced at his men huddled around their campfire. "Now it's a nightmare." For an instant, he saw the sightless eyes of dead Parker stare out at him from the fire. "I'll shovel coal in hell for this," he said.

"Perhaps you have only had the wrong dream," Luzero suggested. Stunned, he could only stare at her. "Buenas noches, Teniente Riley," she smiled, this time flirtatiously. With a swish of whirling skirt and shapely bare legs, she disappeared into the night heading for the wagons. Other women throughout camp were leaving, as well. Riley was astonished at her ability to slash through his blarney with one swipe of razor-sharp insight.

Riley was still staring after her when Ockter trotted up excitedly. The deserters were on their feet, pointing toward the Mexican camp and trying to see something. The sound of cracking bullwhips and creaking wagons signaled the departure of the wounded and soldaderas.

"Captain Moreno needs to see you," Ockter said with a breathless salute. Riley merely offered him the demijon.

"What can possibly be more important," sighed Riley, "than waving farewell to herself."

"Has 'somebody else's daughter' recovered her lost virginity?" Ockter taunted.

"Purge your filthy mind, you dirty Hun," Riley joked as he rose to his feet a bit wobbly. He looked at the demijon. "Damn near good as Irish, this," he said.

"You had better be that good,"Ockter warned. Riley looked concerned, suddenly suspicious. "Moreno says you must recruit from new prisoners," Ockter said grimly. Riley instantly sobered.

Minutes later, Riley stood with hands on his hips and feet wide apart beside roaring flames rapidly consuming a stack of fence rails. The dancing shadows imparted a demon-like quality to his leering image. "The devil himself you'd think I was!" Riley laughed.

The light from roaring flames showed him the faces of angry, defiant U.S. captives. Most were powder blackened and battered from battle. Loosely clustered around a raging bonfire were groups of gray-clad volunteers, Dragoons in their jaunty, dark-blue jackets, and sky-blue regulars.

Seated among these was Conahan, wearing an oilcloth backpack with the neck of a fiddle peeking out. His face was clean, and he sported new white corporal stripes. Riley wondered if he had deserted.

Behind Conahan and calmly smoking a pipe was Dalton, who similarly showed no signs of combat. Riley felt an overwhelming wave of relief wash across his soul. Perhaps they both had seen the light, he hoped.

"You've cursed our race in the eyes of th'native born!" roared an Irish regular shaking his fist. Most shouted to agree. Conahan and a handful remained quietly watching. Dalton looked merely amused.

"As if one curse ain't enough in just bein' Irish!" laughed a mustachioed Dragoon with a gold earring. His mates laughed as the Irish regulars booed.

"Immigrant trash infantry or native-born Dragoon," sneered one volunteer, standing. "You shithouse regulars are to blame!" A hush fell on the rowdy group. "It's soldiering for money that breeds traitors like him!" He pointed at Riley.

"I'd rather burn in hell than serve th'likes of you," vowed another Irish regular, glaring at Riley. "However black hearted the hate of th'native born," he continued, "you've made it 'just' in their eyes!" Others groused in agreement. Riley noticed that Conahan, Dalton, and several more remained silent.

"Play the martyr if you must," Riley soothed. He shifted his attention to the little group around Conahan. "But some of you tortured sons of Erin may realize you're damned well already!"

Conahan and a few seated near him chuckled, though not stoic Dalton. Other prisoners glared at them.

"So if you prefer plump senoritas to the likes of them . . ." Riley roared, pointing at the volunteers; ". . . and tortillas, beef, and beans to prison lice and rats . . ." he continued, pausing to let it sink in; ". . . and three hundred-twenty acres to a swift kick in the arse for being Irish . . ." he added, kicking a spray of dirt in the direction of the volunteers, ". . . then go to the devil you can!" Riley laughed and opened his arms wide, thinking that all he lacked was horns and a tail.

"I'd play a jig in hell for three hundred-twenty acres, I would!" chirped Conahan. He stood and danced a bit of a jig, drawing smiles from his surrounding mates.

"Only damn land you'll ever get is th'bone orchard!" yelled a Dragoon.

While others hooted, howled, and booed, Conahan strutted like a pied piper to Riley with a half-dozen militant Irish regulars following behind him. They returned every insult and taunt in kind as they went.

As Conahan passed Riley, he gave the five-foot fiddler a paternal pat on the head. "You've come up in the world to artillery, you have," Riley taunted. "But Conahan, can you even see over a gun?"

"I makes up in splendor what I lacks in stature," Conahan asserted with a smile, pointing proudly to his new corporal stripes.

Riley laughed as he led the band of defectors away from the campfire. The loyal U.S. troops continued protesting loudly. Riley saw Dalton sitting alone now, quietly smoking his pipe. Riley believed that he must do something quickly.

" 'Tis grand to see some familiar faces," said Riley, still staring at Dalton. He turned to Conahan. "Meet your new employers, so to speak," he added. Riley delivered the defectors to an imperious looking Manzano, grim faced Sergeant Mejia, and eight lethal looking riflemen guards. The defectors looked unsure.

"Come with us, gringos," snapped Manzano, turning on his heels. Conahan looked at Riley with apprehension as they fell in with the squad.

"You'll be safer with them than with the native-born regulars!" Riley called out. He then noticed Moreno walking up in a purposeful stride.

Moreno gave a wave of his arm at the shadows. The company of mounted lancers suddenly appeared from out of the dark brush, trees, and cactus. They completely encircled the remaining U.S. prisoners, who looked intimidated.

"All who would join us of their own free will have stepped forward, Teniente?" Moreno asked Riley, who could not miss his foreboding tone.

"There's one sergeant back there who's a bit thick in the head," Riley said, pointing at Dalton. "Never hears things the same as a sane man."

The lancer lieutenant strode up, anxiously fingering his belt pistol.

"All is ready, sir," he said in Spanish. He eyed Riley with contempt.

"Bring the pipe smoker to this one, alone," snapped Moreno in Spanish. The lieutenant straightened and dared to give Moreno a questioning look, as if to protest. "Now!" Moreno insisted. Cowed, the lieutenant bowed his head and left.

As Moreno stared into his eyes, Riley felt a sudden chill in the humid heat. He did not need to understand Spanish to feel a threat.

"Be most convincing, Teniente," Moreno advised and stepped into the shadows nearby. Riley felt his neck hairs stand to, believing the remaining captives were doomed.

Moments later, Riley found Dalton at Moreno's small cook fire. He was perched atop a rock with a pipe in his mouth and a steaming tin cup of coffee in his hands. He eyed Riley, who drank from his recently filled flask as he walked to Dalton. Riley poured aguardiente into Dalton's coffee.

"I had got myself drunk in camp, I had," Dalton said with a nod of thanks, "and wandered astray." He sipped heavily and rolled his eyes in delight. Riley grinned. "This lancer patrol swoops down and snatches me up." He shrugged and drank again. "I see you ain't yet deserted this bunch," Dalton added wryly. He exhaled a small cloud of smoke with a twinkle in his eye.

" 'Tain't like I've had the chance, is it?" said Riley. He raised the flask in tribute to Dalton. "You Yanks been keeping us too damn busy."

"Beats sloshing through the Florida muck and swamps with Harney chasing Seminoles," said Dalton pensively, almost in reverie. The Seminole War of ten years before had lasted what seemed a lifetime to Dalton, and all for nothing. The most hostile band never signed a treaty. "This time we are winning," he added with soldierly pride.

"You ain't winning now, Patrick," Riley said. He darted a worried look back at the other U.S. prisoners, now being herded roughly by the lancers toward the road. He felt as if a clock had started ticking at an execution.

"Jails and me, we are old friends," Dalton said with a casual air. He gave Riley a discerning eye, tossing a casual glance at the others.

"And I suppose we are not?" quipped Riley.

"Four months ain't a lifetime," Dalton observed, staring at him warily.

"Can be in our profession," Riley mused, seeing Dalton concede the point reluctantly with a grunt. He finished the spiked coffee and stood.

"Thanks for the java Irish, friend," he said, "but it is time to be following my chosen path." Dalton started walking toward the other prisoners now grouped on the moonlit road. "May yours rise to meet you," he added.

"Patrick, I've strayed from my own path too far," Riley suddenly blurted, surprising himself and drawing a look of pity from Dalton, who warned him long ago. "Caught up alone in something what I can't seem to shake loose of."

"No friend of mine asks me to be a dirty traitor," Dalton warned. He puffed his pipe with a vengeance.

"Ain't asking you to be no traitor," Riley implored. "Asking you to be a friend." For all his usual blarney, Riley managed to sound convincing. He hoped it would be enough to save Dalton.

"Some friends ask too much," Dalton said softly, "for nothing in return."

Riley looked again at the hapless U.S. prisoners. The lancers were poking and prodding them into a tighter column and looking restless. Riley had seen that merciless look before in the eyes of the bloody British before they slaughtered some captive savages, too troublesome to take prisoner. "We'd be traitors only to the losing side," Riley urged, "but heroes to the greasers when they win, with money and land to boot!"

"When they win?!" Dalton exclaimed, astonished. "Look around and know what you are seeing!" Dalton laughed. "Regulars just cut through this motley bunch like shit through a goose!"

"This frontier batch ain't nothing but a bluff, a diversion!"

Riley confided. He leaned closer, took a deep breath, and unleashed what he knew was a desperate lie. "Captain Moreno he says they're massing their best troops for the next go in a jolly sucker punch." Dalton furrowed his brow, at last looking intrigued. Riley felt a sudden glimmer of hope. "I tell you, Patrick, they can win," Riley insisted. "All we got to do is survive long enough to become landed gentlemen."

"In all my family history," Dalton dreamed, "from County Mayo to New York, not a single Dalton ever has worked land of his own." He puffed his pipe thoughtfully, staring into the fire. Riley seized the moment, sensing victory.

" 'Tain't looking like much right now," he said, pouring straight whiskey into Dalton's tin cup, "but for starting over, it is someplace else." Dalton cocked his head and unleashed a slow, circling smoke ring. He nodded with a smile.

Within minutes, Dalton, Conahan, and the other new recruits stood around the deserters' campfire tossing their sky-blue jackets into crackling flames. They now wore dark-blue Mexican coatees faced with red, like the others who lounged about staring at them silently. Riley stood apart beside Moreno watching with a few guards. Conahan and Dalton exchanged worried looks.

"Sure and the corpse at a wake is livelier than the lot of you," Dalton pronounced grandly. He began slowly circling the fire as he addressed the deserters. Conahan took his cue and followed.

"A corpse got more to be jolly 'bout than any of us," groused the tobacco chewer, expertly firing juice into the flames with a hiss. "This ain't nothin' but a banty march to the gallows," he said. Dalton darted a look for help at Conahan.

"Not one amongst you regrets more than myself how I come to be in such a fix," Conahan announced in the posture of a bantam rooster.

"Who gives a bloody damn?" grimaced Price. He was painfully re-tying the rag around his wounded leg.

"The warm, willing, and naked senorita what I left in a restive condition, that's who," Conahan declared, grabbing the rapt attention of everyone.

Riley and Moreno stood just outside the circle of light cast by the restless flames. They watched Conahan prance about the campfire mimicking a minstrel as he began his tale.

"None but me tells a better story than Conahan," Riley bragged.

"Perhaps his are true?" Moreno replied. Riley scowled.

"An' so I stole from my post on picket duty into her posted bed at the hacienda, I did," Conahan continued, drawing a few catcalls.

"And there did you do your manly duty, you rogue?!" asked Dalton, easing into the role of "Mister Interlocutor," traditional emcee at any minstrel show. Deserter spirits rose as they waited anxiously for the rest of the story.

"At that most delicate and private of moments," Conahan crooned as he formed the shape of a woman with his hands while leaning back, as if she were sitting atop him, "in burst th'local rancheros, flashing knives longer than my expectant manhood." Chuckles replaced the sexual tittering.

"So sporting pocketknives, were they?!" Dalton interjected to ever more suggestive laughter.

"They may as well have," snapped Conahan, "for that's when 'the long' become 'the short' of this tale!" Rough, rowdy, boisterous belly laughs chased away any remnants of depression.

"And by the time we get our bounty of land," asserted Dalton, "sure and we will all have such ladies in waiting, as it were!"

"I'm blessed if they won't have a long wait," cracked the tobacco chewer. Dalton glared at him while others laughed.

"Do you think me daft," snarled Dalton, "a simpleton what

would leave the winning side just for to lose?!" The tobacco chewer grudgingly shrugged, seeing his logic. " 'Tain't never lost a fight in my life. My sainted mother she would turn in her grave were I to start now," Dalton said to the rest. He still was met with obvious doubt by most, but hopeful looks from a few. "I have it plain," continued Dalton, as if working up a crowd at a revival, "from 'the highest' of greaser officers," he added, flashing a look at Riley, "that we will be joining a grand army of fresh troops just down the road a piece."

Watching, Moreno shot Riley a withering glare. "Your small lie grows huge, Teniente!" he observed in a hot, urgent whisper.

Riley looked every which way but into Moreno's steady, uncomfortable, unsettling gaze. " 'Tis only a bit of blarney for their own good," Riley insisted. "Flags may change, but the blarney never does," he added, a choice bit of his own philosophy. "Besides, I had to save their lives from your lancers." Moreno held his unwavering stare but seemed to be withholding something, Riley thought.

"We will end this brouhaha on our own terms, we will!" Dalton concluded to more cheers. Conahan pulled his fiddle from his pack.

"More harmony might help," Conahan suggested brightly, arching an eyebrow at Dalton.

"As befits the occasion," Dalton announced, "we will seal our fates with a drinking tune. Would that we had something fit to be drinking!"

Dalton looked over at Riley, who gratefully took the chance to escape Moreno by bounding out with the jug of aguardiente.

Rowdy cheers and a few insults greeted Riley as Conahan began fiddling "Derry Down," the tune to which Dalton had sung his ditty back in the provost prison. "Do not let this go to your heads," Dalton chirped, "or to your necks," he added in dark humor, "but the newest damn verse is about you—or, now, us!"

Laughter rippled as Riley passed the jug from man to man. Dalton sang the new words:

> Sergeant, buck him and gag him
> Our officers cry,
> For each trifling offense
> Which they happen to spy.
> 'Til with bucking and gagging
> Of Dick, Pat, and Bill,
> Faith the Mexicans' ranks
> They have helped to fill!

Everyone joined in the rowdy chorus directed at Ockter, who had hoisted the jug and now was drinking with a mighty thirst:

> Drink it down, down, down.
> Drink it down!

Riley sang with the rest but felt more and more remorse as he looked from renewed, hopeful face to face, ending with the buoyant Dalton. Riley gave Dalton a salute with his own flask for the upswing in morale, then left the group. He collapsed onto his blanket beneath the tree, feeling emotionally exhausted and painfully torn. Moreno walked up. Riley looked up at him.

"Men fight hardest when they know fate is against them," Moreno quietly suggested. "Perhaps the truth would be best." Moreno felt a tug of conscience. But was it for Riley or himself? He was no longer sure.

"I tell them what they need to hear," Riley said, drinking again. "If they knew the blessed truth, they'd all be gone. And so would I, had I someplace else to go." He still felt that aching need to escape, though complicated now by his unexpected feelings for Luzero. He felt time would work it all out. It always did.

Moreno merely looked at him, trying to hide the pity that he felt as well as guilt for his own untold deceptions. He turned and walked away.

Riley stared at the laughing, jubilant company he had created, born from nothing but his unabashedly selfish, desperate desire to go back to Ireland. And now he felt trapped into making the band grow strong enough to survive. Riley still felt guilt, could still see Parker's haunting, opaque eyes, asking that eternal question, "Why?" Riley himself had never found the answer and had learned to quit asking. He knew his task would require a steady diet of lies, of whatever was needed to buy enough time until peace was declared. He had to smile at himself. Since when, he wondered, did a little blarney ever bother him? As the deserters broke into another "Drink it down" chorus, this time directed at Dalton himself, Riley lifted his flask to toast them. He found it empty.

"Damn!" he whispered, slamming it hard with a hollow thud onto his blanket. Riley had woven many a tall tale but never one like this: he did not want to know how it might end.

CHAPTER 8
WASHINGTON CITY
FALL 1846

Bone chilling rain poured from a black, thundering sky onto the rural Southern town whose architecture betrayed its struggle to define itself. A rolling cow pasture flanked by primitive wood farm buildings stretched between the Capitol and the future site of the white marble Washington Monument, for which private funds still were being raised. The seemingly endless downpour had transformed this Potomac River grassland into a flooded quagmire more closely resembling a fetid swamp.

As lightning flashed, it reflected in the pooling water and illuminated the squat, copper-covered dome of the edifice where a fractious Congress festered in session. Drenched black livery drivers, mostly slave but some free, shivered in their cape coats. They waited with soggy horses and carriages, parked in the muddy street at the base of the Capitol steps. They could hear applause and cheers resound through corridors of the seat of power of this young, divided republic grappling with its first war on foreign soil. They could not hear the words of recently appointed commanding general of the entire army, Major General Winfield Scott, as he begged for more troops.

"I am too much of an old soldier, gentlemen, to desire to place myself in that most perilous of positions," Scott jested in his soft Virginia accent, "with a fire upon my rear from Washington and a fire in front from the Mexicans!"

Laughter sprinkled with applause ensued from the amused legislators. Crossed United States flags hung on the wall behind

Scott at the podium inside the small House of Representatives chamber. Rows of two-man desks, each with its own burnished brass spittoon, faced the elevated platform in radiating semi-circles, aisles looking like spokes in a wagon wheel, the chairman and dais at the hub. Lightning flashed occasionally through skylights. Thunder crashed like distant cannon. Even in this raging storm, not a desk was empty.

"I urge you to approve President Polk's request for funds to raise ten new regiments of regular infantry," Scott continued, his resonant, commanding voice rising. Congressmen from the twenty-six states had regaled themselves in finely tailored black frock coats or tailcoats and fluffy, vibrant cravats. The sheen from their colorfully patterned silk vests shimmered in the warm glow of oil lamps, lit this day due to the darkness of the angry sky. Surprisingly respectful for this troubled session, they were paying rapt attention to the hero of the War of 1812.

"Disease and surprisingly strong Mexican resistance have decimated our ranks to dangerously low levels," he warned. "Though we have won battles in the north, we still have much work to do. We must be strong enough to strike at the heart of Mexico."

To face this assemblage with such a costly request, Scott knew he must cut a fine figure. Though mid-sixties, his large frame and towering height still looked powerful in uniform, especially now in the unique full-dress attire prescribed for the ranking major general. His double-breasted, dark-blue cutaway tailcoat looked dashing with buff collar, cuffs, oak leaf embroidery, and sash, the same facings as worn by General Washington in the Revolution. He sported a gold embroidered sword belt and massive gold epaulettes with three silver stars, one extra star to denote him as the newly ranking major general. His fore-and-aft cocked hat was topped with a bright yellow plume, alone in all the army. Scott would wear this full-dress uniform even in the field in Mexico. He began to close his eloquent remarks, an appeal to the obstinate, growing anti-war faction.

"General Taylor has won a resounding victory at Monterey, but let us not waste it," Scott concluded. "You and President Polk have given me the honor of overall command. Now, give me the tools with which to crown General Taylor's success with that most satisfying of laurel wreaths—victorious peace!"

Ringing cheers, shouts of "Huzzah!", and applause erupted from most congressmen, many rising to their feet. Toward the back, however, a knot of fourteen representatives traded looks of disdain. They clustered around a petite, white-headed states-man distinctive in a bold plaid cravat tied in a jaunty bow. Former president John Quincy Adams, eighty years old, leaned to the gangly, somewhat disheveled younger man next to him.

"He has not exactly come 'hat in hand,' has he?" Adams asked with a sly smile. Abraham Lincoln, thirty-eight and a first-term representative from Illinois, sported an unruly shock of black hair and an amused expression.

"With that hat, how could he?!" Lincoln cracked, drawing chuckles from the others. "The men in ranks don't call him 'Old Fuss and Feathers' for nothing." His high-pitched Illinois twang made his jokes even funnier. This group of beleaguered anti-war congressmen increasingly rallied around Lincoln's humor as if it were a flag in a losing battle.

The chairman pounded his gavel and announced a recess. Scott bowed and left the podium, heading for a door to the hall.

Minutes later, Adams, Lincoln, and the others huddled in a cold marble corridor as young pages served them hot, steaming coffee from silver trays. Adams, short and frail, shivered with a woven, fringed shawl on his shoulders.

"General Scott has made his sincere, public appeal as a soldier," Adams said in an aside, looking up at the looming Lincoln. "I believe he will make his appeal to us more personal." He turned to address the group at large. "Gentlemen, General Scott's mere presence in these halls strengthens our hand for immediate peace," Adams asserted. "It just may prove to be the undoing of President Polk."

"By letting the Mexicans off so easily after Monterey with only a truce," Lincoln suggested, a twinkle in his eye, "it will surely undo General Taylor." The group was still chuckling when booted footsteps announced Scott's approach.

Scott drew himself up straight. He knew that this confrontation would be difficult. But he felt he owed it to his army, his primary allegiance. "Former President Adams, Representative Lincoln, the 'Immortal fourteen' who vote steadfastly against this war," Scott said graciously as he bowed, "I salute you, gentlemen, for having the courage to stand your ground."

"Thank you, General Scott," said bemused Lincoln, the only one tall enough to stare Scott level in the eye. "If we continue to stand, you will soon be out of a job!"

Scott forced himself to join Adams and the rest in a laugh at his own expense. All of Washington knew he had not been Polk's first choice for overall command; neither had been Taylor. The president had wanted to appoint a political general who could push his agenda through Congress. But Taylor, though a regular, almost forced Polk's favor when he practically won the war at Monterey. But then he let the enemy get away. To sustain momentum, Polk chose speed over politics.

"Any true soldier prays for the shortest route to peace," Scott said. "If you deny me these new regiments, it will tie my hands. I shall have enough troops to continue the fight but not have enough to win complete victory. This war could drag on indefinitely."

"General, the shortest route to peace is simply to quit fighting," Adams said flatly. "If we keep this Mexican land in Texas and what we've now seized in California, as well, we will only kick awake that sleeping tiger, the question of slavery." The group shared dour looks.

"Gentlemen, I need those regiments!" Scott declared. "My army is imperiled by being so under strength! Politics are not my concern."

"General, politics shall be everyone's concern," cautioned Lincoln, "when this nation is forced to decide if these newly acquired lands shall be admitted as slave or free states."

"You know President Polk has nullified General Taylor's truce," Scott pressed. "Leaving that defeated Mexican army in the field killed any hope for a limited war, Polk's first strategy. Now there can be no cheap, quick victory."

"Better to hold our illegally gained ground and start peace talks than expand this immoral war," Adams said. "New regiments mean new fighting."

"When the British invaded our land in 1812," Scott said, "I fought them through ongoing peace talks, even through the burning of this very Capitol, until we gained victories enough to negotiate better terms."

"Yes, General," Adams said. "But this time, we are the invaders."

"And it is the Mexicans who feel they must keep fighting," added Lincoln. "Perhaps they learned from you, General." Scott cast a wary eye at Lincoln, thinking him too clever for such a newcomer.

"If you vote to raise these new regiments," Scott countered, "you can do so in good conscience. I believe it would in effect be a vote for peace." Scott, a master politician despite his protestations to the contrary, surveyed their incredulous reaction. "President Polk has informed me of a change in Mexican leadership, gentlemen," Scott continued in a peculiar, clandestine tone. "It is expected, almost guaranteed, to give both peace and victory."

Scott knew that now was the time to play this trump card. President Polk had arranged what amounted to a coup in Mexico. Scott detested what Polk had done, bribing with gold a notorious former Mexican leader who agreed to sue for peace in exchange for a return to power from exile. To Scott, it seemed both immoral and dishonorable. But if it gave him a chance to end this war more quickly and with fewer casualties, he would do his duty.

The "Immortal Fourteen," those congressmen under Adams who had braved public scorn to vote against Polk's declaration of war, stiffened in polite, wary discomfort. Lincoln, though a freshman in the House, was a rising star who traded skeptical looks with his mentor, Adams.

"Would that we could so easily change our leadership, General," said Lincoln, "and produce so sure a happy outcome."

"Who is this new leader?" asked Adams, sounding as dubious.

"He is hardly 'new,' gentlemen," Scott explained, feeling a bit like a school marm imparting a history lesson. "Do you remember the Alamo?"

CHAPTER 9
SAN LUIS POTOSI: ARRIVAL
OCTOBER 5, 1846

Shortly after dawn, Riley's band of deserters and their ever-present guards emerged from a pass thickly timbered in pine trees. They had trudged all night through a maze of narrow canyons. At times, darkness had been so thick that each man had to hold onto the blanket roll of the one in front just to keep from stumbling. Riley felt increasingly weighed down by the shadows looming in the mountain forest. With no distractions in the dark, he was forced to confront his own conscience. But then he wondered if he even had one anymore. For that he would feel thankful, were it only true.

On horseback, weary Moreno raised his hand to halt the dusty column. It had been a grueling ten days of hard marching. Sergeants bawled commands as the disheveled, dejected men strained to see what awaited them below.

"And the dead shall rise and be seen by many!" Riley exclaimed, having trotted up front to stand beside Moreno and look below. He gawked, amazed to see his lies transformed into truth. He wondered if he somehow had acquired an evil gift of prophecy. His weight of conscience vanished like a hangover cured.

The old mining town of San Luis Potosi lay nestled below against the base of craggy mountains blanketed with green pine trees. A silver cross gleaned from its mines glistened atop a stone cathedral awash in warm sunlight. The tents, wagon parks, and horse picket lines of an immense army camp stretched across adjacent slopes in the lush valley. It is big enough for thousands, Riley surmised. Brightly clad regiments were forming for drill to the melodious brass band, bugle, and drum music of the Mexican reveille, "The Diana." Cavalry platoons were trotting out of camp for morning patrol, their red pennons dancing gaily just beneath the gleaming tips of their deadly lances. Smoke from morning campfires enshrouded it all in a dreamlike haze. Stunned, Riley felt witness to a miracle.

" 'Tis cut to the quick, I am!" Dalton shouted, satisfied by the amazed looks of the deserters pushing to the front. "How could you have doubted the devil hisself?!" he laughed, pointing at Riley. Shouts and guffaws drowned him out.

"How could we not?!" yelled the tobacco chewer with a spit.

"Bloody well right!" grumbled Price, standing beside him but no longer on a crutch, having healed like the other walking wounded.

"Behold our new Army of the North!" Moreno shouted. However, Riley thought his enthusiasm sounded forced, as if waiting for the other shoe to drop.

"Huzzah!" the deserters shouted, more in relief than joy.

Now they felt they had a fighting chance, Riley thought, because he felt similarly. For the first time since his desertion, he believed his original plan still might be made to work. And now it could even include Luzero.

Surprised and yet proud, Manzano echoed the news in Spanish. Mejia led his riflemen guards in a shout of "Viva!"

Riley looked up curiously at Moreno, who seemed strangely guarded. *Was he holding something back?* Riley wondered. The rumble of pounding hooves drawing nearer pulled his attention to the road ahead.

A squad of Tulancingo curaissiers rolled to a dusty, spur-jingling halt just ahead of a luxurious maroon coach pulled by six well-groomed mules. The curaissiers wore metal breastplates and helmets with plumes, sky-blue coats, and cherry-red trousers. Unlike the lax frontier troops, these hard riders cut a strict military attitude: terse, grim, deadly. But they looked oddly antique to Riley.

"Ain't Napoleon dead?!" he joked, drawing chuckles. On cue, Conahan started fiddling "The Bear Went Over the Mountain," a French marching tune.

An intense curaissier lieutenant frowned at what he assumed was disrespect, Riley thought, since he probably did not understand his words. He spurred his horse forward, roughly bumping Riley back.

"Didn't you see me for your horse's arse?" Riley snarled. Scowling, the lieutenant gave a crisp salute to Moreno, who returned it. Riley was astonished at this sudden air of military decorum. "Ockter," he crooned, "you're gonna like this new greaser army." Ockter snapped to attention and returned a salute to muffled laughs. The lieutenant glared at the rowdy deserters, turned to the coachmen, and nodded. One opened the carriage door.

"I have orders," he said in a cultured Spanish accent, "to take Captain Moreno and the Irish gringo, Riley, to our new commander . . ."

"To my old commander," Moreno corrected with an upraised hand. "We are summoned for you to meet 'the Napoleon of the West,'" he added with a knowing little smile at Riley. He lowered his hand. "Continue."

". . . His Excellency, General Antonio Lopez de Santa Anna," the lieutenant finished, looking slightly exasperated. The name sounded familiar to Riley, but he could not quite put his memory to it, remaining too astonished at the lieutenant's excellent English. He must remember, thought Riley, to no longer assume greaser ignorance of the language. It could become a tactical disadvantage.

Riley followed Moreno into the coach, which had doors crested with gold Mexican eagles. They departed with a lurch, the cavalry pounding hard behind.

As the coach slowly wound through the canvas maze of tent streets, Moreno and Riley observed regiments of infantry and cavalry at drill wearing a rainbow of rakish new uniforms. They wore dark-blue trousers and coatees with bibbed lapels in Napoleonic tradition, each regiment with different color lapels from the universal red for cuffs and most collars.

As they neared Santa Anna's headquarters complex of red-and-white striped tents, they saw dashing young officers whose uniforms glittered in gold or silver embroidery coming and going with urgency. At the entrance, they beheld menacing Grenadier Guards of the Supreme Power. In deep red coatees faced in sky blue with white bib lapels, they reminded Riley of the British Grenadier Guards in tall bearskin caps, or even Napoleon's Old Guard. They presented arms smartly.

"Now this is more like soldiering!" Riley exclaimed. Moreno merely lit a cigar. "Whenever you fire up a smoke," Riley said warily, "it's soon I got cause to be nervous." Moreno blew a smoke ring, remaining silent.

Inside the tent, Riley saw two buxom, beautiful teenage mistresses lurking in the shadows of the sleeping quarters. One, no more than sixteen, sat primping herself in front of a mirrored washstand. Her smooth, creamy, chocolate skin showed in stark contrast to her lacy, revealing, white underclothes. Riley could not help but wonder if Luzero looked like that. The other girl, darker and perhaps two years older, stood fully dressed in silk finery, lace mantilla, and shawl, as she prepared a silver tray of fresh bread and fruit. Riley nudged Moreno, who looked at the girls with a bored shrug.

"I have seen this before," Moreno said nonchalantly.

"And once was enough?!" Riley blurted, astonished.

175

An adjutant ushered Riley and Moreno into a room where Santa Anna worked impatiently with several junior engineer officers doubling as artists. They clustered around easels that displayed colorful renderings of new uniforms.

Santa Anna, clean shaven with a white complexion, wore tight white pants, vest, and shirt beneath a dark blue coatee faced with red. It glowed from pounds of gold bullion braid and massive epaulettes with silver Mexican eagles. Though in his early fifties, Santa Anna remained charismatic, fit, and military. He limped in obvious pain on his left leg as he walked from easel to easel.

"Not enough flair!" he insisted in Spanish as Moreno and Riley entered. A hapless ensign withered under his patently lethal glare. "Each battalion must wear a different color for plastrons than the red for facings!"

"With so many new regiments, Excellency," the officer replied meekly, "we have exhausted all possible colors."

"Then create new colors!" Santa Anna snapped. "Do not come back until you have done so!" He waved them out. They hustled to leave with all the renderings but one, remaining covered on an easel.

Santa Anna regained his composure instantly when he saw Riley, who stood at attention, cap in his hand beside Moreno, who held his shako. Riley fidgeted as Santa Anna studied him. He pulled out a gold snuff box, popped it open, and dabbed white opium powder on his tongue. He snapped the lid shut.

"Teniente Riley, I need your help to do something about all these pesky *norteamericano* prisoners," Santa Anna said flatly in perfect English. Riley stared at him in shock and confusion. "It is costly and cumbersome to keep shipping them to Mexico City. And they eat entirely too much."

"Your worship ain't been killing them?" Riley asked, still feeling guilty about snaring Dalton with the "huge army" lie, though now magically it had become the truth. Nevertheless, he glared at Moreno, who smiled innocently.

"He thinks us barbarians," Santa Anna said in Spanish, frowning at Moreno.

"I use what he thinks to get what we want," Moreno replied. "He falls for it every time."

"They always do," Santa Anna said. He smiled thinly as Riley shifted on his feet, uncomfortable with the Spanish.

"I have never needed help to kill anyone," Santa Anna said icily to Riley. "I want you to recruit them. Use this." He handed Riley a document. As he read the hand-written decree, Santa Anna paced. "Ever since that small affair at the Alamo . . ." he groused, perhaps drifting into some morose fog of history.

Riley looked up. Now he remembered the name and its infamy. "Then the tales of torture and execution ain't nothing, your worship, but sordid lies?" Riley ventured. Moreno rolled his eyes.

"Most of the time, Teniente," Santa Anna warned. His dark mood brightened. "Once, like you, I also switched sides. In the middle of a battle against the Spanish," he bragged, "I joined the victor—Mexico."

" 'Tis my fondest hope that soon I can boast of having done the same, sir," Riley said. Unless, he thought, I can first escape.

"You already have, Teniente Riley," Santa Anna said. He held up a U.S. newspaper snatched from his field desk. "The victor in this war will be decided here, in their press. And you are helping us take and hold the high ground."

"Begging your worship's pardon, sir," Riley said, "but we been too busy losing so far to notice that we been winning."

"Subtlety is not among his strengths, Excellency," Moreno cautioned in Spanish. Santa Anna smiled knowingly, nodding in patient understanding.

"The *norteamericano* writer Henry David Thoreau refuses to

pay taxes that finance their war on us," Santa Anna explained, dropping the tabloid, "just as you have refused to fight in their invasion to take our land."

"In my own way, Excellency," Riley responded sheepishly, "ain't I after your land as much as the Yanks?" Riley stared pointedly at Moreno.

"Curb your insolence," warned Moreno. Santa Anna calmed Moreno with a casual wave of his hand.

"Others justify opposition with Thoreau's book *Civil Disobedience*," Santa Anna continued, studying Riley as he showed him the thin volume. "Their former president, John Quincy Adams, leads the fight against the war in their Congress. He is gaining more and more support. Of course, I would be forced unfortunately to execute such a traitor," he warned, dropping the book.

"One side's traitors can be the other side's heroes," surmised Riley.

"Just so, Teniente!" Santa Anna said. "Your name in their press could fan this spark of guilt into a blazing fire!" he exclaimed, as if experiencing a vision. "It could be worth battalions to me on a battlefield! But first they must know exactly who you are."

Riley watched him limp to the covered easel. Only then did he realize that Santa Anna's left leg was wood with a carved and painted boot as his "foot."

Santa Anna unveiled the rendering to reveal a bold new artillery uniform for Riley's men: dark-blue trousers and coatees with black bib lapels; red collars, cuffs, and piping; yellow buttons, trim, and epaulettes; and tall, black shakos.

"Something about a grand looking army can make you believe your own blarney," Riley gasped in wonder. Santa Anna looked pleased.

"Picture a regiment of Rileys," he announced, staring up at Riley, "towering symbols of *norteamericano* treachery!" Santa

Anna frowned as he suddenly realized how much shorter he was than Riley.

"Few see eye to eye with me, as it were, your worship," Riley said, staring down uncomfortably at Santa Anna, who stood barely 5 feet 10 inches tall. Moreno hid a smile. Riley was easily four inches taller.

"You did not tell me he was so large," Santa Anna said in Spanish. He picked up the tall, black artillery shako from the table and held it up to Riley's head. The hat would make Riley a giant.

"His ability to coerce followers seemed the more important quality," Moreno replied. He had learned to deal with Santa Anna's vanity.

"I must be the tallest soldier in my army," Santa Anna insisted. He put the shako down. "Do not issue them shakos, only barracks caps. That will cut them down to size."

"Yes, my general," Moreno replied laconically.

"Begging your pardon for the intrusion, sir," Riley said, uncomfortable with too much Spanish. "Mightn't the cost of this finery instead buy us a heavy gun or two?" Moreno frowned, but Santa Anna remained placid.

"You should find it humorous that your new uniforms, indeed, those for all my new army, were paid for by the United States," replied Santa Anna with a satisfied, small laugh. Riley looked confused. "For the weapons," he added, "strongboxes of Church pesos travel north from Mexico City even as we speak."

" 'T'would be gratifying to fight with more than just the blessing of the bishop, sir," Riley joked, but with an edge to his voice.

"However reluctantly given, eh, Captain Riley?" smiled Santa Anna, announcing an unexpected promotion.

"Thank you kindly, sir!" Riley said, snapping a salute.

"Church gold will get you the best cannon in my army, Major

179

Moreno," Santa Anna added, upping Moreno as well. He bowed in gratitude. "You both must show appropriate rank to lead such important troops."

"Excuse my ignorance, sir," Riley said, clearing his dry throat, "but exactly what portion of those strongboxes might a new captain be expecting?" Riley's audacity shocked Moreno, but Santa Anna merely smiled.

"I would expect nothing less from Captain Riley, Major," he said. Turning to Riley, he replied, "You will receive sixty-seven pesos a month."

"And the land?" Riley persisted, his eyes growing wider.

"As agreed," Santa Anna nodded. "Of course, all land promised to you lay in the frontier provinces, the very land norteamericanos want to steal."

"That is very clever, sir," Riley said frowning, sensing a deal going bad. Santa Anna and Moreno looked insulted. "As an incentive to keep fighting 'til we win, I mean," he added quickly. Riley had never felt such an urge to raid his flask.

"Promote one other *norteamericano* to lieutenant and Manzano to captain," Santa Anna said curtly to Moreno. Santa Anna's scowl faded as the teenage mistresses glided into the room. They carried silver trays of food and facial expressions equally tempting. Santa Anna instinctively looked in a silver shaving mirror to adjust his silk cravat. Riley saw a twinkle in his cold eyes.

"Vanity and glory have never moved me, gentlemen," Santa Anna said jokingly, "but we all have our sinful weaknesses." He glanced pointedly at Riley. "You must excuse me," he said with a dismissive wave of the hand.

Returning in the brougham coach, Riley and Moreno passed a smartly marching column of the 1st Line Regiment in new uniforms, dark blue trimmed in red with yellow bib lapels. Their bayonets gleamed atop well-oiled British Brown Bess muskets with shining brass hardware. A fifer and drummer played a jaunty tune. Riley tapped his toe, feeling nostalgic.

"With each beat of the drum, I feel my raging hemp fever going down," Riley said. Moreno remained distant and eyed him enigmatically. Riley naturally grew suspicious. "So why did the Yanks pay him off?"

"To assume power in Mexico and end the war," Moreno replied matter-of-factly. Such corruption, Moreno knew, always accompanied Santa Anna.

"And in return he'd give them the land they want . . . ," Riley said, feeling the anger of betrayal suddenly rise, ". . . the land me and my lads were to get, or so it would seem." He waved Santa Anna's recruitment decree tauntingly at Moreno. He felt the magical euphoria of this morning evaporate, along with the promised bounty of land, unless, of course, Mexico continued to fight and win.

"They brought him back from exile in Cuba through their own naval blockade," Moreno nodded, lighting a cigar. "And they gave him fifty thousand dollars in *norteamericano* gold."

"That could buy a fine-looking army," Riley said, amazed. He felt lost in a maze. No matter which way he turned, another false avenue opened. "But why spend the gold if only to parley for peace? Ain't it a waste?"

"You must dig deeper than merely new uniforms, Captain," Moreno warned. "Our work now must become a matter of life and death, for us all." He flicked Santa Anna's decree, still clenched in Riley's fist.

"Always thought that was a given, sir," Riley said too sweetly, "in our chosen profession." His cocky attitude hid confused, rushing, conflicting emotions that juggled his desires with the unusual sensation of growing guilt. He wanted to help Dalton and the rest survive, land or no land. But he also wanted to plot his own escape, with Luzero, if ever he saw her again.

Chapter 10
SAN LUIS POTOSI: CAMP
OCTOBER 1846

Over the next several weeks, the deserters pitched tents, dug latrines, felled trees, and implanted a stockade of rough pine logs around their resulting camp, supposedly to keep it separate from the rest of the army for their own protection. Riley felt it served more as a prison, something in the British army with which he was not entirely unacquainted. Four twelve-foot-high platforms rose above the fence to offer their Mexican guards a clear view and, if necessary, a clean shot. The grueling, demeaning labor only fueled his burning desire to escape. He lay awake at night in his tent, imagining various scenarios until it became a raging obsession.

Riley, Dalton, and a sweating crew in shirtsleeves just had finished implanting the final stockade logs when two wagons rolled through the gated entrance. Moreno and Manzano led the convoy astride horses, some guards marching behind. Riley and his workers lowered their picks and shovels to watch. Riley leaned on his shovel as if it were a musket. "What's this," he grumbled, "a damn firing squad?"

A small group of seamstresses walked into view from behind the wagons carrying sewing baskets. Among them was Luzero! Riley tried to hide his sheer joy at the sight of her, but Dalton noticed. He fired up his pipe and blew a billowing cloud of smoke into Riley's face with a laugh. Riley looked sheepish. He knew that Dalton could read him like a drill manual.

Deserters began to gather, walking from chores throughout

the camp. Moreno and Manzano reined up by Riley and Dalton. Salutes were exchanged.

"Excuse me for asking, Major," Riley said, wiping sweat from his forehead, "but the lads are a bit confused on their status, as it were." He leaned on his shovel. "Exactly, what are we?" His tone was toxic.

"Only peons dig in the dirt like chickens," Manzano said to Moreno in Spanish. Moreno shot him a look that commanded silence, then stared at Riley.

"Put on these new uniforms, Captain," he said, "and you shall have your answer."

"Well, I am digging deeper than the uniforms, sir," Riley retorted, drawing a glare from Moreno at the sting of his own words. Riley played to his growing audience of deserters disgruntled by the stockade. "Are they uniforms for soldiers or for prisoners?" he asked. The men grumbled to agree.

"Guards surround all our camps," Moreno replied. "It is General Santa Anna's way of insuring 'patriotism.' "

"And this damn stockade?!" asked Riley, flinging his arms toward the surrounding palisade.

"To protect you as much from our native troops as from your own tendencies to desert," Moreno replied cooly.

"Ah, sweet Jesus, I begin to understand!" Riley sang out. "So, the only difference 'tween us under guard and them under guard is themselves being 'native born'?" Moreno nodded. "At last," Riley exclaimed, "we're being treated as equals!" The deserters laughed and cheered as Riley raised his shovel above his head. He led them to the wagons, where guards handed out tied bundles of uniforms.

"For such impudence," Manzano fumed in Spanish, "we should cut off his balls and stuff them into his mouth, like we would for any common bandit."

"That might be the only way to keep Captain Riley from

183

speaking his mind," Moreno replied with a smile. "But if we did that, then who would keep this rabble together?" Manzano merely straightened in his saddle, frustrated.

Soon the deserters donned new uniforms topped by jaunty blue and red wool barracks caps with tassels. Rough laughter abounded as they traded hats and coats, many too small, in search of a better fit. Conahan and Ockter sported yellow-fringed epaulettes as sergeants. The new lieutenant was Dalton, who fidgeted and fussed in his officer coatee. Riley watched, amused.

"Look what you have done to me!" Dalton moaned. "And I your best friend!" He flicked the dangling fringe of his gold epaulette.

"Elevated your Hibernian arse to the level of a gentleman's," Riley replied, squirming in his own tight tunic. It was exactly like Dalton's but with two gold epaulettes.

"No friend of mine calls this new lieutenant a 'gentleman,' " Dalton warned, blowing smoke furiously from his glowing pipe.

Riley saw Moreno and Manzano slip into their own new coatees with the help of Luzero and other seamstresses, who received pesos from the officers for their handiwork. Both coats were like their old ones but more richly embroidered in gold bullion scrollwork to reflect higher rank. Riley frowned at his comparatively plain coat. Obviously, the women had supplied the craftsmanship.

"Not only is the fit too tight," Riley observed, "but ain't it a tad tame for my new, elevated stature?" This could be an opportunity, he hoped, to see Luzero.

"Indeed," Dalton chimed, "our newest whorehouse pimp should dress the part." He blew another cloud of smoke at Riley's scowl.

"How do I obtain a more spirited version?" Riley wondered aloud, already knowing the answer. Dalton nodded suggestively behind him.

"I can add 'spirit' to anything," Luzero said, having overheard.

Riley turned around to see her, his eyes merry with the amusing thought that she had read his mind. The spark between the two was immediate and obvious. "In our army, officers decorate their own coats per rank," she explained, trying to hide her feelings. She fumbled inside her sewing basket.

"And could you add a bit more room for the spirits consumed by himself over the years?" Riley asked, puffing up to show the tight fit. Luzero laughed as she made quick, expert chalk marks on the wool. Riley unbuttoned the coat and handed it to her. He pulled a few pesos from his vest pocket and offered them. "Now that Holy Mother Church has at last coughed up her coffers to his worship Santa Anna, I can pay for the new pretties," he said.

"De nada," she smiled, waving it away. " 'For nothing,' like a favor returned for your wonderful stories!" She hesitated, unsure, then forged ahead anyway. "Besides, I have missed seeing you." She stared unflinchingly up into his clear, blue eyes.

"And I you, darlin'," Riley managed, amazed at his own sudden loss for words. Her searing, black eyes seemed to burn through his self-delusional blarney and throw warm light onto his dark, lonely heart. If they were alone, Riley knew, he would kiss her. Instinctively, he started to lean into her.

Feeling the moment and fearful, Luzero suddenly turned her head aside. Thankfully, she saw Ockter frantically waving at her. The prim German was pointing down at his feet. They were almost being touched by the tails of his new, overly large sergeant's coatee. He flapped his arms helplessly. Grateful for this excuse, Luzero gave Riley a fleeting smile and flitted away toward Ockter.

"Your frontal assault was outflanked by the Prussians, I see," Dalton observed.

Riley could only toss him a heated glare. Why was it that Dalton was always right? he wondered. Riley watched Luzero sashay to Ockter and begin making chalk marks on his coatee.

"I am the senior sergeant here," Ockter announced. "Why is it that only the newest of sergeants enjoys a good fit?!" he blustered, much to the merriment of surrounding deserters. Ockter glowered at Conahan as Luzero worked.

"I do stand in the pink of perfection!" Conahan crowed, his sergeant tunic fitting the diminutive fiddler as if tailor made. He pulled at his snug barracks cap and flicked the tassel dangling in front, cocking the cap rakishly to one side.

"It fits 'cause Conahan's already shrunk down to greaser size!" roared Riley, triggering general laughter.

Riley could not see the pained expression that crossed Luzero's face, her back to him as she worked with Ockter's coat. But Dalton could see how Riley continued to stare at her longingly.

"A young woman like that, she could breathe life into a dead man," Dalton whispered with a leer. "And even the likes of you."

"Mind your mouth, you dirty old sot," Riley said. "I'll not have you lecher what could be my own daughter." Riley feared anyone knowing his true feelings, about anything or anybody. Such knowledge could be used against him.

"Aw, the poor lass, she must be terrible confused about her family tree," Dalton taunted.

Riley frowned as Dalton sauntered away, whistling an old Irish love ballad. Riley knew that Dalton was right, as usual. But he did not want his growing feelings for Luzero to complicate his plans. She would make it more difficult to leave, unless he could convince her to go with him. Still, his idle moments remained overwhelmingly consumed with thoughts of her.

That evening, deserters sat glum and depressed in their new

uniforms around campfires. They could hear female laughter and buoyant music from the surrounding Mexican camps, but within the stockade all they could see were stark walls and intimidating guards on platforms. Riley walked among his men.

"Latrine diggers an' fence builders, that's us," groused the tobacco chewer, "disguised in fancy clothes." He spat a hissing glob into the flames.

"We got greaser spondulicks t'spend," added Price, jingling his coin purse for emphasis. "But they don't let us in the bloomin' town to spend it!"

"Better things are coming, lads," Riley said, trying his best to hide the truth. "Got it from the mouth of the grand greaser himself."

"What's greaser for blarney?" the tobacco chewer asked, ignoring Riley.

"Ain't it 'Juan O'Riley?' " Price growled. Others chuckled.

Riley ignored the slights and walked to his own campfire, per army tradition set apart from the enlisted men. He shared coffee and tortillas with Dalton, Ockter, and Conahan. The tents and cookfires of the guards were visible outside the stockade entrance. Moreno, Manzano, and Mejia stood warming their hands and drinking coffee.

"They'd best give the lads something meaty to chew on soon," Riley nodded, "else they'll climb the damn walls and storm the gate." He poured from his flask into his coffee cup.

"The gate is barred tight as the bodice of a nun," Ockter warned.

"I will give you this," said Dalton, " 'tis a finer jail than what you sprung me from on the other side."

Riley frowned, hiding much more than Dalton knew.

"Aw, stow the blow," Connahan suggested, pulling out his fiddle. "Sure and we've shed th'buck and th'gag," he added brightly. He started to play a soft Irish lullaby, "Connamara

Cradle Song."

Outside the gate, the Mexicans could hear the music at their campfire.

"They are all the same," Mejia scoffed in Spanish. "What difference if we shoot them in our uniform or that of the gringo?"

"It would be a costly waste of precious new uniforms," Moreno said, allowing a small laugh to escape his usual stoic demeanor.

"This is all a waste!" Manzano snapped. "We are here out of love for Mexico. They are here only out of greed!"

"Each of us must fight only for what we feel here!" Moreno urged, passionately striking his chest. "The rest is lies." He looked across to Riley's campfire where Conahan continued playing. "That they are here to fight at all is what matters," he added, "not why."

"What will history say if we lose?" Manzano worried. He shivered from the cold mountain air and pulled his officer's cloak tighter. Moreno knew the odds, knew Santa Anna's penchant for treachery. He looked at stoic Mejia.

"If we cannot be victors," Mejia said, "then we will be martyrs."

"History is only a cruel joke, played by the living upon the dead," Moreno counseled. Manzano and Mejia nodded, familiar with the old Mexican saying. A pack of wolves howled in the looming, dark mountains.

The next day, Moreno and Manzano rode at the head of a lumbering column of four huge cannon, ancient cast-iron guns on creaking double trail carriages. Two could fire cannonballs weighing thirty-two pounds; the others, twenty-four pounds. Yokes of oxen struggled to pull them as Mexican teamsters cursed and cracked whips above their heads.

When they creaked to a stop outside the stockade, the

company of deserters assembled into ranks. Dalton and Riley, still without his coat, stood at the end of the line. They traded looks of stunned disbelief. Moreno walked his horse to Riley as the guns were unhitched from the oxen.

"General Santa Anna sends you the largest guns in our army," he announced. "They are also our oldest, left by the Spanish when they departed rather hastily in 1821."

Riley's eyes widened. He stared in dismay at the heavy, improvised wooden carriages, several with solid wheels like oxcarts. Leather thongs held aged, cracked sections of the carriages together instead of iron nuts and bolts. The barrels were rusted; the blue and red carriage paint, peeling.

"Glad the Romans never occupied your land, sir," he said. "You'd have us flinging stones from catapults."

"Mexicans make do, Captain!" Moreno snapped. "And, like it or not, you all are now Mexican!" He wheeled his horse and left with Manzano.

Riley turned to his men, many obviously unsettled by Moreno's outburst and not a few highly insulted. "Well, you been bellyachin' for female companionship," he shouted. "The 'ladies' have arrived! Get acquainted!" Riley nodded at Ockter.

"Company, break ranks!" Ockter shouted, waving the men to the cannons.

They explored the guns with curiosity, disbelief, and humor. Each barrel was different and ornately sculpted with dolphin handles in the old style. Ockter took to them as if they truly were women. Conahan noticed, his eyes, gleeful. "We must clean up these old girls," Ockter said to Conahan. Ockter gently caressed a buxom naked mermaid sculpted onto one barrel, nestled between the two dolphin handles. "Under Marshal Blucher, my father opened the ball at Waterloo with guns such as these."

"Sure and that day he made th'Frenchies dance to a new

tune," Conahan said, sprightly squeezing the mermaid's breasts with a look of exaggerated orgasmic pleasure. Outraged, Ockter shoved him back amid boisterous laughter.

Dalton saw Riley watching, apparently preoccupied, and sidled up to him. "Ockter must like his women a bit older than your own wicked self," he whispered merrily.

Riley frowned as Dalton fired his pipe. "I'll keep Luzero's spirited intentions on the high road," Riley snapped.

" 'T'ain't Luzero's intentions I am doubting," Dalton replied. Riley could only stare in reply, wondering which "intentions" Dalton was questioning. Dalton turned and sauntered toward Ockter and Conahan, now forming gun crews.

Riley strode to Moreno and Manzano, watching on horseback near the gate. Mejia stood beside them afoot. Riley saluted smartly and stood at ease in strict military formality. Moreno looked suspicious.

"If I'm to officer this bunch, sir," Riley said, "I'd best start looking the damn part. Surely my coat must be ready by now in the ladies' camp." He cocked his head to Moreno. "Need to go there, sir."

"You will need a guide, Captain," Moreno replied with a smile, knowing Riley's attachment to Luzero. He beckoned at Mejia. "Take him wherever he wants," Moreno said in Spanish, "but never leave him alone." Mejia nodded as Moreno turned again to Riley. "Your path should take you through the heart of our new army," Moreno added pointedly. "Remember, dig deeper."

"Given my first chance to roam, sir," Riley said, "I'd be daft not to learn all I can about soldiering greaser style." Riley saluted, turned, and left with Mejia.

Fuming, Manzano turned in his saddle to Moreno. "I should slit his throat for using that insult so freely," Manzano said in Spanish.

"Kill him for using 'greaser' as you use 'gringo,' Captain," Moreno chided, "or for attracting the woman you never could?" Manzano straightened in his saddle, nodded in respect, turned his horse, and trotted away. Moreno produced a cigar, struck a match on his rawhide saddle horn, and lit it. He watched Riley and Mejia walk over a small hill leading toward the main camp. A squad of lancers thundered past them in the opposite direction, making them vanish in dust. Riley and Mejia coughed in the flying cloud of dirt but kept walking.

"Kiss my arse you shithouse adjutants!" Riley screamed, turning and shaking his fist at the galloping riders. At the same moment, Mejia turned and shook his own fist.

"May your horses mount your virgin sisters!" Mejia screamed in Spanish.

The two looked at each other in surprise.

"Don't know what you said, Mejia," Riley said with a wry grin, "but 'tis plain any flavor of foot soldier hates th'damn cavalry."

Mejia grunted, apparently to agree. They dusted themselves off and continued walking. The sprawling, smoky Mexican camp loomed ahead.

Riley stopped. "Take me to the ladies' camp," Riley said, adding in bad Spanish, *"comprende?"* Mejia shook his head. Riley feverishly imitated the motion of a woman scrubbing clothes. "Senoritas?" he tried again.

"I know what you want, gringo," Mejia said in Spanish, playing dumb. "Let us see if you do!" He cupped his hands at his chest as if hefting two large breasts. "Luzero?!"

Riley nodded with a laugh and followed Mejia off the road into the trees. They waded across a shallow brook and entered an open meadow cut by a sparkling stream. A cluster of tents, mud and twig huts, and brush arbors lined the banks. Freshly washed laundry hung everywhere, on lines and in trees.

"At last, 'tis the ladies' auxiliary!" exclaimed Riley, wandering beside Mejia into the camp. Native women of all ages washed shirts and brushed wool uniform coats strung on lines. He stared amazed at the naked, nubile breasts of teenage women as they knelt to grind corn and roll tortillas, their camisas tugged down off their shoulders to keep their blouses clean. Other soldaderas tended pots of boiling pinto beans. Rows of women rolled musket cartridges from raw black powder, lead balls, and thin paper. Riley's eyes widened when he saw the size of the charges, nearly twice the standard amount. "Jesus, Mary, and Joseph!" he exclaimed. "That's enough powder to fire a siege gun!"

Mejia did not understand. He beckoned Riley to follow him deeper into the maze. Small children romped and played among the tents and the trees. A few new mothers suckled infants even as they worked. Riley had seen camp followers around the world, but nothing to compare with this. They reached Luzero's small wall tent, pitched on a slight rise that afforded a view of much of the bustling camp. She was hanging wash on a line outside when Riley and Mejia approached. She greeted Riley with a beaming smile.

"Never seen war waged in such a family way," Riley said.

"This is my family," she said. "Mexico has never known peace, so we know no other way of life." She opened her tent flap to invite Riley inside. Mejia plopped down on a tree stump outside to roll and light a cigarette.

As she took Riley's coat out of a small, wooden trunk, he looked around the interior: a sewing table, a cot draped with woven blankets; some colorful, finer clothes in a half-open steamer trunk; a few candle lanterns; and a shrine. A small miniature painting was propped beside a votive candle and a wooden statue of the Virgin of Guadalupe: A handsome, dark-skinned Mexican sergeant in his late thirties stood holding an older style shako beside a beautiful, white-skinned Spanish girl. Riley's heart quickened when he saw the crumbled remains of a red rose in a clay saucer nearby. He hoped it was the blossom he gave her back in Monterey. As Riley slipped into his coat, he nodded at the painting.

"My father and mother," Luzero said. "He was killed at Vera Cruz fighting the French with Santa Anna," she added. "She died of fever."

"Look to be about the same age," Riley said, pointedly. He could not help thinking of both Dalton and Ockter's comments on his and Luzero's ages.

"Yes, but he was better looking," she teased. They laughed together as Riley looked in a hanging mirror and marveled at the beauty of his revamped tunic. Gold embroidery had been worked into entwining scrollwork around the black bib lapels to form shamrocks in each corner. Embroidered gold flaming bombs glistened on his red collar, symbols of the Mexican artillery branch.

"In those tiny fingers, darlin'," Riley exclaimed, "you got the magic of the little people."

"There is only one thing missing," she said, obviously pleased at his response. "It is special." She rummaged through her trunk and produced a small package wrapped in flannel. "I had it made for my father," she said, carefully unwrapping it, "when they said he would be promoted to capitan."

Luzero revealed a gleaming gorget, a burnished brass crescent moon designed to grace an officer's neck as a sign of rank. A shining silver Mexican eagle was affixed to the front. She placed it gently on Riley's chest and slid behind him, caressing him softly with her fingers as she tied the silk ribbon. Riley grew very aware of her caresses.

"Before I could give it to him," Luzero said softly, "his promotion was denied. An Indian cannot rise above his class," she added bitterly. "Now I want you to have it."

Riley was touched and a bit relieved. " 'Tis the sweetest gift what I ever been blessed with," he said. "But I really shan't keep it."

"Maybe it shall keep you," she whispered. She impetuously hugged him, holding on. Riley increasingly noticed his manhood asserting itself.

"And I'm honored for you to think of me as you do," he said in a huskier voice, guardedly, "as maybe your sainted father." He could feel the soft warmth of her breasts push into his back. Luzero gently released him from her bear hug.

"I am pleased you are so pleased," she said, turning to repack her trunk. "But you should know that in our land, perhaps because so many young men die in so many wars," she teased, "young women expect to marry men old enough to be their fathers." Luzero knew he felt the difference in their ages.

"Surprised if the old duffers survive the wedding night," he said, squirming a bit. Luzero laughed. He pulled at his tight three-inch-high collar.

"Young girls look to them for security and wisdom," she said.

"Well, darlin', then sure I'd be doomed to die single," Riley said, wiping his brow playfully. "No one's ever accused me of being 'wise.' "

Outside the tent, Mejia jumped to his feet as Riley and Luzero emerged, laughing together. He stood at attention and waited for Riley's next command. Riley looked at Luzero amazed. Mejia's constant look of disgust was gone!

"Now you look like officer!" Luzero explained, beaming.

"He'd sooner slit my throat as take an order from the likes of me," Riley said, frowning and feeling confused.

"What he thinks does not matter," she said. "Many of our officers are frivolous dandies; they treat the army as a social club. But they do have the look of power. Our men most respect power."

"Least we got that in common," Riley said, "and I need to see some up close. Could you be walking us back through the big camp?" Luzero nodded. "Mejia don't savvy gringo and me no greaser," Riley added.

She sagged at his use of the offending word even as she led the way, Mejia following. They walked in silence. Riley could feel a palpable change in her earlier lighthearted mood. He wondered if he had said or done something wrong but hesitated to ask, fearful as to what it might be.

"Why do you call my people 'greasers'?" Luzero finally blurted out near the edge of the soldadera camp.

Riley looked puzzled, as if he'd never thought a reason worth pondering.

"Comes with the damn job, it does," Riley said in a matter-of-fact tone.

"To use hateful words of disrespect?" Luzero pressed.

" 'T'ain't like that," Riley said. "Never killed a fighting man what I didn't respect. 'Tis somehow easier to kill a 'what' than a 'who,' someone you don't know, like a 'heathen,' a 'wog,' a 'fuzzy wuzzie,' a 'wooly head,' a 'redskin' . . ."

"A 'greaser'?" Luzero interjected, her tone sharp as a finely-honed blade.

"Afore I got the chance to send up a greaser," he replied, "I switched sides." Left unsaid, of course, was that Riley would not have hesitated had it been necessary. He hoped that she would not reach this conclusion.

"Yet you do not call me 'greaser,' " Luzero said, staring at him unblinking, searching deeply into his eyes, striving to see any truth that might be lurking there. He felt the need to squirm.

"Well, darlin'," Riley replied innocently, "I know you." He felt extremely uncomfortable, his lifelong attitudes never having been challenged. It seemed to him the most honest of answers and, in a curious surprise, refreshing.

"If you know me," Luzero said, "then you know my people."

Riley stared at her as she led on, moving ahead toward the treeline on the crest of the ridge. The thought of Luzero being a "greaser" had never crossed his mind. Regarding her, it did not matter to him. So why, then, he wondered, did it still matter for all the rest? Give it time, he thought. And he shut the lid once again to his mental footlocker, that strongbox where he kept troubling matters of conscience safely out of the way. Riley felt it steadily growing heavier.

They passed through the tree line and beheld the sprawling, dusty, noisy Mexican camp stretched out below. Its cacophony of military sounds attacked their ears. Dozens of bugles for different colorful regiments combined with drums for varying drill calls. The distant rattle of musketry could be heard sputtering beneath it all with a dull crackle.

"Nothing shows the caliber of a soldier better than the crack of his musket," Riley observed, arching an eyebrow at Luzero.

"He wants to see them shoot," she said to Mejia in Spanish.

Mejia laughed and waved them to follow. His laugh alone was enough to make Riley suspicious. There should be nothing funny about musketry drill.

At the firing range, Riley watched a regiment of recruits trigger a roaring, smoky volley. The rows of square-framed wood targets on posts with painted black bullseyes showed little resulting damage. And the powerful recoil nearly knocked over a few of the smaller soldados. Only a few hits splintered the wood. Most of the lead balls whizzed past the targets and spit up dirt in the hillside behind. Riley stared open mouthed as Mejia looked amused. Another company of soldados stepped up. They raised their British Brown Bess muskets only waist high and fired. Their aim was even worse. Mejia just laughed.

"What's the damn joke?" Riley asked, grim faced and apprehensive.

Luzero translated and Mejia replied in Spanish, all the while Riley watching the recruits re-load clumsily. He doubted if they could load and fire more than one shot a minute, far less than the rate of fire of three shots per minute necessary to hold a line of battle under attack.

"Mejia says that they must shoot from the hip," Luzero said, "to avoid the pain of the recoil." She held a hand to her right shoulder.

"Hope they can work a bayonet," Riley replied, worried. Mejia added something in Spanish with a sneer. Riley looked at Luzero.

"If you are man enough, he says, you endure the pain to aim well," she translated. "It is a challenge to you," Luzero added flirtatiously.

Never one to avoid a martial contest, Riley agreed with a cocky nod.

Mejia stepped to the firing line. He deftly raised his Baker rifle, cocked it, and fired a bullseye.

"Not bad for a greaser," said Riley, immediately regretting his old habit. Luzero frowned at him and did not bother to translate. There was no need, judging by Mejia's scowl.

Riley pulled his flask from his vest pocket and took a swig as Mejia quickly re-loaded with precision. Riley swapped his flask for the rifle, stepped up, and fired a bullseye beside Mejia's mark. In Spanish, Mejia said something.

"What'd he say?" asked Riley, rubbing his sore shoulder from the strong recoil. He knew the cartridges were overcharged, remembering what he saw as he passed through the soldadera camp.

"Not bad for a gringo jackass," Luzero said with a giggle. Riley laughed. He gestured for the sergeant to take a swig from his flask. Mejia hesitated. Riley looked at Luzero.

"He feels it would not be proper," she explained.

"Tell him it's a damn order," Riley said with an emerging grin, "from his Irish gringo jackass officer."

Luzero said it in Spanish. Mejia laughed and finished the flask in one long gulp. Riley was impressed, though he looked dismayed as he re-pocketed his now empty vessel. "Why do the soldier women overload them cartridges," Riley asked, "if it makes the lads shy of aiming properly?" While Luzero and Mejia conversed in Spanish, Riley observed the arrival behind the firing range of a motley group of recruits. Veteran infantry guards prodded poor Indians, civilian convicts, cutthroats, and vagrants, many barefoot and in ragged clothing, to a row of tables. They were issued simple white uniforms, caps, and straw brooms for drill. Corporals carrying wooden batons freely beat them.

"Our powder is so weak," Luzero finally explained for Mejia, "that it takes twice as much to get proper range and impact."

"Only thing it seems to impact is the dirt," Riley grumbled, now absorbed by the recruits behind them. Mejia looked amused by this. "Where are their muskets?" Riley asked. Luzero translated as Mejia answered in Spanish. Riley watched the conscripts march away at the point of the bayonet.

"He says convicts and lower classes are merely 'food' for gringo guns," Luzero said. "Target practice would be a waste of precious powder for them. They are not worthy of shooting bullets, merely for stopping bullets."

Barely hiding his dismay, Riley gestured with a casual wave of his hand for Mejia to lead the way back to the deserter compound. As they began walking, Riley felt that familier shroud of gloom descend upon him once again. He understood now that many of Santa Anna's new troops were ill-trained, poorly equipped, and unmotivated conscripts.

He wondered if Santa Anna intended to fight with this motley bunch, or merely use them for show while he pursued peace, per his deal with the Yanks. Either way, Riley knew he was in a losing situation, one in which he had ensnared not only himself now but his comrades as well. He looked at Luzero, walking beside him with an almost lighthearted air to her step. *Damn!* he thought. That mental footlocker was growing to an unbearable weight.

"Darlin', remember my tale of the little people and the red bandannas?" Riley asked. How best could he tell her he needed somehow to escape?

Luzero looked up at him with a girlish smile. She fondly remembered their long interlude at the watering hole during the retreat from Monterey. It had given her hope for a possible future in Mexico with Riley, that his "pot of gold" might change, as she already suspected, from leaving to staying—with her.

"Again, dug up the wrong bush," Riley said gently, with a note of foreboding.

Luzero gave him a stinging stare, as if she had been slapped. She shook it off, looked up the road, and stopped in her tracks. "Just follow Mejia," she said. "He will not let you become lost, no more than you already are." She turned around and began walking back to her own camp.

Riley could not understand her reaction. He stared helplessly after her, then heard Mejia shouting at him in Spanish to hurry and catch up. He turned around and jogged to join him, pondering what he would say to Dalton, Conahan, and the others; or if he should say anything at all.

CHAPTER 11
SAN LUIS POTOSI: SPORT
LATE OCTOBER 1846

On a cold, misty morning with ground fog hugging the muddy road, Riley led a recruiting detail toward a livestock corral hemmed by a crumbling adobe wall, seemingly held upright only by sturdy, prickly pear blossom cactus. He accepted that he had done deeds over the years of which he was ashamed. But Riley's conscience had been mollified later by sure knowledge that his actions had been born of his own stupidity with no malicious intent. But with what he was about to do, he felt he had fallen to a new low. He cast a glance over his shoulder. Dalton, Ockter, and Conahan tramped steadily behind him. Moreno and Manzano marched just beyond with a squad of guards led by Mejia. As they approached the corral, troubled Riley fell back to walk with Moreno. He thrust the new recruitment decree from Santa Anna under Moreno's nose.

"How can I ask them to join an army of the lost?!" Riley pleaded in a frantic whisper.

"It has never stopped you before," Moreno quipped.

Riley looked guilty, knowing it was the cold truth. He stared ahead at Dalton. "That had to be done for friendship," Riley said, "pure and simple."

"Then put your heart into it, Captain," Moreno urged, looking at Riley as if beholding a madman, "and keep your friends alive."

Riley shot him a glare, then trotted to catch up to Dalton just as they entered the smoky compound, guarded by a squad of grim Grenadiers.

About eighty U.S. prisoners had segregated themselves into three distinct groups, each huddled around their own campfires against the walls. There was regular infantry in dingy sky blue, Dragoons in dusty dark blue, and volunteers in drab gray. They all looked ragtag, filthy, and hungry. In startling contrast, Riley and his men looked dashing in their brilliant new uniforms and jaunty caps.

"Perhaps Luzero overdid it a bit," Riley worried. He fidgeted with his gold braid as they strode into the compound amid hateful stares.

"Faith they would flock around if you dressed as the hangman," Dalton said, firing up his pipe. Riley frowned but had to agree.

Manzano led his guards to one side and pointed angrily at the adobe walls. They were covered in soldier graffiti. He watched one young volunteer scrawl his name and unit on a wall using a burned charcoal stick from a fire.

"They deface our walls, everywhere," Manzano said in Spanish.

"They are proud of what they have 'conquered,' " Moreno replied wryly. He gestured at the muddy, dung-littered corral.

Manzano smiled tightly at the small jest. "But how can one calling himself a man so imitate a dog lifting his leg?" he asked.

Catcalls, insults, curses, jeers, and boos exploded in a verbal barrage at Riley from the prisoners, many of whom shook fists, when he held up Santa Anna's decree. Manzano's guards kept them all at bay with fixed bayonets.

" 'Irishmen! Listen to the words of your brothers . . . hear the accents of a Catholic people!' " Riley read in his brogue.

"Sounds more to me like an Irish traitor!" hollered an enraged volunteer. Others shouted to agree.

" 'Can you fight by the side of those who put fire to your

churches in Boston and Philadelphia?!' " Riley persevered, looking anxiously at the angry faces. He knew that some would
recall the anti-Irish riots in U.S. cities a few years earlier. Then
he spied Conahan's old friend, the German giant, Morstadt,
amid a quiet group gathered to one side. Morstadt was translat-
ing Riley's words into German. " 'If you are Catholic, the same
as we,' " Riley continued reading, " 'why are you seen sword in
hand murdering your brethren?' "

" 'Cause they're stinkin' brown greasers!" shouted one regular.

"I'm here t'serve me new country, you heathen bigot," snarled
an Irish regular who shoved him. They tangled briefly, but
comrades separated them.

Riley pulled the stoic Ockter close to him.

"Could use a few big Germans on those big old guns,
couldn't we, Ockter?" he whispered, nodding at the hulking
Morstadt and his hefty comrades.

"Germans take to artillery like moths to a flame," Ockter
replied with an almost comical confidence.

" 'Are Catholic Irishmen,' " Riley resumed reading, pausing
thoughtfully, and then continuing with a pointed look toward
Morstadt's group with his own addition, " '. . . and Germans . . .
to be the destroyers of Catholic temples, the murderers of Catholic priests, and the founders of heretical rites in this pious
nation?' "

Riley saw the spunky Irishman and his pals fall silent at these
words. Other regulars and volunteers continued to howl and
berate Riley.

"Are West Point drill instructors supposed t'turn traitor?!"
yelled an outraged young Dragoon. Riley stared at him, aware
of the ridiculous stories now abounding about his past. Moreno
had told him the rumors were created to fuel fires of outrage
through the Yank newspapers, as Santa Anna had hoped.

"Were that blarney true, boy-o," Riley replied in a mocking tone, "do you think I'd ever have left?!"

Dalton stepped up beside Riley. "The Yank press want to make you out as something better than what you are," he said with a wicked grin, "to make it even more hateful that you left." He blew smoke at the nearby Dragoons. "Imagine the fuss if they had labeled you 'native born'?" A Dragoon leaped up and took a wild swing at him. Dalton dodged and flattened him with one blow, then calmly re-lit his pipe. "The blaggard would have spoilt my smoke entirely," he calmly asserted. Conahan barely contained a laugh.

Riley waved Conahan to him and nodded at Morstadt. Conahan appeared to feel a mix of joy at seeing his old friend and embarrassment, for having joined the other side. Riley knew exactly how he felt, casting an eye again at Dalton.

"What would best snare your old mate?" Riley whispered. " 'T'would be for his own good, don'tcha know."

"Land," said Conahan. "He lost his farm to the German tax-man. Come across to start anew." He let loose a sad little sigh. "Like most of us, I s'pose."

" 'May Mexicans, Irishmen'—and Germans," Riley resumed reading, again embellishing Santa Anna's prose, " 'united by the sacred tie of religion, form only one people!' " Riley lowered the decree and added solemnly, "And if you come over to us, once hostilities have ended, you get three hundred-twenty acres of land to boot!" He chose not to mention the proviso of having to win the war to get the land. Riley clung to the belief that Santa Anna would instead negotiate a peace to keep the frontier land now in question. The thought helped assuage his growing guilt.

With a yell, Morstadt and his dozen Germans charged Riley to escape the wrath of the outraged loyal troops. The spunky Irishman led an even larger group of Irish through the gauntlet of flying fists. In total, thirty recruits followed Riley, Dalton,

Conahan, and Ockter out of the corral amid angry boos and shouts.

Moreno backed out with Manzano, Mejia, and the guards, rifles at the ready. He felt Riley had done well enough to satisfy Santa Anna for the moment, always a tricky task.

"You and your men wait here until the transport wagons arrive," Moreno told Mejia in Spanish.

"These gringos will wait out the rest of this war in Mexico City," Manzano said with arrogant satisfaction.

"Mexico's best hope," Moreno said, "is that it will be a short wait."

Days later, the original deserters manned their four big guns in a field facing a blasted mountainside, nearly denuded of brush and cactus. Charred stumps encircled patches of surviving pine trees. The refurbished artillery pieces now sported new spoked wheels, sparkling clean bronze, and repainted red and blue wood carriages. The fresh recruits in new uniforms awaited their turn at the guns with Conahan. As designated master gunner, Ockter walked the crews through a modified Mexican drill. He called commands in English as he looked at drawings in a printed Mexican manual. Dalton and Riley stood at the end of the line of guns. Riley felt his sense of professional pride soar above his now almost manic depression.

"Drop that next little move, Ockter!" Riley yelled, pointing it out to Dalton in his manual. " 'Tis another one of them pretty flourishes the greasers seem so fond of. Does nothing but take up precious time."

"We have cut their moves in half!" Ockter beamed proudly. "We can out fire any Mexican crew!"

" 'T'ain't saying much," Dalton said, blowing a smoke ring.

Riley looked at him curiously as Moreno and Manzano walked up. Dalton sauntered away toward Ockter. Riley felt a twinge of fear in his heart. He wondered if it was possible that Dalton had uncovered his deceit, that he knew this new grand army was nothing but a sham, a ploy for negotiation, a deathtrap.

"They ignore our drill manual," Manzano said to Moreno in Spanish. "If Mexico is to be their new country, they should learn our language."

"I do not have the patience nor our country the time to teach them," Moreno replied, an edge to his voice. He had tired of Manzano's attitude.

"We should not coddle them!" Manzano insisted indignantly.

Riley stepped up, flourishing his Mexican drill manual.

"By trimming your drill down to something the lads can savvy," Riley said, "we can load and fire these old girls twice as fast."

"In Mexico, Captain," Moreno said, "not only is Catholicism the national religion, but Spanish is the national language. You serve in the national army." He tossed a deferential look at Manzano.

"See Morstadt there?" Riley asked, getting the point and nodding at the towering Teuton. "His lads only speak German, 'cept whatever Yank drill they had to learn in English." He held up the Mexican manual. "We put your pictures here to English drill that they understand, so's the job gets done. And ain't that the damn point?!"

Moreno eyed Manzano, who stubbornly remained unmoved.

"Ready!" Ockter shouted, turning to Riley. The four crews stood at their posts by the loaded guns.

"Luzero's been coaching me in a bit of your lingo, though," Riley said. "Says I put too much of a brogue into it." He turned and bellowed, *"Fuego!"*, which came out sounding *Foo-way-go!* Riley saw Moreno cringe.

The guns roared in a thumping, rumbling boom of billowing white smoke and orange flame. Each heavy gun slowly, irresistibly rolled back nearly ten feet in recoil. Four large explosions ripped away surviving pine trees on the mountainside, some boughs bursting into flames. Immediately, the crews leaned on the wheels and rolled the two-ton guns back into their initial positions.

"New crews!" Dalton shouted. Conahan waved his bunch forward as Dalton ushered the first crews aside.

"Doubt the damn guns would've fired any better had they been loaded to Spanish, sir," Riley quipped. Manzano conceded with a silent nod.

"Your men have done well, Captain," Moreno said. "They have earned a night in town."

"Gracias kindly, sir!" Riley beamed with a salute. He turned and rejoined his troops.

"You see," Moreno said to Manzano in Spanish, "as they go, they pick up the words most important to them." Moreno almost smiled.

"Aguardiente *mucho*, por favor!" Riley shouted later that night, raising an empty mug in a smoke-filled cantina. Amused by his odd accent, a sweat-encrusted barkeep brought over a jug and poured more. Dalton was seated with Riley. "See, Patrick?" Riley continued, "Just need to pick up a few of th'more necessary bits of greaser lingo." Dalton looked unimpressed.

Mejia and several guards stood near the door with their weapons, but the overall mood was jolly. Guards or not, for the first time after months of isolation, the deserters were outside their stockade. Conahan played his fiddle and led a drunken group in "Rosin the Bow," an Irish favorite.

As Ockter, Morstadt, Price, and the tobacco chewer all sang along on the chorus, Dalton spied a seductive woman in her early thirties named Bel. A soldadera as well as a server, she danced flirtatiously among the tables in folkloric style even as she delivered drinks. Dalton looked captivated.

"I'd wager that dusky lass can sing in my key," Dalton observed. Like the dark, smoky, and aging cantina itself, Bel was irresistible in an earthy fashion. Her long, black hair fell in billowing tresses over her bare shoulders and across her breasts, trying their best to escape her camisa. She danced to Dalton and brushed her bosom past his face. He blew pipe smoke down her cleavage. Her black eyes flashed. She placed his drink onto the wood table with a challenging thud.

"She could light your pipe with only a smile, she could!" Riley laughed.

"To flaming women what light the fire that don't burn!" Dalton roared, standing for a toast.

The deserters laughed, raised mugs, and shouted "Huzzah!" in drunken delight. Conahan played and sang. Bel danced and brought sloshing mugs of potent aguardiente. This triggered more verses of the interminable song. It related the impending demise of an alcoholic Irish fiddler and the funeral he planned for himself, just prior to his inevitable meeting with the Devil.

Riley grew depressed the more he listened and watched his men. He felt weighed down, unable to shake off or drown his feeling of foreboding. He could tell that Dalton noticed the mood. Riley turned away and emptied his mug, then refilled his bottomless flask.

"Sure and you have seen a banshee," Dalton said. Riley sat silently. "Worse, then, it must be the girl!"

Riley looked at him in surprise. "Luzero?" he asked, shaking his head. "Says her name means 'the early light of dawn.' " He admitted to himself that just the thought of her lifted his spirits, though lately she had seemed more withdrawn, even a bit distant.

"Is her light so damn blinding you cannot see our new army ain't nothing but sham and smoke?" Dalton said, exhaling for emphasis into Riley's face.

"Hoped you hadn't noticed," Riley managed, squirming. *At last,* he thought, *we can get this out and into the open.* Already he felt better.

"Faith we all got eyes," Dalton said, nodding at the room. " 'T'ain't one of these lads what would trust them greasers in a fight."

" 'Bout as much as they'd trust us, I'll wager," Riley said, nodding toward Mejia and his squad.

"We got twice as many men as guns to serve," suggested Dalton. "And most of us are trained as infantry, anyway. If we had our own muskets . . ."

". . . We could protect our own guns in a fight!" Riley said, completing Dalton's thought. "Could open our own 'back door' if we'd a mind to!"

"Leave it to himself to find the way out," Dalton said knowingly.

"You know, Patrick," Riley gulped, "I need to get a weight off my chest."

"Sure and the lass don't give a damn about your age," Dalton interrupted jokingly. "You ain't that much older than her, 'tis just your licentious life."

"What?" Riley asked. He needed to clear his conscience, empty a bit of weight from his mental footlocker. But Dalton had diverted him.

" 'Tis obvious to all but himself that she loves you, saints preserve us," Dalton teased.

Riley just stared and downed another drink. "There's more," he said. " 'Tain't my age. I lied . . ." he started weakly but stopped, losing heart. "There's my mum and sis back home. Need to go back."

"The dear old family on the dear old sod, is it?!" Dalton scoffed. "And you think after all these years they would give a damn if you suddenly showed up? Ah! The grand arrogance of the man!"

"In all my life," Riley admitted, "nothing's ever felt right, always been something missing, or so it seemed."

"Until now, you say?" Dalton taunted. Riley nodded.

"She is the most elegantly pure creature what ever I met," Riley said. "But I know my own self. I can't let her saddle an old war horse what's someday gonna put her afoot." Riley hated using Luzero as an excuse not to tell Dalton that he had ensnared him with a lie. But he comforted himself with the knowledge that at least he had admitted the truth about his feelings for Luzero.

"Sure and you mean 'dumb jackass,' " Dalton said. "Have you never once figured, in all your failures over the endless centuries, that the only thing missing was the will to stick something, anything, out to the end?!"

Riley felt as if he had been blindsided by a thundering right cross. He sank back onto his stool to consider this revelation.

Dalton laughed it off and resumed tracking Bel, who was now smoking a cigarette. Dalton's pipe had gone out. He cursed when he found his tobacco pouch empty. She saw and glided over to him. She bent over in front of him, drawing his eyes to her bosom as she unrolled another cigarette. Dalton barely suppressed a gasp as he beheld two pear-shaped, heaving, light-brown breasts with taut, pink nipples and all glistening with sweat. She smelled of sweet cinnamon.

"Apparently, Mexican women have never heard of undergarments," Dalton exclaimed breathlessly. Bel filled his pipe bowl with the tobacco. Then she ignited his pipe with her burning cigarette. "There are times down here when I feel like white goat cheese floating atop a bowl of simmering brown beans," Dalton mused. She kissed him softly, tantalizing him with pliable, sensuous lips. They easily parted, and he tasted the sweet essence of her darting, curious tongue. "But then, cheese can melt," he gasped. She smiled.

"Maybe 'tis time to put more wood on the blessed fire," Riley mused.

Bel plopped onto Dalton's lap as a Mexican flute player, seated at a table of native townsmen, walked to Conahan and joined him. The haunting wood flute combined with the fiddle to create an eerie, melancholy undertone to the song as it droned on with its seemingly never-ending verses.

"To our own 'little' Rosin the Bow, his own self!" Dalton shouted, raising his glass to Conahan. Another "Huzzah!" resounded amid laughter as all joined to sing the final verse, recounting the inevitable encounter with Death itself.

Riley quit singing halfway through the last chorus. He surveyed the room, staring at Conahan, Ockter, Morstadt, and the others. Finally, he looked at Dalton, engrossed happily with Bel purring on his lap. More than ever, Riley felt weighed down. He had turned tail and run, shirking from his duty to tell Dalton the truth of their situation. He gulped a drink, slammed down the empty glass, stood, and staggered toward the door. A Mexican guard followed him out and shadowed him all the way back to the stockade. The ongoing music faded into the distance.

On the following warm Sunday afternoon, the deserters played the new American game called "Ball" with the guards, some camp women, and a few native children. The game moved slowly, partly because few knew its rules except Ockter. He had learned it from Lieutenant Abner Doubleday of his 4th U.S. Artillery section. Ockter stood as umpire behind Conahan, who was pitching. Bel stood at bat with Dalton cuddling behind her, his pipe smoking.

"Get out of th'bloody way, Dalton!" Price yelled from first base.

"I'm firing my curve!" Conahan warned, winding up.

"Sure and he already got enough curves over that plate,"

cracked the tobacco chewer as catcher. He fired a glob of juice toward Conahan.

"I am instructing her," Dalton pleaded with a straight face, "on how to properly fondle the stick to make it work better!" He adjusted Bel's grip on the rough-hewn bat as the deserters unleashed a barrage of guffaws and laughter. Conahan pitched. Bel swung and missed.

"I could have hit it if you would just quit mauling me!" she said in Spanish. Not understanding a word, Dalton merely offered a lecherous leer. She liked his look. "Until later," she purred with a sexy smile.

Watching within earshot, Riley brooded on the sidelines. Moreno walked up, pulling out a cigar.

"This sport you call 'ball' is too dull," Moreno said, lighting up. "Where is the honor with no shedding of blood?"

"Soon enough we'll be awash in our own," Riley snapped.

"So now you think that you understand, eh, Capitan?" Moreno asked, using the Spanish word for "captain" to emphasize Riley's predicament.

"Your new army speaks 'soldier' about as well as I speak 'greaser,' " Riley replied. "Got a few crack regiments, but they ain't nearly enough."

"It is your new army as well," Moreno quipped. "Not all are conscripts," he said, "but even they will do their duty."

"Patriotism at the point of a bayonet don't win wars," Riley said. "It just fills graves."

"If dying is their duty," Moreno replied, "then that is what they must do."

" 'T'ain't my blessed duty!" Riley insisted. He pointed to the deserters at ball. "And it sure as hell ain't theirs!"

"If any of you truly understood what duty meant," Moreno said, "you would all still be on the other side." To Moreno, duty now transcended right or wrong, win or lose; it was a hard mistress.

"Got them into this for the money and the land," Riley said. "I owe them at least a fighting chance." Riley straightened to formal attention. "I request that we be issued our own muskets, sir."

"Our infantry can protect you and your artillery," chided Moreno.

"And didn't they do a grand job of it at Monterey?!" Riley scoffed.

"Raw recruits," Moreno said. "But this is the flower of our army."

"Nothing's changed except the uniforms," Riley persisted. He could tell that Moreno knew he was right, but he merely smoked, watching the game.

"Much the same can be said of your men," Moreno observed. Riley squirmed and drank from his flask. "Ours cannot speak of it, simply because they do not know the words. But at least here they know the truth." Moreno struck his chest. "They will stay until the end. Will you and yours?"

"What's in it for them?" Riley asked. "Nobody ever does nothin' for nothing." Moreno looked at Riley's hard glare and sighed.

"We need an afternoon of Mexican sport," Moreno replied with a slight smile, sounding resigned. "It could prove . . . instructive."

Dalton had stepped back, pipe belching like a chimney. Bel eyed Conahan with steely determination. The grinning fiddler lobbed the ball. She hit it with a resounding crack whose beefy tone left no doubt that it would clear the bases. Dalton roared with delighted laughter.

Later that day, a huge crowd erupted in cheers and applause at the traditional Sunday afternoon bullfight in San Luis Potosi.

The entire town was present and on its feet. The matador had just narrowly escaped being impaled by an enraged bull, wounded and bleeding but still charging with fury. It was dust, blood, and glory. It was war with a picnic lunch, thought Riley.

He, Moreno, Manzano, and Dalton watched by the wood palisade fence that enclosed the ring. Riley and Dalton were awed by the spectacle. They saw upper class patriarchs, their wives, children, and grandchildren dressed in fine Spanish style attire; middle class merchants and their families; priests and nuns from local churches and a convent; and dashing vaqueros with flirtatious women on their arms. The upper class sat apart on wooden bleachers.

The lowest class of peon farmers and miners sat in the grass on a small hill overlooking the bullring. Their families sat with them on blankets and shared food and drink from baskets. Groups of Mexican soldiers and camp followers also mingled on the grassy hill.

Ockter, Morstadt, Price, and the tobacco chewer were among the knot of conspicuous deserters perched on the crest. Gaudy soldaderas surrounded them, all laughing. Little Conahan, pointer fingers beside his temples like horns, was chasing a buxom soldadera around the grass like a charging bull.

A Mexican military brass band played Italian opera arias as food vendors hawked tortillas through the stands. Suddenly, the band paused, then launched into a heroic Mexican march entitled "Sangria de Patriota" or "The Blood of the Patriots."

The expectant crowd looked to see Santa Anna, in flamboyant uniform with a silver-trimmed blue cape, take his seat in a special box. Several other Mexican generals sat with him. A squad of Grenadier Guards positioned itself around the box. The crowd cheered for Santa Anna even more loudly than for the matador. Soldiers stood to attention. Riley thought it could have been the entrance of a Roman emperor.

"You'd think he could walk on water," Riley said, an edge to his voice.

"They believe that he can," said Moreno. "He saved our republic three times in war and revolution." He let escape an almost imperceptible smile. "And just as many times, he was driven into exile for corruption."

"And I see he left the harem back in the tent, as it were," Riley laughed.

"A married man never appears in public with his mistress," Manzano asserted, assuming an arrogant stance. "It would show disrespect for his wife."

" 'Tis plain we look at 'respect' from opposite ends of the word," Dalton laughed, firing up his pipe.

"No gringo could understand," Manzano replied.

"I do understand betrayal, boy-o," Dalton said ominously. "There is no greater disrespect than a lie."

Riley straightened at this, turning from Dalton with an urgent need to watch the bullfight more intently. He appeared to be watching but saw nothing, instead chewing on Dalton's words like stale beef jerky.

"It is seldom a secret," Moreno advised. "So long as the wife receives her public respect and the man provides for her and her children, affairs simply are not seen as important." Moreno, however, had never been unfaithful to his own wife, safely ensconced in Mexico City. He felt that doing his duty, however distasteful, would keep her safe there.

The crowd again cheered as it jumped to its feet. The matador had just teased the bull into charging him while kneeling and deftly avoided being gored. He turned his back to the bull and bowed, removing his hat and drawing yet another cheer. The crowd saw him as brave for ignoring the snorting, pawing, horned danger lurking just behind him. Riley saw him as more stupid than brave.

214

"Some lies are more honest than others," Riley suggested weakly, thinking of how best to defend his own betrayal, if necessary.

"This sport itself is a lie," Moreno nodded, gesturing at the arena, "because, of course, the bull must lose. But he is respected for his courage in fighting to his inevitable end." Moreno stared pointedly at Riley.

"The bullfight celebrates hopeless valor," Manzano explained. "It cannot be a mere game of chance, mere sport. It is more like religion."

"Sure and the blessed bull got no chance," said Dalton. "What if the bull says, 'I ain't going up today, thank you very much' and breaks ranks for the rear?"

"Some must be held to their duty," Moreno said, pointing at mounted vaqueros with lances who surrounded the ring.

"If the beast knew his fate, he'd find the damn back door," Riley said. "A bit of the blarney gets any job done better than the damn truth," he blustered, downing a heavy shot from his flask.

Dalton turned to face Riley, suddenly taking note. He hoped that his suspicions might be wrong. "It is one thing if the bull knows he is going up. Then it is his choice and it is suicide plain," Dalton said. He stared harder at Riley, who looked increasingly uncomfortable. "But if he don't know, so he is thinking he has got himself a wisp of a chance to survive, then on the part of persons unknown it is murder, plain." Dalton's pipe was churning.

Suddenly, the crowd erupted into wild, continuous cheers of anticipation. All four looked at the ring. The matador was poised with his sword above the bleeding, exhausted, half-dead bull. The wretched beast looked as if death would be a blessing, Riley thought. Somehow, he began to identify with it.

"Ah, the moment of truth," said Moreno smoothly.

Riley knew Moreno was not talking about the bull. He glared at Moreno, then looked at Dalton, who folded his arms, chewed on his pipe, and stared at him unblinking, expectantly. But the drama in the ring pulled them all back.

The matador thrust his sword into the bull. It dropped stone dead with one stroke, rolling over onto its back, its lifeless legs thrusting straight up into the muggy mountain air in a grotesque tribute to valor. The matador faced the crowd and bowed to their cheering. The brass band played a tribute.

"Viva! Viva!" shouted Manzano, with hundreds of others.

"Without muskets, we got about as much chance in this fight as that poor dead beast," Dalton said icily.

"Major Moreno and me, we got us an audience tomorrow with himself the excellency," Riley offered, tossing a look at Santa Anna. "We're going for to get us muskets."

"Still and all, Fate ain't yet smiling upon us," Dalton continued. "My question to you, mate, is did you know the deck was stacked against us when you dealt me this losing hand?"

Riley looked desperately at Moreno, who showed no sympathy. He had been preaching against Riley's deceptions all along, though he felt somewhat hypocritical about his own misrepresentations. But it was his duty.

" 'T'was in my darkest moment of weakness," Riley blurted helplessly. Dalton's face first registered hurt, then dangerous, simmering anger. Riley took refuge in another shot from his flask. "Back in Rinconada Pass, thought them damn greasers was gonna slaughter th'lot of you!" he pleaded. Moreno felt a twinge of guilt even as Manzano sneered. "Didn't want to see my old mate march off to certain death! Besides . . . I need him at my side," Riley concluded softly. Dalton looked impassive, turning to Moreno.

"Thank you for taking me on this splendid scout of your

culture, Major," Dalton said as he braced to attention. He glared at Riley. "But I fear there is a traitor in the ranks." He turned on his heels and joined the crowd as it exited the ring. A guard fell in behind Dalton to shadow him back to the stockade.

Riley watched Dalton until he disappeared into the milling crowd. He had never felt so bone-chilling cold on such a warm day, and so desperately alone. Even the fleeting thought of Lu-zero had no effect on his overwhelming despair, wrapping itself around him like a funeral shroud.

That night in the compound, Dalton sat on a stump by the fire with Bel, smoking a cigarette as she cuddled beside him, watching sparks soar into the crisp, black, high desert night. Conahan and Ockter sat on logs nearby. Two girls seen earlier at the bullfight flirted brazenly with them, passing an earthen-ware jug.

"I could light my pipe with his flaming lies!" roared Dalton into the blazing fire. "The poor dumb greasers find honor in losing so they are bound to make it a fact, like some devilish kind of self-fulfilling Fate. And Riley, the black hearted blaggard, wants us to go to hell with him, so's he won't be lonely!" Ockter and Conahan laughed, which infuriated Dalton even more.

"This is a softer shade of hell than I have known," Ockter said. He was enjoying a gentle squeeze of one swollen breast on a plump, swarthy soldadera perched upon his lap, her military shako cocked saucily askew on her head. She giggled, poured liquor into his tin cup, and played with his eyepatch.

" 'Stead of bein' roasted for the rogues we surely are," Conahan laughed, standing and raising his glass, "we're being toasted for th'heroes we surely ain't!"

He got a warm kiss from his leggy senorita, who stood and raised her glass to him on shaky, drunken bare feet. Arms around her waist, Conahan steadied her while looking up at her, about four inches taller than himself.

"If I could only find one what's shrunk a bit," Conahan pondered.

"If one of these mahogany frauleins could only cook schnitzel," Ockter joked, "then it could indeed be heaven!"

"Bah!" Dalton bellowed. " 'Tis all nothing but a sham! This lovely creature don't speak a word of gringo and me no greaser. But sure and we got more honesty between us than Riley in his whole belly full of blarney."

"Come now to the tent," Bel whined playfully in Spanish. "Soon we must return to our camp." She stood and tugged at him. He rose to his wobbly feet and followed the teasing Bel into his tent, taking the bottle with him.

Conahan took out his fiddle and began playing a love ballad. Looking like a puckish prankster, he nudged Ockter to watch the fun. The melody was lonely, wistful, and lovely. Conahan played louder and louder as heavy breathing, rustling, and feminine moans grew in volume inside Dalton's tent. Suddenly, they stopped.

"And what is that painful malady you are scratching at, Conahan?!" Dalton roared from inside the tent.

"You know it's that darlin' romance from the old sod," Conahan taunted. "I'm blessed if they don't call it 'John Riley.' "

The only sound for a long moment was the crackling fire. Suddenly, the empty jug of aguardiente flew out from the tent and shattered at Conahan's feet. He and Ockter burst into laughter with their female companions.

At the far end of the tent line, Riley sat alone at a dying campfire. He drank heavily, heard more laughter and music as Conahan began playing a different tune. Other deserters throughout the compound were singing along, telling jokes, imbibing, and generally unwinding from the day's festivities. Riley identified more with the wolves, howling mournfully in the mountainside woods.

"Do not feel so sad," advised the voice of Luzero. Riley turned to see her emerge from the shadows with a plate of hot tamales. She sat beside him on a log and hugged him tenderly. "My father said that to be officer is to stand apart. You can be close to them no longer," she said, looking at the shadows silhouetted by other campfires. "How else can you order them to die?"

"With a clean conscience," Riley admitted. "Didn't I know from the get-go we got no chance? Hell, Moreno's the blaggard what first told me, and then too damn late." He held back that his plan all along was to desert anyway.

"He hates what he must do, I think," Luzero said. "But he is a patriot."

"I ain't no damn patriot!" Riley gnarled, shocking Luzero with his passion. "But I am feeling a lot like a black hand murderer."

"Then there is but one thing to do," she said in simple faith. He looked at her. "Give them the best chance you can to survive."

"Thank you, darlin'," Riley whispered, taking the food. He ate in silence, lost in a maze of conflicting questions: Would obtaining muskets be enough to soothe his guilt? How would he know when to cut his losses and go missing? And what of Luzero? Would she even go with him? Should he even ask her?

"I should go back to camp, now," she said quietly, rising slowly. She knew that he wanted her to stay, perhaps satisfy his longings as did the other soldaderas. But she was not yet ready for that. One day, she felt, maybe she could share her secret with this man. First, he must prove himself worthy.

Riley looked up at her with mixed emotions. He ached to take her inside his tent but somehow kept fighting the urge, trying perhaps to retain a shred of integrity. "Wolves are prowling the woods," Riley said.

"I have a gruff old bear to protect me," she said. Luzero smiled warmly and held out her hand.

Riley stood and took her warm hand but looked at her sternly, feeling oddly paternalistic. "I'll be coming back here directly," he said, in case she had something more on her mind than mere protection. At least, Riley thought, he would try and keep one thing pure in his blighted life.

"I might like you to stay with me tonight, some night," she admitted, thankful for his patience. "But I would not know what to do with you if you did."

Riley looked at her searchingly, wondering if she meant to sound so innocent or even if she could be. After all, she lived among the licentious horde of soldaderas. She tossed her hair back with a girlish laugh and led him into the surrounding darkness. Riley wondered how far Luzero would have to take him until he could disappear completely, if only he could.

Chapter 12
SAN LUIS POTOSI: MUSKETS
NOVEMBER 1846

Inside Santa Anna's headquarters, Riley and Moreno stood at attention in front of the radiant general. Bugle calls resounded outside. Riley felt strangely uneasy in the presence of this pompous peacock who presumed to compare himself with Napoleon. Riley had heard stories in Ireland as a lad from Irish veterans who had fought the great soldier himself on the Continent. He had seen nothing yet in this greaser imitation to inspire his confidence in anything other than learning how to dress well. But Riley knew when to play along.

"Before business, gentlemen, always comes pleasure," Santa Anna said in what seemed to Riley almost a catlike purr. His two teenage mistresses glided into the room carrying silver platters with glasses of wine and fresh Mexican breads. Santa Anna said tauntingly, "Care for one?"

Riley did not know if Santa Anna meant a glass of wine, a piece of bread, or one of the swarthy, seductive girls, exactly the dilemma Santa Anna had intended. Riley felt and looked uncomfortable with his own indecision, as always. He managed to clear his throat and eye Moreno with a pleading look.

Santa Anna smiled knowingly. "When you cannot choose, Capitan, do as I do," he advised. "Take it all."

"A toast, my general," Moreno suggested. "Perhaps, to victory?"

Santa Anna looked as if a toast was unnecessary to something so surely in the cards. He gestured the girls forward and took a glass, followed by Moreno.

"May you be half an hour in heaven afore the Devil knows you're dead," Riley toasted, taking a glass and trying to inject some humor.

Santa Anna and Moreno exchanged hesitant looks. Riley appeared hung over and obviously had not slept. They wondered: was this a new insult? Not getting the joke, they let it pass.

"To the bloom on new roses," Santa Anna said, eyeing his blushing girls, "and to those with the wisdom and courage to ignore the thorns." They drank together, Santa Anna all the while studying Riley. "I understand you are requesting muskets," he said, sending the girls out of the room with a dismissive wave of his free hand. "Muskets are at a premium."

"The difference 'tween us and the rest of your lot, sir, is that we actually know how to use them, your worship," answered Riley, an edge to his tone.

"Indeed!" Moreno snapped, aghast at Riley's audacity. "Some in this army still question on whom you would use them."

Santa Anna shook off Moreno's reprimand. "These wolves hunted with a different pack, Major," he said in Spanish. "Now they run among those they have had the instinct to kill and whom they despise because of our breed." He sipped his wine. "And our pack feels much the same about them." He munched on a sweet bread, eyeing Riley, braced and fidgeting. "Muskets could be welcomed by both packs as a sign of trust."

"Are we then to remove the guards and tear down the stockade?" Moreno replied. Santa Anna flashed him a look of displeasure at the sarcasm. "What have they done to earn such trust?"

"As I have done in my day," Santa Anna said with a sly smile. "They have chosen to join the other side." Moreno bowed his head slightly in acquiescent respect as Santa Anna turned to Riley. "You doubt the abilities of my infantry?" he asked, resuming English.

Santa Anna walked to a tent flap and flung it open. Infantry regiments at drill lined the sloping hillside, trembling from the thunder of drums as if from a distant earthquake. Legions of cavalry trotted into formation, their heavy sabers jingling louder than the pounding horse hooves. "They are simple, and many are poorly trained," he said. "But they make do. They have heart."

"They got numbers, I'll give you that," Riley observed, pulling slight smiles from Moreno and Santa Anna.

"Ten years ago, men such as these marched fifteen hundred miles through blizzards to surprise Texian pirates at the Alamo," Santa Anna said proudly. He looked at Moreno and Riley. "There is nothing they will not do for Mexico . . . for me." To Riley, it sounded as if they were one and the same in Santa Anna's mind.

"Yank regulars roll like a well-greased wagon going downhill, your worship," observed Riley. "You'll be hard pressed to stop them. You'll need every lad you got! Let us defend our own guns and free up that many more soldados for your own self, sir."

Santa Anna looked at Moreno. "You were right, Major," he said in Spanish. "In his crude fashion, he can be refreshingly persuasive."

"Thank you, excellency," Moreno replied with a bow. "So you agree with his request?"

"Tempered with appropriate prudence," Santa Anna said, arching an eyebrow. He looked at Riley, looking uncomfortable with the Spanish. "You shall have your muskets, Capitan."

"Thank you kindly, sir!" Riley beamed, relishing success, though he still harbored nagging doubts about Santa Anna as a general. It was one thing to overwhelm a small band of untrained frontiersmen trapped in a crumbling adobe fort. But it was quite another to plan and fight a set piece battle, a brutal chess game in which the mangled, fallen pieces never again rise.

The following morning, Riley strode with renewed purpose to a wagon just arrived inside the compound. Mexican guards were handing British surplus "Brown Bess" flintlocks to the deserters. Dalton looked surly as he worked with Ockter and Conahan, making sure each man received his .75 caliber musket, triangular bayonet and scabbard, black leather cartridge box, and white leather shoulder slings. Dalton ignored Riley when he picked up a musket to inspect it, handling it as if it were an old friend.

"I'd wager this veteran took a few shots at the real Bonaparte," Riley observed. The gun was circa 1812 and well used, brass trimmings dulled with patina. Moreno said Santa Anna had bought thousands.

"Where's th'bloody ammunition?!" Price raved, staring into his empty cartridge box.

"Same place as our blessed three hundred-twenty acres," said the tobacco chewer, walking beside him back to their tent. He spat casually toward Riley as they passed. Once again, Riley felt the bile of betrayal rise in his gullet.

Riley eyed Ockter and Conahan, both looking helplessly uninformed. Dalton merely lit his pipe, exhaling an angry cloud of smoke. Riley thrust the musket into Dalton's hands, turned, and stormed toward Moreno and Manzano, presiding over the process with some guards at the wagon. A table was piled with cartridge boxes and slings.

"Tell me if this ain't a joke, sir," Riley said icily after saluting. "Not only are the muskets older than our big guns, but they got no bite!" He grabbed an empty cartridge box from the table and opened it upside down in Moreno's face.

"Your men already know how to shoot," Manzano said

sarcastically, "as you never tire of telling us."

"Ammunition will be issued when you need it," Moreno snapped.

"Make sure that's afore th'damn ball opens, else we might miss the last waltz," said Riley. He grabbed a musket and thrust it above his head, waving for Dalton, Ockter, and Conahan to follow him. " 'Tis time to fill our dance cards with Miss Brown Bess here!" he yelled. Dalton looked hesitant but reluctantly joined in. But he lagged, puffing his pipe as he went. Riley sensed trouble.

Moreno and Manzano watched the foursome walk toward Riley's tent.

"They have so little respect for us," Manzano observed in Spanish, "they think these few muskets in their hands will protect them better than our entire army. What arrogance!"

"I did not want the muskets," Moreno admitted, "but without them, they might hold back like a bull whose horns have been dulled." He lit his cigar. "This bull must enter the arena snorting and pawing, eager for the fight."

Outside his tent, Riley laid out a plan he had devised to best use the muskets. As he expounded, Conahan perused his rumpled paperback copy of "Scott's Infantry Tactics," a quaint memento he had kept of his U.S. service. Ockter leafed through a leather-bound Mexican manual of arms, a gift from a soldadera, comparing pictures of drill movements to those in Conahan's manual.

"The maneuver of which you speak is the same in both books!" Ockter exclaimed. "Your plan might work!"

"Wellington's little Waterloo jig has proven popular," mused Conahan, "even with the greasers."

Dalton sat back on a log disinterested, puffing his pipe. Riley recognized signs of a gathering storm: He hoped to avoid the imminent squall. "We'll not lose these guns," Riley vowed, still smarting over the fiasco at Monterey. "Our big guns can shred any line of infantry, but if they send them damn Texas Rangers at us again—or even the native-born Dragoons—we got to be ready. So, start drilling the lads both on the guns and on our new infantry tactics."

The sergeants nodded as Riley eyed Dalton, who looked unimpressed, even bored.

"Well, Patrick," Riley offered, "leastwise I did get us the blessed muskets." Dalton puffed his pipe and stared unblinking at Riley. As usual, he felt the old soldier could read his mind.

"You put me in this coffin and handed me the nails," Dalton said. "I will do my damn job and hammer the lid down tight. But I will not kiss your arse for giving me the privilege."

"Take charge of the companies," Riley said wearily with a slight wave of his hand. He watched Dalton, Ockter, and Conahan walk to the deserters, gathered and waiting. Riley had held the same doubts as Dalton for far longer, which he rationalized gave him good reason to stick to his plan to desert. But after mulling over Luzero's words and losing sleep from a nagging conscience, he had at last decided on a commitment, of sorts: He would remain long enough to lead his deserters out of this deadly maze before leaving himself. Anything less would be murder on his part. And he had determined at last that the only way to accomplish this noble feat was to fight and help win at least a truce for Mexico. Anything less would be suicide, on all their parts. As to Luzero, he would do what he always did: He would give it time.

Weeks passed amid a blur of fast-paced, intensive infantry and artillery drill. The deserters were divided into two companies, each practicing a routine devised by Riley to both work the guns and protect them. Once the routine was mastered, the companies would trade places and drill on the other's assignment. At last, seeing his command work the plan like well-drilled professionals, Riley felt it was time to inject one final tactic.

On the first day of this new maneuver, which Conahan called "the Waterloo jig," Riley's company loaded and fired the big guns with crisp precision. Each crew had stacked its muskets with bayonets fixed behind their gun. At a shouted command by Riley, the gun crew dropped their cannon implements, fell back from the guns to grab their muskets and form a line of battle. Riley bawled, "Charge, bayonet!" As if one, they instantly assumed the lethal stance of muskets waist high with bayonets thrust forward, ready for anything. Riley felt strangely proud, recalling with bittersweet reverie how he had demonstrated the position for the honorable Captain Merrill, seemingly a lifetime ago now, just to allow himself to enlist so that he could desert.

The other company, under Dalton, executed the second half of Riley's support tactic. They shifted from a marching column two men abreast into a fighting line two men deep, then divided quickly into two small platoons, each the rough length of Riley's line already formed from the gunners. At the given command, one platoon swung into a right angle to Riley's line, then the second platoon formed another right angle to the first. They had formed three sides of a square—only three sides. Riley, Dalton, Ockter, and Conahan stood and stared in futility at one another: They could not complete the tactic.

"Ain't enough lads for your brilliant plan, sir," observed Dalton that night with undisguised contempt. He chewed on his pipe at the meeting around Riley's campfire with Ockter and Conahan. "But then not being a military genius such as himself," he said, "I would find it hard to fill the vacant ranks with blarney." Riley ignored the disrespect. He looked across the compound to the guard campfire, where Mejia was holding his own nightly meeting. He brightened.

"There ain't enough of us," Riley said, "but there's damn well enough greasers!" The others exchanged surprised, worried looks. "Can't get rid of them. May as well put our darlin' brown shadows to work," he added.

"Even if th'lads are willing to drill with them, which maybe they ain't," said Conahan, "what makes you think greasers would 'lower themselves' to soldier in ranks with us gringo jackasses?"

"From the beginning, has it not been best to be keeping us apart?" asked Ockter, "except, quite nicely, for the soldaderas I mean."

"Could be a tune with too many sour notes," injected Conahan.

"Got to admit, a lot of my brilliant plan's been losing its shine of late," Riley said, offering a discreet, sheepish look at Dalton. He hoped Dalton would detect this oblique admission of guilt as an apology, but he seemed to ignore it. Riley grunted, then glanced toward the Mexican guard campfire just outside the compound gate. With everything in the pot of this game of brag, he decided to draw to an inside straight. "Sargento Mejia!" he bellowed.

The Mexican turned and saw Riley ask him to come over with a wave of his flask. Mejia smiled and began walking to Riley's campfire with a spring to his step. Always better, he thought, to drink gringo whiskey than pay for his own.

"With the few bits of greaser we've all managed to pick up, and some help from our 'translator' here," Riley said, brandishing his flask, "maybe we can yet fill our ranks and stand to when the damn time comes." He hoped there would be time enough. He knew that survival depended upon it. Riley felt desperate, like a condemned man waiting for a pardon while climbing the gallows.

CHAPTER 13
SALTILLO
NOVEMBER 1846

Dusty sky-blue columns of U.S. regulars swung jauntily down a narrow dirt street lined with one-story, flat-roofed adobe and stone buildings. Dark-blue regimental flags flapped and flaunted the angry eagle that grasped arrows of war. Rowdy voices sung out lustily, "Green Grows the Laurel," as fifers and drummers played the shrill music. The veterans tramped loudly in a solid lock step under heavy, full packs as they happily left squalid Saltillo behind them.

Squads of sullen, scornful Arkansas, Indiana, Illinois, Kentucky, and Tennessee volunteers watched from stone sidewalks and narrow, dark alleys. Their dull, gray jackets and battle shirts mirrored the lead-gray winter sky and their anxieties. False bravado aside, they knew that now they were on their own.

Watching from the flat, dirt rooftops, Mexican women wrapped their rebosas more tightly as a blustery, cold wind blew across. They had heard rumors of rape in narrow alleys, private homes being ransacked and pillaged. Looking fearful for their town to be left to the occupying rowdy volunteers, the few grim old Mexican men with them stared down anxiously at the regulars. They, at least, had stopped the atrocities whenever possible. Children ignored it all and played, laughing and giggling among cactus and tumbleweeds growing on the roofs.

The noisy children drew a quick glance and smile from Captain Merrill, passing below and just behind the color guard of the 5th U.S. Infantry. Their six-foot square U.S. flag and regimental colors snapped sharply in the crisp breeze. Merrill, sword tucked against his right shoulder as he tramped beside Company K, suddenly recognized someone up ahead.

"Company! Eyes right!" commanded Merrill, now sporting a broad-brim, tightly woven Mexican straw hat instead of his regulation blue cap. He kissed the hilt of his sword and lowered the blade sweepingly to his right. The men turned their heads to the right with practiced precision in salute, continuing to march.

Astride his white horse, General Zachary Taylor held a return salute until the color guard had passed. Then he slumped in the saddle. Crossing a leg over the pommel, he settled in to watch one more regiment of his reliable regulars leave. Taylor pulled his linen duster tighter in the cold wind and tugged his wide-brim sombrero down snug on his head. On one side of Taylor was Colonel Harney, warm in a dark-blue cape coat; on the other, bespectacled and bookish Major Bliss, Taylor's adjutant, clutching a wool cape. Behind them in capes and overcoats were staff officers and a young Dragoon, Lieutenant John Richey.

"Shit," growled Taylor, watching the troops. "That pompous prig Scott cuts off my balls an' Polk still expects me to plow th'whole damn brothel!" Taylor had been ordered to send all his regulars to Scott for a march on Mexico City from the sea while Taylor held the north. Taylor suspected political treachery on the part of Polk, who hastily approved Scott's strategy as a way to deflate Taylor's growing popularity in the press. He suspected that was why Polk gave overall command to Scott, to dim Taylor's rising star.

Harney merely grunted as Bliss blanched at the general's usual foul language. Astride his horse, Bliss held up a pencil while struggling to hold a writing tablet with his other hand still gripping his reins.

"General Scott expects a reply, sir," Bliss ventured.

"Bah! He's President Polk's trained lap dog now," Taylor snapped. "If he'd left me even one regiment of my regulars, he knows I'd have cut through th'damn greasers clear to the capitol." Bliss perused a handwritten order.

"Sir, General Scott says he's shortening the war by taking the shortest route to Mexico City," Bliss observed, "from the coast at Vera Cruz."

Taylor looked incredulously at Bliss and joined Harney in a wry, knowing chuckle. In this unpopular war, both understood that generals now had to be politicians as well as battlefield leaders.

"Major Bliss," Harney said in a condescending tone, "President Polk also sees that the shortest route to the White House is through Mexico City—and neither General Scott nor General Taylor are in Polk's party." Bliss rolled his eyes sheepishly, finally understanding. Politics was not his strong suit.

"Them greasers'll mass to stop Scott's march from the sea," said Taylor sadly. "Ain't much glory ahead for us up here in th'north 'cept swattin' flies."

"And the butts of the damn unruly volunteers," added Harney, eyeing a particularly noisy bunch across the street as they exited a cantina. Bliss cleared his throat. Taylor and Harney looked at him.

"Lieutenant Richey is waiting, sir," Bliss pressed, "to take General Scott your reply."

Taylor turned in his saddle to size up the boyishly handsome Richey, dashing in his dark-blue Dragoon officer's jacket.

"I hear you're one helluva horseman, Lieutenant," said Taylor. Richey flashed a shy but cocky grin.

"Some have said so, Gen'ral," he replied in a soft southern drawl.

"You'd better be, son," Taylor warned, "or th'damn greaser

guerillas'll stuff your dick in your open dead mouth."

"Yes, sir," Richey blustered. "I mean, no, sir!" Taylor and Harney laughed.

Bliss frowned, putting his pencil to paper. Taylor's vulgarity always made him uncomfortable.

"What shall you say, sir?" Bliss asked tactfully.

"Word for word, Bliss," Taylor commanded, continuing to eye his veteran regular troops as they tramped past, "read me our beloved commander's latest larceny." Bliss struggled to read Scott's order as the page rippled in the breeze.

" 'For my march on Mexico City, I shall be obliged to take from you all the gallant regulars you have so nobly commanded,' " Bliss managed. " 'I rely upon your patriotism to submit to this sacrifice with cheerfulness.' "

"Fine," Taylor growled. "Tell General Scott he's a damn imperial son-of-a-bitch. He's stole my best troops like a common horse thief, but they march to him today. And I'd more cheerfully kiss his bloated Virginia ass!"

Harney, Richey, and the staff officers burst into raucous laughter. Bliss sighed patiently and began writing something on his tablet. As usual, he would make Taylor sound literate and like a gentleman.

"With just my Dragoons and the regular artillery to count on, sir," Harney said glumly, "we can't press the greasers or even get at them damn Irish traitors."

Taylor frowned, looking at Harney curiously. "Harney, there ain't enough of them to make the gas of a good fart," he said. "Forget 'em."

"Respectfully, sir, they're a yellow piss stain on our flag and a threat," Harney insisted.

At this, Taylor cocked his head, intrigued. As he had warned Polk before the war, half the regulars were Irish. But aside from these few deserters, nothing massive had occurred. What threat?

Did Harney know something new?

"I am aware of exactly which men serve in our ranks," Taylor replied. "What is your concern?"

"If Riley's band survives," pressed Harney, "what's to keep our Poper Irish from skedaddling to join him?!" Taylor looked at Harney with a curious blend of respect and pity in his hesitant smile.

"They've taken an oath before God, Harney. That alone will keep our Irish doing their duty," Taylor insisted. "You're a mile long on guts, Harney, I'll give you that. But you are damn short on faith, God knows."

"Then God can have mercy on them Irish turncoats, sir," Harney vowed. "I cannot."

Taylor grunted dismissively. Harney indeed was a hard hater, he thought. But that can serve him well in a fight. He turned in the saddle to look at Bliss.

"Do I sound proper yet, Bliss?" he taunted. The others smiled knowingly at what apparently was a familiar routine. Bliss held up his tablet.

" 'In reply to your note summoning my entire force of four thousand regular infantry,' " Bliss read, looking up cautiously a moment before continuing, " 'I beg leave to protest but accede respectfully to your request.' " Some officers stifled laughter.

"Perfect Bliss," Taylor said sarcastically. "Perfect." The others chuckled at Taylor's little joke: Staff officers long ago had taken to calling the adjutant "Perfect Bliss" behind his back. Taylor took the pad, signed the message, ripped it off, and handed it to Richey. "Harney may not need Him," Taylor said, "but God go with you, son."

Richey saluted, spurred his horse, and expertly trotted his way past the marching regulars and up the dusty, wind-blown street.

"Better get our volunteers out of town and back into camp,

Harney," Taylor commanded. "There's a storm comin', an' I wouldn't want th'dumb bastards to catch a chill. That's about th'only threat they'll ever have now."

In his heart, Taylor felt abandoned by Scott and betrayed by Polk. He had given the country three major victories: Palo Alto and Resaca de la Palma in Texas, and Monterey. Effectively, he had conquered northern Mexico.

His reward was to be stripped of the power to remain on the offensive and acquire more laurels, which would have made him a political threat to Polk and his party. Taylor had no political ambitions, thinking himself nothing more than a simple soldier. So now, he resigned himself to merely watching the show as Scott would proceed to win and do the same thing. Taylor felt he would enjoy heartily that last laugh.

CHAPTER 14
SAN LUIS POTOSI
DECEMBER 1846

A night procession of Mexican townspeople in colorful holiday attire snaked along the narrow dirt path that led to the deserter compound. Small paper bags with burning candles inside had been set on the ground to light their path. Women and men of all ages carried torches, sacred statues, Christmas decorations, platters of food, tables, chairs, and musical instruments, everything possibly needed for a fiesta. Excited children tagged along.

The anxious deserters had gathered in rowdy anticipation to receive their guests. Moreno and Manzano stood with an amazed Riley as he watched enchanted near the entrance. Riley beamed with martial pride: His command looked crisp and clean in their newly brushed uniforms. Angelic melodies seemed to float down gently like musical "snow" from the brilliant stars above, Riley mused. He felt amazed at his oddly poetic sentimentality.

Riley cast a more cynical eye upon the true source of the music: The ethereal harmonies of Ockter, Morstadt, and the nine burly German gunners, looking hardly heavenly as they stood in a choir formation to one side of the open gate. Ockter was leading them in a reverent rendition of a popular German carol, beautiful for its simplicity. Only they could understand the German words, but its message of peace seemed to transcend language. Ockter had translated its German title for Riley. It was called "Silent Night."

Riley was surprised and delighted when he spied Luzero in the column costumed as the Virgin Mary. Mejia walked beside her dressed as a protective, lethal Joseph and led the small burro upon which Luzero sat.

A bevy of other camp women marched in the procession, as well. Bel walked along demurely with the two camp whores who had attached themselves to Ockter and Conahan. Gone were the tawdry, saucy soldadera outfits. The women were clad in their finest Spanish-styled silk gowns and adornments. The men had never seen them looking so angelic.

"This is the ninth and final night of the Posada," explained Moreno. "A different house has been visited each preceding night, seeking room for Mary and Joseph."

"I'd find room for her, I would," Riley said with an eye on Luzero. "But th'blessed sergeant might be walking a bit further."

"You should not make light of such an honor," Manzano said curtly.

"This is Christmas," Moreno said with a patient smile, weary of Manzano's antagonistic attitude. "You should be less 'restive' and more 'festive.' " Riley laughed at the jest. Manzano merely nodded in obedience.

"The last house visited has the honor of giving them shelter," added Manzano.

"Ain't this place a tad drafty for the baby Jesus?" Riley asked, looking around the compound.

"Perhaps," Moreno smiled. "But it is a perfect place for a fiesta."

Later that night, the entire compound was ablaze with torches and merriment. A papier-mâché manger scene had been set up in one corner. A few grandmothers knelt before it, praying fervently with their rosary beads. It seemed to Riley that old Mexican women always seemed to be praying, as if they knew some calamity always was about to befall their people. He suspected that they might be right. But tonite he decided to put it out of his mind.

Elsewhere, civilian musicians were playing Mexican and Spanish dance airs. The local women were trying to teach the rough gringo deserters how to move with Latin finesse, tough duty in anyone's drill book, Riley thought. Conahan was playing his fiddle with the locals. Ockter, Morstadt, and other Germans helped children play with various holiday piñatas.

Mighty Morstadt easily lifted two small, blindfolded brown tikes up at one time to the height of the piñata, so they could smash it to bits and fling small candy surprises everywhere to the other children.

Price gorged himself at the tables of tamales, enchiladas, burritos, tortillas, beans, fruits, vegetables, and the lethal aguardiente. Curious locals crowded him for the chance to meet a gringo deserter, now considered someone of celebrity.

Price looked suspicious at all the attention. He softened when a plump, young senorita walked up, took his arm, and pulled him onto the dance floor. He put down his food and meekly followed, seduced by the flirtatious giggle she tried to hide behind her fan.

The Irish tobacco chewer ambled up to them on the dance floor with a darkly handsome woman of his own on his arm. "We got more in common with some than most," he said. The woman and he spat tobacco juice together. All four laughed and joined in a Mexican folkloric dance for couples. Conahan played along with the Mexican musicians.

Bel had managed to get Dalton onto the dance floor, where he had applied Irish jig movements in the place of Mexican male steps, making Bel laugh as she glided expertly around him. He was captivated by her grace and charm; she, by his outlandish antics and devilish humor. The song ended, and he bowed to her graciously and deeply. Then he flashed his grin at Conahan.

"Conahan, give us the reel!" Dalton yelled. The Irishmen clapped and cheered. Dalton looked at Bel. " 'T'ain't fair not to give us a shot at showing off in our own way," he said, knowing Bel did not understand a word. "Hard-shoe dancers!" Dalton cried, "Form ranks!" Laughing, the Irishmen left their confused female partners and formed a line.

"Are they going to dance or to fight?" Bel said in Spanish, the girls beside her giggling and hiding their smiles with their fans.

"Here's an Irish jig called 'Gobby O,' " yelled Conahan, "which the Yanks've stole and renamed 'Jefferson and Liberty'!" Conahan ripped into a rousing fiddle rendition of the ancient melody.

With a shout, the Irish discarded any genteel civility just acquired for the Spanish dancing. Dalton led the Irishmen in heel stomping hard-shoe dancing, with their arms held rigidly to their sides as they leaped, bobbed, and weaved with broghan stomping fervor. They sent a small dust cloud up into the torchlit night, punctuated by wild Celtic yells.

Riley stood alone and watched from the sideline, tapping his toe as he poured himself more of the lethally alcoholic punch. Luzero stepped up, having changed her Virgin Mary costume for a brilliant Irish-green, raw silk ball gown. Her hair was combed up and covered with a Spanish mantilla, revealing her long, graceful neck. She was lush with rustling petticoats, and her tight-fitting bodice was cut daringly low. Riley took her hand, bowed low, and enjoyed a long, lingering view of her nearly exposed breasts. When she curtsied, his heart beat faster at a fleeting glimpse of rose colored nipples.

"Were the Virgin Mary contemplating a change in status," Riley gasped, kissing her hand, "this would be the dress to get the job done." She squealed and bashed his head with her folded fan.

"It was my mother's," Luzero pouted, feigning outrage. "I wore it for the sentiment, not the style." But secretly she was pleased at his reaction.

"Lookee there," Riley chuckled. "Our 'Teutonic terrors' are showing their own sentimental side." He led her to a corner of the palisade where a ten-foot high, bushy, and sweet-smelling pine tree stood upright on a wooden stand. It was ablaze with small, burning candles perched atop the end of each branch. The German gunners were helping the local children, their eyes shining brighter than the candle flames, hang small, papier-mâché decorations.

"Morstadt! Fill in that gap!" Ockter ordered in German, pointing to a bare spot. As usual, he had taken charge of operations, mused Riley.

"At your command, my sergeant!" Morstadt replied tersely in German, mocking Ockter's military attitude. The other Germans laughed as Morstadt turned to Riley and Luzero. "Ockter, he thinks he directs artillery fire, ja!" Riley and Luzero joined the laughter as Morstadt lifted a beaming little girl, radiant in a white lace dress with red and green ribbons. Looking reverent, as if discovering something magical, she fit a papier-mâché star atop the tree.

"It is so beautiful!" Luzero sighed. "What a lovely German tradition!"

"Heard that Queen Victoria's German husband, Prince Albert, sets one of these up in the palace every Christmas," Riley said. " 'T'won't be long afore the whole world follows suit, like they do everything else she takes a fancy to."

Conahan struck up a melancholy Irish waltz, "Fiddlers Green." In his cups, Dalton staggered up with Bel in tow and began to sing along. The maudlin lyrics spoke of an old fisherman facing his demise and bidding his mates farewell, until he would see them again above, in "fiddler's green."

Riley suddenly felt as if the words had grabbed him by the throat and made him gag on guilt. His merry mood deserted. He downed more punch.

Luzero placed her hand on his arm, giving him an understanding squeeze. "Why are Irish songs so sad?" she wondered aloud.

Riley smashed his punch glass into a bonfire and led her toward the dance floor. He forced a sardonic little smile. "For the great jails of Ireland are the men who God made mad!" Riley declared, quoting an old poem. "For all their wars are merry and all their songs are sad!"

She laughed as they swirled onto the dance floor with other couples already gliding around and around in the dizzying Viennese waltz. Riley and Luzero floated gracefully as one with an obvious magic between them.

Manzano and Moreno watched them from the food tables. Moreno appeared at ease, relaxing with a cigar. Manzano looked on typically in anger.

"In the north, our women who take up with gringos are despised," Manzano said in Spanish. "They call them, 'Yankedos.' "

"These gringos now wear our uniform," Moreno replied. "Would you kill them all?" Moreno pointed at the dance area, filled with deserters dancing with Mexican women of all ages.

"Their blood is not ours!" Manzano insisted.

"The gringos justify their crimes against us using those very words!" Moreno replied hotly. Chastened, Manzano bowed and left. Moreno stared after him, wondering if this experiment could ever succeed.

Past midnight, the compound was nearly deserted. Campfires burned low. The ground was littered in confetti, broken glass, and dismembered piñatas. Mexican guards stood drowsily in the towers and leaned on their rifles for support. A few deserters sat drunk and huddled around the dying fires. They hummed dance melodies to keep awake. Here and there, a disheveled woman would emerge from a tent to scurry back toward town.

The sounds of passionate, noisy lovemaking rose from one tent as Riley and Luzero walked past, arm in arm. Riley flushed, embarrassed for Luzero. "The Blessed Virgin shouldn't hear such foul noise," he said, playfully cupping her ears.

"It is the sound of life," Luzero said nonchalantly. "I am used to it."

Riley looked around at the debris from the fandango. " 'T'ain't like you folks don't know how to live," he said. She laughed as they reached his tent. "I'll call for a guard to walk you back," he said. She gave him a look that said he should not be so stupid and walked into his tent. Riley sheepishly followed.

Inside the large wall tent Luzero beheld Riley's spartan existence: a crude wood rope bed, a chiseled table and twig chair, and a pitcher and wash basin. Several candle lanterns burned low. His sword and sling hung from a tent pole. She watched Riley take off his coat, hanging it on a hook.

"There is nothing of you in here, only your work," Luzero said flatly, looking around. She yearned to know him better but found no clues.

"Whatever there was of me, I left long ago back in Ireland," Riley said, turning to face her. She looked magnificent and somehow darkly magical in the candle glow. The green silk of her gown shimmered like the placid lake waters back home on a moonlit night. Riley was reminded of many an Irish colleen.

"So that is why you want to return there," she mused, fully aware of his growing passion as he stared at her. "Perhaps you will find what you seek here."

"I should burn in hell for what I'm seeking right now,

darlin'," Riley said, a huskiness in his voice. "You'd best be on your way," he said tenderly.

She shook her head very slowly. Stepping to him, she stared into his eyes steadily. "Just hold me, por favor," she said. Luzero deftly removed her mantilla and hair comb, her tresses cascading over her shoulders onto her bosom.

"You don't got to say please," Riley choked out breathlessly. He put his arms around her. She enfolded him, squeezing tightly.

"Kiss me," she whispered, her heart beating faster. She was pleased to feel his own heart pounding hard against her. And she was embarrassed to feel his manhood growing to press hard against her as well.

He hesitated briefly, then surrendered to a long, lingering kiss. To Riley's surprise, her soft lips parted beneath his. Her tongue swirled tenderly and caressed his own. She tasted softly sweet, and he grew aware of the aroma of cinnamon oil, with which she adorned her hair. They stared at one another in wonder as they pulled apart.

Luzero had satisfied some question deep inside. "You are trembling," she said shakily, perhaps even referring to herself.

"I can't be leaving it at that," Riley managed hoarsely. He wanted to rip off that shimmering dress and take her into his bed then and there.

"I like how you hold me, as if I might easily break," she said softly. Luzero pushed gently away from him. "But with me, this kiss must be all." She laughed lightly at his confused look and stepped to the tent flap. She would continue to keep her secret, for a while.

"You're wiser than your years, darlin'," Riley said. "You know I'm too old and battered a ship for you to book passage on." Riley wiped his brow, feeling strangely relieved.

"No more such talk!" she scolded, a twinkle in her eyes. Luzero stepped outside, turned back, and gave him a taunting grin. "I never kissed my father in that way!" She laughed, tossing her mane of raven hair as she turned and left.

Riley stared after her and sighed. He dropped his face into the washstand, splashed cold water onto his neck, and stood erect, refreshed and confused.

"Another mystery of faith," he marveled, plopping down on his bed. He fell back and drifted off into the deepest sleep he had enjoyed in months.

Just after dawn, Riley strolled to a campfire where Dalton, Ockter, and Conahan were sipping coffee and nursing hangovers, as was Riley. Morning drums to assembly began beating throughout the camps. It was a painful roar.

"Leastwise all we got on our plate this fine Christmas day is roll call," Riley said wearily.

" 'Tis pot and th'kettle sure," moaned Conahan, holding his head, "but somebody please shoot th'damn musicians."

Riley looked around as the half-dressed deserters stumbled out of their tents. They began to form ranks in their two companies.

"All the ladies out of camp, per regulations?" Riley asked. Conahan and Ockter nodded yes. They looked at Riley, inquisitive. "I'll have you know that my lady did not stay the night," he said pertly, feeling somehow noble. "Did the decent thing."

For the first time, Dalton looked up from his coffee. "Than turn her down with another damn lie, 't'would be more decent to give her a good poke," he said.

Riley frowned and fired a look at Conahan and Ockter. "Tend to th'lads while Dalton and me have us a little chat," Riley said with an ominous tone.

Conahan felt he knew what was coming. He nudged Ockter, and they walked to the deserters. But the two companies merely milled about at ease in their ranks. They looked expectantly back at Riley and Dalton. A few made bets and exchanged coins, each company betting on its own officer.

"Patrick, I'm trying to do the proper thing," Riley said.

" 'Tis another sham," Dalton replied, anger rising, "another excuse to skip out on what you have started. You would leave us all flat, you would. And himself lying to me all the while!"

"I never meant no harm," Riley pleaded. "Thought you were all doomed."

"Sure and you never turn around to see how many bodies litter the path behind you," Dalton asserted.

" 'T'ain't like I didn't see them at Monterey," Riley gnarled, his own anger rising. He would never forget the innocent, sightless eyes of poor young Parker.

"But you are afraid of Luzero," Dalton taunted. "You like her too much, and that might mean tying your own self down!"

"Don't want to hurt th'lass," Riley said, knowing Dalton was right.

"You don't want to be trapped is more like it," Dalton said, rising to his feet. "But that ain't stopped you from getting the rest of us locked up good and proper, has it?!"

"This ain't nothing like what I thought it would be," Riley admitted.

"I'm blessed if you didn't think a whit about any of this beyond your own skin!" Dalton roared. "Another morning shall not find me here," he added quietly.

Dalton pushed Riley out of the way. He started walking toward the assembled deserters.

Riley grabbed his shoulder and jerked him around. "I'll not let you leave!" he warned. "They'll shoot you to doll rags!"

"Better them than my old mates on the other side!" said Dalton. "Remember, I was proud to be an American soldier!"

Dalton pulled loose and started to walk away. Riley chased after him. The money between the assembled ranks was changing hands fast and furiously now. Ockter and Conahan joined the betting, both on Riley. Price and the tobacco chewer favored Dalton.

"I'll not have your cursed death on my head!" Riley roared.

"Sure and it already is!" Dalton retorted. He turned around to face Riley, who suddenly charged him like a bull.

Riley tackled Dalton in mid-body. They fell together into the campfire, scattering embers and ash everywhere. They pummeled each other, rose, and engaged in a gouging, biting, kicking, slugging, rough-and-tumble frontier fight. They rolled over the camp like a tornadoe. Tents were flattened. Clothes and equipment flew. The deserters gave a cheer, broke ranks, and surrounded the two fighting officers as they sent a swirling cloud of dust skyward. Conahan orchestrated the dusty battle by playing jaunty jigs and reels on his fiddle.

Finally, Dalton broke a clay jug of aguardiente over Riley's head just as Riley smashed a twig camp chair to bits across Dalton. They both dropped to their knees, exhausted but still trying limply to swing at each other.

Suddenly, a half-dozen fixed bayonets were held to their throats. They froze instantly. Moreno and Sergeant Mejia had come running to surround them with a squad of guards.

"I must stop you before you destroy any more tents," Moreno said calmly. "Tents are expensive."

"Damn if it ain't a draw!" spat the tobacco chewer in disappointment.

"Leave it to th'bloody greasers to spoil a good fight," groused Price.

"Fiery men are soon put out!" Mejia said in Spanish. His guards laughed.

Riley and Dalton looked sheepish as they rose unsteadily to their feet. Faces and knuckles bruised and bloody, lips puffed and cracked, hair encrusted with dirt and thistles: They more resembled street beggars than soldiers, Moreno thought. He lit a cigar, surveying them both with disappointment and disgust.

"Clean yourselves up," Moreno snapped. "I will not be embarrassed by the shabby appearance of my officers," he added. "Then bring your men under arms. We have a *norteamericano* prisoner of some importance."

Riley and Dalton traded suspicious, surprised looks, eyed one another, and gave a penitent shrug. They left together to assemble their men. As usual, Riley felt as if a good fight had lifted the smothering weight of his guilt and cleared his head, as well. Refreshingly battered, he likened it to having done penance after Confession.

In an open area on the fringes of the Mexican camp, Manzano and Mejia's guards were drawn up in ranks on one side of a dirt road. The deserter contingent, carrying muskets and accoutrements, marched into place on the other side, facing the Mexicans.

"Bring in the prisoner!" Manzano shouted in Spanish. From out of the nearby woods came the throaty pounding of horse hooves. A dozen Mexican guerillas rode up at a gallop. They stopped amid jingling spurs and a cloud of dust. Moreno and Riley had to turn away from the choking dirt.

"Bah! Guerillas!" coughed Moreno. "In peace, we call them 'bandits' and hunt them down as a scourge. But now," he admitted, "war has made them allies and even heroes."

To Riley, the guerillas looked like colorfully clad Mexican versions of the Texas Rangers with long hair, heavy armament, and the calm look of cold-blooded killers. Their leader was Romeo Falcon, who sported a silver accented Mexican saddle. He took the reins of a horse and pulled it forward from the group. Tied to the horse was a hapless young Dragoon lieutenant. Frightened but bravely trying to show bravado, Lieutenant Richey managed to maintain his courage. Falcon took notice of Riley and his Anglo troops. He could not disguise an immediate look of contempt. He tossed Moreno a pair of U.S. saddlebags.

"His gringo dispatches," he stated in pointed English for Riley's benefit. "Our job we have done. Now, we take our prisoner to issue Mexican justice."

"Hold!" Riley commanded. He stepped forward and grabbed Richey's reins. Falcon's men immediately put hands on their pistols and swords. Riley flashed Dalton a commanding look, instantly understood.

"Battalion!" Dalton bellowed.

"Company!" Ockter and Conahan shouted to each of their units.

"Charge, bayonet!" Dalton commanded. As a unit and with the crack precision of regulars, the two companies of deserters snapped their muskets with bayonets fixed to waist high, pointed at the guerillas. As they did so, they unleashed a threatening, guttural shout. The guerillas paused, looked at Falcon.

"We patrol roads between Monterey and Saltillo," Falcon said, an edge to his voice. "This gringo pig and his fellow invaders rape our women, kill our men, plunder our homes. They desecrate our churches." He spat in Richey's face. "For these crimes he must die."

"That may be," said Riley, "but, if so, he'll die by the rules of war."

"This war has no rules!" Falcon shouted. "He is our prisoner," he added. "We are not military."

Moreno stepped up to Riley with Manzano, leaving Mejia with the guards.

"Captain, we must let them have their prisoner," Moreno cautioned quietly. "It is General Santa Anna's arrangement with them, a kind of favor."

"We'll not be party to murder, sir," Riley snarled. He looked at Richey. "Is what he says true, lad?"

"You're Riley the traitor, aren't you?" Richey managed, obviously nervous. The sweat of fear beaded on his forehead and face, dripping into his eyes. With hands tied, he could only suffer the discomfort.

"That's the least of your worries at this delicate moment," replied Riley. "Answer the damn question."

"I'm a regular Dragoon and native born," he asserted proudly. "Colonel Harney has us arrest any disgraceful volunteers who commit such outrages."

Riley looked at Moreno. "As I thought," he said. " 'T'ain't the regulars but the volunteer rabble doing th'damn mischief."

"They are all under the same flag," said Moreno.

"There's a difference!" Richey yelled at Riley. "Make these yellowskins understand!" Everyone blanched, even Riley.

"Careful, lad, else I'll kill you myself for dubbing these fine greasers 'yellowskins,' " Riley snarled.

Moreno rolled his eyes at Riley's unfortunate choice of words. Riley himself felt a twinge of regret almost as soon as the words left his mouth.

"Once arrested, how are these disgraceful volunteers punished?" Riley asked, clinging to the hope that Richey's answer might mollify the guerillas.

Richey hesitated a moment. "General Taylor has always released them," he admitted in shame. "He has too few men under arms to do otherwise."

Riley instantly knew that he had lost. He read the hardened faces of the guerillas. Richey sensed the moment. He was as young as Manzano and just as immortal in his sense of self. He looked at Manzano, as if sensing a kindred soul.

"Why do you keep fighting us?" Richey asked, looking perhaps for a reason to the death he knew now was imminent. "You cannot win! Why?!"

"Because you are here, gringo!" Manzano snapped. Calming himself, he added, "But why did you even come down here?"

Richey felt a leather riatta drop around him from behind, tossed by one of the guerillas. Another cut the ropes tying him to his saddle with expert use of a short Spanish sword. "I . . . I don't know, really," Richey said. "I guess it was just the old flag."

Riley felt a ripple of recognition run through the ranks of his deserters. Even Dalton's face stiffened. Their sudden pang of remorse was palpable. "I can't let you do this!" Riley yelled. He stepped beside his line of deserters, muskets at the ready.

Moreno tossed Manzano a curt nod. Perhaps, Moreno feared, this entire hopeless experiment will end here, badly. Surprisingly, he thought, he would regret it.

"*Preparen!* . . ." Manzano shouted.

"*Apunten!* . . ." Mejia ordered, almost looking joyful. With crisp style, the Mexican guards cocked and aimed their rifles at Riley's men.

"Ready! Aim! . . ." Dalton countered. The deserters executed the same maneuvers, pointing their cocked muskets at the now nervous guerillas.

Manzano held up his hand to postpone the final command. A long moment of silence hung heavily. Richey's eyes darted in fragile hope from one group to the other. Moreno was calm as he lit a cigar. Riley wondered where Moreno managed to obtain them all, a seemingly endless supply.

"Captain," Moreno said to Riley in a tone gentle with chastisement, "you should remember one important thing." Riley looked at him with almost frantic intensity. "Only our weapons have the bullets."

Riley looked stunned, recalling the empty cartridge boxes. Moreno gave a nod to Falcon. Richey's wide eyes locked with Riley's for a terrified instant as he was yanked off his horse. With shouts and yips, the Mexican guerillas rode away at a gallop into the mesquite, dragging Richey behind them. Richey screamed as first his uniform and then his flesh was ripped off across the cactus beds. Both guards and deserters stared in grim, morose silence. Young, proud Lieutenant Richey disappeared over the near horizon in a cloud of dust and blood.

That evening, Riley and Dalton met with Moreno and Manzano inside Moreno's headquarters. The large wall tent sported a Persian carpet on the ground; the rope bed had a feather mattress; finely hewn camp furniture was evident; a British officer's camp chest contained Moreno's spare uniforms; and a silver framed, family tintype rested on a table beside the cot.

Riley lingered at the photograph of a beautiful, raven-haired Mexican woman and two small children: a little girl, her displeasure at standing still for the camera evident in a pout; and a 12-year-old boy, looking sternly into the camera in a proud stance and wearing a small military cap. Riley smiled. "Would that I had an image of me mum and sis from back home," he mused. "When I left, this camera magic didn't exist."

"They are my Mexico," Moreno said softly. "I fight to keep this horror away from them."

Riley stared at Moreno, then at the picture again. "Don't even know if they're still alive, what with the damn famine and all," Riley brooded. He looked up at Moreno. "I still write to them regular," he said, then caught himself. "Or rather, I used to."

"Sure and they would be proud to hear of your latest glorious adventure," Dalton injected, lighting his pipe.

Riley glared at him as Manzano opened Richey's saddlebags. He pulled out some documents on U.S. Army stationary and handed them to Riley.

"We cannot believe what these letters say," Manzano said. "Do you think they are genuine?"

Riley and Dalton each perused the letters, trading looks of surprise, even shock. "General Scott is cutting Taylor's army in half!" Riley exclaimed. "By God, he's pullin' all the regulars to his own army, for to march on Mexico City from Vera Cruz, where he plans to land by sea."

"And my family lives in Mexico City," Moreno said, casting a look of concern at the tintype.

Dalton looked incredulous. "Taylor's supposed to hold the whole north of Mexico with four thousand volunteers, a few Dragoons, and his regular artillery," he said, looking at Riley. They both stared excitedly at Moreno and Manzano.

"Do the gringos hold us in such contempt," asked Manzano, "that they believe we would let rabble terrorize half our country and not react?"

"Or do you think this is a perverse ruse, a trick to set a trap?" added Moreno.

"The mind of the native-born Yank is such he'd never even consider he might lose to a 'lesser race,' " observed Riley. He caught himself in the sobering realization that he once felt the same way.

" 'Tis just arrogant enough to be genuine," chimed in Dalton.

"Then, my friends," said Moreno with a smile, "perhaps we all must be guilty of having too little faith. General Santa Anna will surely pounce on Taylor. Mexico's chance for victory now shines as bright as the Bethlehem star."

Riley and Dalton left Moreno's tent, each striding with the confident strut of professional soldiers once again on an assured path. Dalton cast Riley a look of amused wonder.

"The good Lord must love a liar, boy-o," Dalton said, "else why would He go to such great lengths to straighten out your twisted path."

Riley unleashed a healthy laugh. They traded swigs from his flask. Riley felt the dull, leaden weight that had settled months ago in his stomach suddenly vanish. For mystical reasons, well beyond his understanding, it seemed to him that Providence had provided a way to victory. And victory meant salvation for his friends and redemption for himself.

Riley could not help but wonder if his reverence for young Luzero had been part of this "heavenly bargain." By holding his base desires in check, had Good Fortune smiled upon him? Riley had always found it best not to question these things too deeply but merely to ride the horse as far as it would take him, else the luck might fade away. Magic, he felt, should always remain a mystery.

ABOUT THE AUTHOR

Ray Herbeck, Jr., is a writer whose passion for history began with a Civil War musket ball. A California native, Herbeck at age ten visited his maternal grandfather in Arkansas. Together they walked what was then a poorly maintained state park, a battlefield called Pea Ridge. Young Herbeck left ecstatic with a calcimined lead ball. He still cherishes the relic that fired his imagination and led to a unique career.

Herbeck graduated from California State University at Long Beach with a degree in journalism, became a copy editor and reporter at *Billboard Magazine,* and the editor of *On Location,* a film and TV production trade magazine.

In 1984, producer Paul Freeman met Herbeck on the set of *The Chisholms,* a western TV mini-series Herbeck was covering for *On Location.* On the set, they talked about Herbeck's hobby as a Civil War buff. Months later, Freeman phoned and asked him to be historian and technical advisor for David L. Wolper's *North & South: Book I,* at that time the biggest mini-series ever envisioned.

In quick succession came *North & South: Book II, Gone to Texas,* and, elevated to associate producer, *Alamo: The Price of Freedom,* a destination IMAX film shown daily in San Antonio.

As associate producer of triple Academy Award–winning *Glory,* Herbeck at last penned a historical script as writer and producer for a SONY Pictures DVD companion documentary, *The True Story of Glory Continues* (narrated by Morgan

Freeman). Also, he was writer and producer of "The Gunfighters" and "The Soldiers" episodes of a ten-hour documentary series *The Wild West* (narrated by the late Jack Lemmon). Late in his career, Herbeck wrote destination scripts for the National Park Service, including *Days of Thunder* for what had become Pea Ridge National Battlefield Park, *It Took Brave Men: U.S. Deputy Marshals of Fort Smith*, and *Manassas: End of Innocence* (narrated by Richard Dreyfuss), which Herbeck also produced for Manassas National Battlefield Park in Virginia.

Herbeck retired from active film production in 2005. He resides in Prescott Valley, Arizona, where he still writes true stories drawn from history.

The employees of Five Star Publishing hope you have enjoyed this book.

Our Five Star novels explore little-known chapters from America's history, stories told from unique perspectives that will entertain a broad range of readers.

Other Five Star books are available at your local library, bookstore, all major book distributors, and directly from Five Star/Gale.

Connect with Five Star Publishing

Visit us on Facebook:
https://www.facebook.com/FiveStarCengage

Email:
FiveStar@cengage.com

For information about titles and placing orders:
(800) 223-1244
gale.orders@cengage.com

To share your comments, write to us:
Five Star Publishing
Attn: Publisher
10 Water St., Suite 310
Waterville, ME 04901